HO FENG SHAN

‿❧ A NOVEL ❧‿

HO FENG SHAN

THE CHINESE OSKAR SCHINDLER

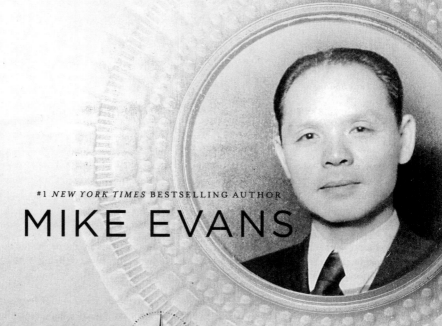

#1 *NEW YORK TIMES* BESTSELLING AUTHOR

MIKE EVANS

TIME**W**ORTHY
BOOKS

P.O. BOX 30000, PHOENIX, AZ 85046

Ho Feng Shan:

Copyright 2018 by Time Worthy Books
P. O. Box 30000
Phoenix, AZ 85046

Design: Peter Gloege | LOOK Design Studio

Hardcover: 978-1-62961-187-7
Paperback: 978-1-62961-188-4
   Canada: 978-1-62961-189-1

This book is dedicated to
*his excellency President Xi Jinping
and to the Chinese people*

who so courageously saved the lives of
thousands of Jews during World War II.
Thank you for your bravery in the face of evil.

İNTRODUCTİON

❧ ⚘ ☙

FOR MOST OF MY TIME in Vienna, I had issued visas to people who were attempting to flee a ruthless Nazi regime. As news of my willingness to be of assistance spread, more came to our offices seeking help. For every visa we issued, two more requests took its place. And still, after months and months of round-the-clock effort to address their needs, as I left the office for the final time I passed applicants standing in line from the building to the street and up the block. As much as we did, there always was more to do. And I began to wonder if I had done anything at all. If my life had made a difference. If I really had helped anyone at all. There were so many. . . . But there was more I could have done, too. I could have stamped one more passport. Issued one more document. If I had slept less. Eaten less. Spent less time in the District and more time at my desk. Or if I had taken the office *to* the District. If. . . if. . . if.

CHAPTER

&&s~ 1 ~&&

AFTERNOON SUNLIGHT filtered softly through the slats that covered the window, casting streaks of light and dark across my father's face. As I sat watching him, cool damp air seeped through the walls and gave the room a chill, but I was determined to remain with him, savoring every moment left to us. It was a dreadful time—for him and for me—but it was a wonderful time, too.

My father spent his life as an academic—a scholar in the teachings of Confucius—as had his father. As he lay there on his bed, unable to move, facing an end we both knew was rapidly approaching but neither of us dared acknowledge, he poured out his mind and soul to me in a manner I, in all of my seven years of living, had never known. Compressing a lifetime of conversation, teaching, and instruction into the little time that remained.

A time shortened by tragedy and compounded by poverty and the ignorance of the times in which we lived.

A few days earlier Father had come upon a Master beating a servant. True to the teachings of Confucius, Father intervened on the servant's behalf. In the ensuing struggle, the Master struck Father on the side of his head with the handle of a broom the servant had been using. The blow sent Father to the ground and as he lay there, the Master stomped his foot on Father's leg, a little below the knee. The bone snapped in two with a sharp end protruding through the flesh. Blood spurted out.

Our physician, one of Father's former students, set the bone as nearly as could be done by traditional methods, but lacking modern equipment, training, or medicines, he was unable to properly address the wound. A week after Father's leg was broken, an infection developed. Ten days later, the infection had spread throughout his body. Already confined to bed with a broken leg, the infection spread to his lungs.

Many people witnessed the incident between Father and the Master but the Master, an influential merchant who dealt in linens and rare herbs, was known to have a vicious temper and had taken retribution in prior incidents against those who spoke against his interests. Because of that, no one would identify the Master as the assailant. Hence, the visit of Chen Bocheng, whose arrival we awaited.

Father turned to look at me. "I am thirsty."

A glass half filled with water sat on a small table next to his bed. I took it and eased it to his lips. He took a sip, then smiled and closed his eyes. "Perhaps you should light the lamp," he added.

A coal oil lamp was on the table next to where the glass had been sitting. I walked to the front room, lit a small stick from the fire in the cooking stove, and brought it back to the bedroom. By the time I removed the glass globe from the lamp, the flame at the tip of the stick was almost gone. I blew on it gently and the flame glowed as the wick of the lamp caught fire. Suddenly, a flame leapt up, glowing with a combination of orange and red. I watched a moment, then turned the wick down, forcing the flame to burn lower.

Just then, we heard Mother open the front door. There was the sound of muffled voices and then footsteps approaching. In a moment, Chen Bocheng appeared in the doorway and came to stand at the side of Father's bed, opposite where I stood.

Chen Bocheng was an elder in our village of Yiyang, a thriving community on the outskirts of Changsha, the capital of Hunan province located in south central China. Even then, during the closing days of the Qing dynasty at the beginning of the twentieth century, neighborhoods like ours were self-organized. Everyone lived in small homes known as *siheyuan*—constructed of wood and arranged in a square with houses on four sides and a court-yard in the center. Each siheyuan chose a representative to the prefecture that consisted of one hundred siheyuan. The prefec-ture was presided over by an elder. Chen Bocheng was our pre-fecture's elder, responsible for maintaining peace and order and for resolving disputes that could not be decided at a lower level. Someone had reported Father's difficulty. Chen Bocheng came to investigate.

"You have a broken leg," Chen Bocheng pointed to the lower portion of Father's body.

"Yes," Father replied.

"They say you intervened to stop a beating."

Father shrugged but did not speak.

"We must find the person who did this," Bocheng said.

Father did not want to press charges. Not because he was afraid of the man who hurt him, but because he was committed to his view of Confucius's teachings. If he identified the Master and formally accused him, the Master would be detained and questioned. Ultimately, however, he would be set free. That is how justice worked back then. When wealthy and influential people were accused of a crime, authorities made a show of investigating—often detaining them in an abrupt and confrontational manner. But they were always set free and always with the explanation that the accused had proven his innocence.

Servants, however, were another matter. Once the Master was released, the servant Father intervened to protect from a beating would be accused of lying and beaten again by the Master. Perhaps even killed. And all of it with impunity. Nothing would ever happen to the Master. Father knew that, and so he kept quiet for the servant's sake.

"Have you questioned the others?" Father asked finally.

"They say they did not get a good look at him," Bocheng replied. "They only turned in that direction after the fight started. Are you certain you could not identify him?"

Father looked away. "I was too busy fending off his blows with the stick." I could tell from the fleeting expression in his eyes that he most certainly knew the identity of his assailant and detested the charade of the investigation Bocheng was conducting. They both knew how this would turn out and the part they had to play.

Chen Bocheng continued to ask questions, but Father avoided them. After a while Bocheng grew tired of the effort and departed. When he was gone, Father looked over at me. "Remember the four pillars."

"Of Confucius?" I asked, knowing full well what he meant.

"Yes." Father sighed heavily. He had a look in his eye as if he were seeing far into the future and after a moment he said, "Feng Shan, your mother is Christian." There was a hint of resignation in his voice.

"Yes," I replied.

"She will lead you in the direction of her beliefs. And perhaps it must be so. But you must always remember the four pillars."

"Yes, I will remember them."

Indeed, Mother was devoutly Christian and participated in worship services with the Lutheran missionaries at their compound near our home, the same location where I attended school. At her behest, I went with her to the weekly services and sat quietly beside her. But even then, when I was only seven years old, there was a tug-of-war in my heart between traditional Chinese culture and beliefs—steeped in Buddhism, Taoism, and the philosophy of Confucius—and the Christian beliefs Mother attempted to instill in me. Father recognized this tension in me very early, before I was old enough for school. Yet he did his best to help me work through the struggle without telling me the answers and without forcing me to believe one way or the other.

"Tell them to me," he instructed. "Tell me the four pillars."

"Morality, respect, justice, sincerity," I replied.

Father smiled. "Now I shall die in peace." Father's words hit me hard. He was sick. So sick that even I, a young boy, could not ignore it. The thought that he might die soon left me devastated. Father seemed to sense that I was upset and looked over at me with a kind smile. "Do not let it trouble you. Jesus taught the same thing, though He . . ."

"I am not worried about that," I blurted out, tears streaming down my cheeks by then.

"Then, what?"

"I do not want to lose you," I sobbed.

Father reached out and touched me gently on the arm. "You cannot lose me. I will always be with you." He took hold of my arm and tugged me toward him. I leaned over him, taking care not to bump his leg and felt comforted by the feel of his closeness. Father wrapped one arm around me and hugged me with what I am sure was every bit of his strength. "You must find your own way," he whispered. "It is the way of manhood. We all have followed the path. You must follow it, too. I had hoped this moment would come later for you, after years of tutelage at my side, but I have every confidence you will be a success. You have gifts and intellect I never had. You will do well."

After a moment, Mother entered the room. I heard her footsteps and then felt her hand on my shoulder. "Come," she said. "We must let your father rest."

I did not want to leave Father's side but when I hesitated, Mother pulled at me all the more. "Come," she repeated. "He needs his rest. You can see him again tomorrow."

Father nodded and gave a thin, tight-lipped smile. "I will be here," he whispered. "Bring your books and we will study together."

With that assurance, I relented and followed Mother from the room.

In the weeks that followed, I continued to attend the Western-style school operated by the Lutheran missionaries. They were from Norway and worked as an extension of the Norwegian Lutheran Church. The compound where the school was located was known to us as Sin I or, in its complete form, Chung Hwa Sin I Hwei—a school of the Lutheran Church in China.

Each morning I said good-bye to Father and Mother and walked to school with friends who lived near us. In the afternoon I returned home, lit the lamp on the table beside Father's bed, and sat in the room with him, positioning my stool as close to him as possible.

The missionaries were kind to us and gave us instruction we could not receive anywhere else, tutoring us in Western literature, mathematics, and classic Christian teachings. But many said that what they taught was merely Western lifestyle and ideals. They argued that because we would spend our lives in China we should learn the Chinese way, not the ways of another country or another people. Mother told me to ignore the critics. Father said it was good to learn many things and to learn them from every point of view.

Classes at the missionary school were taught in English, which I learned very quickly, but at home with Father I practiced Chinese letters—the ancient art of calligraphy—and listened as he instructed me in the traditional Chinese way. We spent many hours with the Five Classics of Confucius—the subjects he stressed with his students—Poetry, Documents, Rites, Changes, and Annals, which were a collection of ancient poems, hymns, social traditions, and the like. In this way, contrary to the concerns of those who criticized the missionary approach, I received the best of both traditions.

Father told me, as he had the day when Chen Bocheng visited, that Confucius did not teach religion but merely a way of organizing one's thoughts and world view. However, the Classic Poetry and I Cheng—the Classic of Changes—opened the way to ancestor worship and divination. Mother was squarely opposed to those practices. She permitted me to study the poems while in Father's presence but forbid me even to mention the subject of I Cheng, a prohibition she conveyed to Father. Consequently, he avoided the topic with me.

When Father and I concluded the traditional lessons, I completed my school homework assignments from my teachers at the missionary school, still sitting on the stool beside the bed, while Father dozed. The rhythmic sound of his relaxed and unlabored breathing was like music to me. I loved him more than life, as he did me, and in spite of Father's condition, those were some of the most peaceful, exhilarating days of my life. Just the two of us. Alone in his room. Studying. Learning. Enjoying each other's presence.

In the weeks that followed, however, all of that changed. Father began to cough and then to wheeze. The doctor visited and listened to his chest, then shook his head. "You have pneumonia."

"Is there anything we can do?" Mother asked.

"If he is able, he can try sitting up or walking some, but there is not much else to do."

Over the next several days, I helped prop Father up in bed to elevate his head. And once or twice Mother and I helped him to a chair in the corner of the room. But the broken bone in his leg made even the slightest movement excruciatingly painful and he could sit upright for only a brief period of time. He was obviously very sick.

Once, when Father was feeling particularly alert, my uncle,

Tian Yutang, came to the house and moved him from the bed to a chair we'd positioned in the courtyard between the houses. Father sat for almost two hours, basking in the warm sunlight. He did so well, we thought he'd taken a turn for the better and would ultimately recover.

A few weeks later, though, I returned home from school and found Uncle Yutang standing outside the house, waiting for me. He had a serious look on his face and my heart sank at the realization of what his presence might mean.

As I approached the house, Uncle Yutang stepped forward to meet me. He put an arm around my shoulder, and the sinking feeling inside told me the worst had happened.

"This is a day for bravery," Yutang said softly. "Your mother needs you to be strong."

"Why?" I asked, sensing the truth already in my heart. "Has something happened?"

Yutang looked down at me and suddenly grief struck my heart. I knew then that Father was gone, but I did not want to accept it.

Instinctively, I broke free from Yutang and ran into the house to Father's room. He was lying on the bed, right where I'd seen him early that morning. Only, now he was dressed in white. His eyes were closed and his hands rested peacefully on his chest.

"Father!" I shouted, but he did not answer.

I leaned forward to rest my head on him and take him in my arms, but just then Mother appeared behind me and took me by the shoulders with both of her hands, restraining me but not leading me away. "He is not here," she whispered. Mother was crying, too. I could hear it in her voice and turned toward her, burying my face in her abdomen. "He has died?" I asked, stating the obvious as only a child could do.

"Yes," she sobbed. "He has died." She wrapped her arms around me and held me in her embrace with a gentleness she had not always shown.

After a moment, Uncle Yutang entered the room. I did not look up to see him but felt his arms tighten around us both and smelled the musky scent he always gave off.

CHAPTER

᎒Ꮗ 2 Ꮗ᎒

FATHER'S PASSING brought a profound sadness. It also brought dire physical and circumstantial consequences.

Throughout my childhood, our family lived in financial distress. Father was a brilliant intellectual with a nimble mind and many original ideas and insights regarding the work of Confucius. During the Qing dynasty, however, the imperial examination system held the key to advancement. It was the means by which everyone rose to a higher status. Questions on the test were crafted with the help of European advisers and drew upon the latest advances in Western thought.

Yet Father, for all his intellectual prowess and understanding of the ancient customs, was unable to score well enough on the exams to secure an important position. He taught privately, but without the benefit of an academic appointment or the financial stipend that came with it. Moreover, most of his pupils were from poor rural families and there were not very many of them, either. Many times we faced the night with no assurance of anything to eat the following day. But after Father's death, Mother and I were plunged into even more extreme poverty.

I did not mind our situation too much. School at the missionary compound was offered to me free of charge and the teachers fed us a light meal at noon each day. In the evenings, I returned home and sequestered myself in Father's room, sitting on the stool beside his bed. When we had coal oil for the lamp, I would light it and stare silently at the empty cot. When we had no oil, I sat alone in the darkness and wept.

Mother remained at home during that time, unwilling to surrender the daily life she'd known since marrying Father. Thinking about it now, I can understand that she, too, was grieving his loss and expressing that grief in her own way, just as I did. We subsisted during that time on handouts from friends and gifts from Uncle Yutang. In the daytime we did fairly well but at night we usually ate only rice, though sometimes we were able to add a few bits of dried fish. Once in a while we cooked fish head soup, which Mother and I thought of as a delicacy. But most of the time we were hungry.

After several months with no prospect of a change in our situation, Mother relented and took a job as a housekeeper at an orphanage operated by the Lutheran missionaries. The orphanage was located in the same compound as the school I attended.

Many mornings Mother and I walked to the compound together, but occasionally she was required to work at night. Those evenings when she worked, I remained with her at the compound, not returning to our home but sleeping in a room near the missionaries' offices. Because of this, the missionaries came to know me quite well.

One of them, Karl Torvik, made a point of befriending me, teaching me to pitch and catch an American baseball in the afternoons after the other students had gone. Torvik seemed to like Mother, too. He was not married and visited us at home on the days we did not stay over in the compound. When he came, he always brought food and books and talked to me about the lessons our class was studying.

Afterward, while I continued with my studies, Torvik sat with Mother and talked as adults do. Unlike some Western missionaries, Torvik had a good command of the Chinese language. He and Mother enjoyed each other's company, and I liked him, too.

The school day routine at the missionary compound included a chapel service at which the basic tenets of Christian belief were taught. In the days following his death, I remembered the conversations I had with Father during the final weeks of his life. Conversations about Confucius, Chinese culture, Buddha, and how many of the concepts Jesus taught were embraced by Confucius. Remembering those days as I sat on the wooden pew during the chapel service heightened by a sense of loyalty to him. Consequently, I resisted the teachings of the missionaries.

The thought of accepting the missionaries' teachings appeared to me a betrayal of Father. As if by agreeing with them in their propositions about Jesus I felt that I would be forsaking Father and saying good-bye to him all over again. I was not prepared to do that. The emotional wounds from his passing were quite raw back then.

After school, on the days we returned home, I would again go to Father's room and sat on the stool beside his empty cot. Even though he was gone, I lit the lamp that sit on the table beside the bed, as I had when he and I met to talk or study. Then, with the writing board and paper resting on my lap, I practiced Chinese letters and sometimes talked to myself as if talking to Father, even pausing to listen as if he were speaking to me and replying to his imaginary comments. A few times, the line of demarcation between fantasy and reality became quite confused and I could smell him as well as hear and see him.

One day, Uncle Yutang stopped by for a visit. I heard him as he entered the house and sensed him standing at the doorway to Father's room, but I did not turn to acknowledge him and continued my work with the Chinese script, keeping my head down and my eyes focused on the writing board.

A moment later, I heard Mother's footsteps as she approached, then Uncle Yutang said, "He does not need to sit there like that. This is not good."

"Shhh," Mother whispered. "We must leave him alone."

"You agree with this?"

"He is finding his way."

"But what way?" Uncle Yutang asked with an incredulous tone. "I heard him talking to himself when I first arrived. And I've heard him doing it before."

"It is the path to manhood for him," Mother replied patiently.

"The path?"

"This is but the first step," she answered. "Come. Leave him to it." Then she guided Uncle Yutang away from the doorway and left me in peace.

Mother's words to Uncle Yutang reminded me of what Father had said about how I must find my way to manhood. My own way. That all boys do the same and that I possessed the means and ability to do so in a successful manner. I smiled at the thought of that conversation. Then once again, as often happened when I thought of Father, tears filled my eyes.

∽◌◦ ◦◌∾

A few weeks later, at the conclusion of a chapel service at school, Torvik took me aside and asked me to follow him from the building. I did as he requested and we sat together on a bench near a stand of bamboo at the far side of the compound, a place to which I sometimes retreated when I wanted to be away from the other students.

As the other students went back to class, Torvik sat next to me and began to talk. "I wanted to ask you about how you are doing."

"I am fine."

"You miss your father." It was a question, but he asked it as a statement of fact. "I miss mine, as well."

The comment surprised me. "Your father is dead?"

"Yes. He died when I was a boy."

His words were oddly reassuring. He had made the transition to adulthood alone, perhaps I could, too. "Like me?" I asked.

"Yes." Torvik nodded. "Like you."

"And you still miss him?"

He sighed, "Feng Shan, you will always miss your father. And it would be a mistake to attempt to push that loneliness aside. But after a while it gets easier to handle. One day his absence will not be such a burden to you as it is now."

The thought of forgetting Father terrified me. "I don't want to forget him," I replied sharply. "I will never forget him."

"No," Torvik assured. "You won't forget him."

"If I ever forget him," I continued, "he might not be here for me when I need him."

A puzzled look wrinkled Torvik's brow. "Wherever your father has gone, he will always be there."

I knew what he meant. Christians believed people either went to heaven or hell after they died. We heard much about that in chapel. But I was doing my best to refuse those ideas. Father was not a Christian and therefore, as I understood their beliefs, he was disqualified from heaven. "He told me he would always be with me," I stated with as much confidence as a young boy could muster.

Torvik glanced at me. "Is that what he said? Is that what he told you?"

"Yes." I nodded vigorously to stress the point. "He said, 'You cannot lose me. I will always be with you.'"

A kind smile came to Torvik's face. "Your father was an intellectual."

"Yes."

"He taught his pupils the value of learning."

"We studied together every day," I said boldly.

"He studied right along with you. Always learning."

"He wanted to know many things," I said proudly. It was true. Father wanted to know everything.

Torvik thought for a moment, "I have noticed that you pay attention in class." I grinned at the affirmation of being noticed. "But you are distracted in chapel," he quickly added. "You spend most of the time during the service staring out the window with a scowl on your face." He was correct, of course, so I did not reply. He continued. "You don't like chapel?"

The service was important to him and I did not want him to stop liking me, but the question presented a choice between him and Father and my loyalty had already been decided, regardless of the consequences. "I prefer the traditional Chinese way that Father taught," I said.

Torvik grinned. "Well," he said slowly, "I don't think your father would mind if you paid attention. I'm not asking you to agree with what is being said. Just that you give the service your attention. Your consideration. To see if there is something in it that you can learn."

There was little I could say in response. Father valued learning. Not merely studying about a topic that could be applied to the practical needs of everyday life, but learning solely for the sake of knowing a thing as clearly and deeply as possible, regardless of its practical application.

"You know," Torvik continued, "Confucius taught a system of thinking, of processing, of organizing one's beliefs and applying them to one's life through simple principles. He taught a philosophy, not a religion."

That was exactly what Father had told me and I marveled at the similarity, as if the words of one confirmed the other.

"Those principles," he added, "are not in conflict with the teachings of Jesus. They can help you organize your life, your thoughts, the way you encounter the world, just as I organize it in my mind around Western principles I learned from *my* father."

I liked that idea, but it left me with a question. "How would I know the difference?"

Torvik seemed puzzled. "The difference?"

"Between philosophy and religion."

Torvik smiled as if he had been waiting for that question and yet was surprised by it. After a moment, he rose from his place on the bench. "Come with me. I have something for you."

I followed him from the stand of bamboo, across the compound to his office, a tiny room off the hall that led from the classrooms to the chapel. The walls were lined with bookcases that reached to the ceiling and were crammed full of books, pamphlets, and papers. Opposite the door was a desk cluttered with still more papers and more books, some of them lying open and stacked on top of each other.

Torvik reached over the clutter and retrieved a Bible from the corner of the desk, then handed it to me. "Take this. Keep it for your own and read it every day. Let the words soak into your mind and down into your spirit. Then you will know the difference between the things that are compatible with the teachings of Jesus and those that are not. The things that are philosophy and those that are religion."

The book was bound with a leather cover and felt heavy in my hands. I gripped it tightly and tucked it under my arm. In spite of my reluctance to accept Christian teaching, a grin spread over my face. This was my first book in English and I was very proud to have it.

That afternoon when I returned home from school I entered Father's room, lit the lamp on the table beside the bed, and took a seat on the stool, just as I had on every other day. Only this time, instead of holding the writing board in my lap, I held the Bible Torvik had given me.

It seemed like an important moment and I paused to look over at Father's cot, hoping to see him, at least in my mind. To my delight, an image of him appeared and he smiled up at me from his place on the bed, as if he approved of what I was about to do.

Confident that he would not be upset with me, I rested the Bible on my knees and began to read.

As I read, I sensed the mood in the room begin to change. The mood inside me changed, too, and I no longer felt a conflict between what I had heard at chapel—which I now read firsthand from the Gospel text—and what Father had told him. As if the two perspectives—the traditional philosophical approach Father gave me and the spiritual context Jesus offered—were coming together. Words from the pages washed over my mind, my memories, and my spirit, bringing relief to them all.

Later, when I paused to reflect on what I'd been reading, I thought again of Father and once more he appeared in my mind, smiling at me with the same sense of satisfaction he showed when I got my lessons correct. Tears filled my eyes once more, only this time they were tears of joy and relief.

⁂

For the next several evenings at home, I asked Mother questions about the gospel, about Jesus, and about the things Father told me just before he died—about the teachings of Confucius and their compatibility with the teachings of Jesus. "Yes," she said. "The teachings of Confucius inform Chinese culture and define it in many ways. But it is our culture, not our religious beliefs. Why do you ask these things?"

"Because I would like to become a Christian. But I do not wish to become something other than Chinese."

She laughed and tousled my hair. "You do not have to give up being Chinese to become a Christian."

"Good," I sighed with relief. "Is it difficult?"

"To become a Christian?"

She smiled. "It is easier than you could imagine."

At Mother's direction, we knelt that evening in the room beside Father's bed and she led me in a simple prayer to become a Christian, to give my allegiance to the kingdom of God, to become a follower of Jesus.

At school the next day, I told Torvik of my decision to become a Christian. Torvik was excited and began meeting with me in the afternoons after class, teaching me about Jesus. I was about nine years old at the time but had an aptitude for learning languages and reading English at a grade several levels higher than others my age. Studying the Bible in English helped advance my understanding of English as well.

Besides English and Chinese, I also understood rudimentary German and French. One day, Torvik gave me a devotional book to read. We were in his office and I was standing near his desk. "Go ahead," he urged. "Open to the first page and tell me what you think."

I opened the book and saw it was written in German. "I'm not sure I can read this well enough to understand it," I was fearful that I would offend his generosity but equally concerned about making sense of the text.

Torvik took another book from the shelf and handed it to me.

"This is a German–English dictionary," he explained. "Take it with you, too. You can use it for help with the passages that give you problems."

"You think I can do this?"

"Yes," he nodded confidently. "It will help you understand Jesus and help you learn more of the German language. You can practice writing the words, too. Just copy them from the book."

"Very well," I said. "I'll give it a try."

"Work with it some," he urged, "and we can talk again to go over the paragraphs."

Our discussion that day brought to mind the way Father and I used to sit together in the evening. We read the lessons in Chinese, then we both practiced drawing the characters on our writing boards.

I left Torvik's office that day with two books tucked beneath my arm and the confidence that I could master German as well as I'd mastered English. But even more, I looked forward to meeting again with Torvik to discuss what I read.

The years since Father's death had been bleak for me, but the day Torvik gave me the German devotional was another turning point. Together with the Bible and becoming a Christian, a path to the future seemed to open for me. In my heart, I wanted to find out what lay ahead.

CHAPTER

৽ৡ৾ 3 ৽ৡ৾

ONE MORNING when I was ten years old, I was on my way to school, walking with my friend Bo Zhongfa and several other classmates who lived in the neighborhood near our home. As we walked along the street, a great calamity arose behind us with the noise of tambourines and loud shouts. We all turned in that direction and saw a large procession headed our way. A sedan chair carried by four muscular servants was at the center, flanked on either side by rows of guards dressed in the robes of the imperial staff. One, who appeared to be the commander, led the procession. With a stern and demanding countenance, he scanned the people on either side of their path, watching, looking, searching—for what, I did not know. Behind them, I saw imperial attendants stepping in time with the guards, banging the tambourines with each step, and they all were moving at a swift trot.

As the procession drew near, everyone around me bowed low, their foreheads touching the dirt. I was mesmerized by the spectacle and remained standing, watching in awe as the sedan chair passed by.

Seated in the sedan was a single little boy. He wore a silk robe the color of saffron. Lush and ornate, it fell over him in a luxurious, flowing manner and on his head was the traditional headpiece worn for a coronation—a skullcap fitted with a flat board-like piece across the top and had decorative strands that hung from two sides.

The boy in the sedan was very young, not more than three or four years old, and he had a strange look about him. Rather aloof, a little angry, and quite a lot frightened. As he drew opposite my position, our eyes met and his gaze bore in on me with piercing intensity. I had never seen such a thing and found myself unable to move or avert my eyes from him.

Just then, one of the imperial attendants rushed toward me. He had a scowl on his face and held a bamboo cane in his right hand. When he was a step or two away he drew back the cane and swung it toward me, striking me across the back of the knees with a loud *whack* that brought gasps from those around me. "Kneel in the presence of the emperor!" he demanded. And before the words were out of his mouth, I collapsed to the ground, clutching my legs and writhing in pain.

After the procession had passed, the others stood and Bo Zhongfa took me by the arm. "Come," he ordered. "We must be on our way."

"Is he gone?" I asked, unwilling to stand if it meant receiving another blow from the cane.

"Yes," Bo Zhongfa replied. "He has moved on. Are you okay?"

I struggled to lift myself up from the ground, "I think so." There was burning pain in my knees where the attendant struck me with the cane, but I was unwilling to show such weakness to my friends and said nothing of it.

Others crowded around. "What were you thinking?" someone asked.

"I was thinking nothing," I replied.

"Then why did you not kneel?"

I frowned in response. "Kneel?"

"That was the emperor," someone else said. "We must kneel to show our respect."

"Could you not see that he was the emperor?" another asked.

"Yes," I replied. "I could tell that from the color of the robe. But I have never seen an emperor before and he is so young."

"He is Pu Yi," an unfamiliar voice added.

"You have seen him before?" I asked.

"No one has seen him until now."

"Come," Bo Zhongfa said once more. "We must be on our way. Otherwise, we will be late for class." He offered his shoulder for me to lean against, which I readily accepted, and together we hobbled up the street toward the missionary compound.

⟿ ⟾

Even with Bo Zhongfa's help and with several minutes to limber my knees and walk off the pain, I still was limping as we arrived at school. Torvik noticed us and came in our direction. "What happened?"

"It is nothing," I replied, eager to avoid a discussion. "Just an—"

Before I could finish, Bo Zhongfa spoke up. "An imperial procession passed us while we were on our way. Feng Shan did not kneel. One of the guards struck him behind the knees with a cane."

"Is it true?" I asked, attempting to steer attention away from me. "Was the little boy in the sedan really the emperor?"

"Yes," Torvik replied. "Zaitian, the emperor, has died. His cousin, Pu Yi, has become the new emperor of the Qing dynasty."

"He is not even as old as I am," I said.

"Pu Yi is three years old," Torvik responded. He explained a little further about the installation of the new emperor and the necessity of the procession we encountered, then called everyone to the classroom and we all started in that direction. I lingered behind and turned to Bo Zhongfa. "You should not have told him," I said.

"About what?"

"About me and the imperial attendant."

"Why not?" he asked.

"I am able to bear the consequences of my own conduct."

Bo looked angry. "The imperial guards are bullies," he retorted. "My father says they should be opposed at every possibility."

"And how are we to do that?"

"We speak when they tell us to be silent. We stand when they go by."

"And look what that got me," I said, gesturing to the deepening bruise on the back of my legs.

Bo Zhongfa smiled. "And a lovely sight it is," he said with pride.

I could not help but note to myself that it was bruises on *my* legs, not Bo Zhongfa's. And while he claimed that standing was a form of resistance we should embrace, just an hour earlier he had bowed immediately upon sight of the imperial sedan and accompanying procession.

We spoke a moment longer, then Bo Zhongfa drifted off with the others, and another of our classmates, Li Du, appeared at my side. He and I were friends but I was not as close with him as with Bo Zhongfa.

Li Du leaned close and spoke in a voice just above a whisper. "Do not trust Bo."

"And why not?"

"His father is a Communist."

A frown wrinkled my brow. "A Communist?"

"Surely you have heard of them. And if not, you must have read about their plans for us."

I had not read about the Communists. And certainly not about their plans. But Li Du was always showing off how much he knew and I did not like it—which was one of the reasons we were not close friends. Because of that, I was reluctant to admit that Li Du knew something I did not. And besides, I *had* heard people talking about the Communists. Everyone had heard of them, as it was the topic of almost every conversation. I just did not know precisely what the term meant.

So, instead of responding to Li Du's question I simply turned it back to him. "Have you?" I asked in a condescending tone.

"Yes," Li Du replied. "And you will notice, although Bo Zhongfa says we should resist, the marks are on *your* legs, not the legs of Bo Zhongfa."

Of course, I had noted that already but did not say so. Certainly not to Li Du. He had little regard for Bo Zhongfa on many points aside from issues related to politics and the emperor.

"That is the way of the Communists," Li Du continued. "They talk endlessly about the worker's right to protest, but they make no protest themselves. They talk at length about the need to resist, but when trouble comes they push others to the front to take their place while they remain safely out of reach."

It was difficult to refute his point, and the notion stuck with me for the remainder of the day—that others admired my stance and encouraged me to do it again should the opportunity arise, but all of them knelt immediately when the emperor appeared. And none of them expressed an intention to protest in a similar manner, though my actions that day had been no protest at all but rather inspired by a rapturous awe.

According to Chinese history, which Father instilled in me with deep devotion, the ancient Five Emperors ruled our country long before Columbus discovered North America. The last of those ancients was Shun, who handed the throne of leadership to Yu the Great, the first emperor of the Xia dynasty, which lasted until the year 1600 BCE. There followed the Shang dynasty, which gave us our earliest written records dating from the year 1250 BCE. The Shang ruled as kings over the Yellow River valley until 1046 BCE, when they were conquered by the Zhou, the longest of the dynasties.

And so it continued until the year 221 BCE, after a period of internal conflict, when Qin Shi Huang united the country as the state of Qin and established himself as its ruler. His descendants governed for the next fifteen years in a succession known as the Qin dynasty. The Qin reigned for a short period and gave us only two emperors, but they instituted a system of imperial government that lasted until the time of my youth, early in the twentieth century AD. Under their leadership, the nation became the China of history.

All of this was ingrained in me and in my subconscious at a level beyond thought, feeling, or emotion. I had no intention of protesting against that order, no matter what my friends at school might say. How could I? This was my country; they were my people. And, in no small way, this was me; to rebel against the imperial order would have been to rebel against myself.

A few days after the incident with the imperial procession, Li Du met me in the schoolyard and gave me a small booklet. "My father wrote this," he explained. "Read it. It will tell you all you need to know about the Communists."

I took the booklet home and that evening I read it by the light of the lamp that stood on the table beside Father's bed. As I slowly turned from page to page, I read about the Communists and how they had come to prominence in China with the help and aid of operatives from the Soviet Union—Russians—our mortal enemies. The words I read were troubling and I found in them a great unsettling, quite unlike the things I sensed when reading from the Bible or the devotional books Torvik gave me.

The following afternoon when I returned from school, Uncle Yutang was at our house. I already had thought of asking him about the things that troubled me from the booklet and was delighted to see him. As I entered the front room, I showed him the booklet I had received from Li Du, eagerly producing it for him to see.

Uncle Yutang glanced through the first few pages and handed

the booklet back to me, and shook his head. "It is nothing."

As I had many questions, I was not satisfied with his response. "The book gives details about the Communists in China, how they rose to prominence, the things they plan to do."

"It is nothing," he said once more.

Still I continued. "They plan to infiltrate and take over the Kuomintang." I gave Uncle Yutang a questioning expression. "What is the Kuomintang?"

Uncle Yutang refused to look in my direction. "It is none of your concern."

"But what is it?" I was unwilling to let the matter drop and moved to position myself in front of him. "What is the Kuomintang?"

For a moment Uncle Yutang was silent. Then, with a resolute expression he took me by the shoulder and led me to a corner of the front room, away from the windows. "These things must not be spoken of carelessly." His voice was hardly a whisper. "Do you understand?"

"Yes," I replied. "I am not being careless. I simply want to know what it means."

"Very well," he said grimly. "But the things we learn change us. Once you learn a thing, your eyes are opened. You cannot return to the state of ignorance you previously enjoyed."

I nodded. "I understand." Father had explained this concept to me on several occasions. "What is the Kuomintang?"

"The Kuomintang is a. . . shadowy group," Uncle Yutang

replied. "A resistance organization loosely gathered around a leader, Sun Yat-sen."

"I have heard of him."

"I am sure you have."

We continued talking, and Uncle Yutang explained the history of the movement—the emperor unified China long ago, but gradually the imperial government became corrupt. Now, with Pu Yi as emperor, it was totally corrupt and no longer capable of functioning as a government. Instead, it existed only as a means of exploiting the people for the luxury and satisfaction of the imperial family and staff. Sun Yat-sen and his followers—the Kuomintang—were attempting to take us in a better direction with a government that served the interests of the people.

When Uncle Yutang finished his explanation, I showed him the last page of the pamphlet, which contained a list of the supposed Communist factions within the Kuomintang, along with the names of people who were said to be Communist activists. Among those listed was Bo Shu-Nim, the father of my friend Bo Zhongfa. "Do you know this man?" I asked.

"Certainly," Uncle Yutang answered. "He is the father of your friend."

"Is he one of the Communists?"

Uncle Yutang shrugged his shoulders. "These things are not easily decided. Some think so. I am not sure."

"And what about Bo?" I asked. "Is he one of the Communists?"

Uncle Yutang had an indulgent smile. The kind adults often

gave to children who asked simple questions regarding complex matters. "Bo is a boy," he explained, tousling my hair as Mother often did when responding to me. "He is a young boy like you. This is not a fight among children."

Indeed, we were young, just as Uncle Yutang suggested. And as he suggested, the struggle against the imperial government did not involve us directly. But we were not immune to the consequences of that struggle or to the disruptions the struggle brought to daily life.

Likewise, the conversation of adults was unavoidable. As a result, my classmates and I overheard many people talking about the topics of the day—the young emperor who had ascended to the imperial throne, the corruption and profligacy that surrounded him, the need for change—all of which we mimicked in our own conversations among ourselves at school and in the neighborhood where we lived. We repeated the ideas and ideals of our parents and adult neighbors and were quite serious in doing so, even if we did not fully understand the issues or their implications.

CHAPTER

❧ 4 ❧

IN THE WEEKS that followed my conversation with Uncle Yutang about the booklet, I spoke many times with Li Du, continuing to address the question of Communist intentions toward the imperial government and the nature of the Kuomintang resistance. The topic captured my imagination and I longed to know every detail. As a result, Li Du and I became closer. Our friendship steered me away from Bo Zhongfa.

At the same time, I began spending more time with Uncle Yutang, usually in the afternoons or evenings, after I had finished schoolwork for the day. He talked to me about the latest developments in the resistance to the imperial government. He also gave me books to read about Chinese history, democracy, and even the American Revolution, along with several biographies of other great world leaders.

The books Uncle Yutang gave me about China were written in Chinese. The others were in English and French. By then I understood English very well but French was a bit more challenging. Torvik loaned me a French–English dictionary and I soon mastered the language well enough to read the books Uncle Yutang had given me.

One day Uncle Yutang saw me with the two books—a biography written in French resting on my lap and the French–English dictionary lying open on Father's bed.

"You are reading both at the same time?"

"One helps the other," I explained.

"And yet you understand them both."

"Yes," I replied.

"You have a gift for languages?"

I had already reached that conclusion but had not mentioned it to anyone for fear of seeming too prideful or boastful. It was the sort of thing Li Du often flaunted and I did not wish to be like him in that respect. But while reading the books Torvik gave me I noticed that languages came easily to me. I had no understanding of what that meant our how it might affect my life, other than that I enjoyed reading and found great pleasure in reading other languages.

As the weeks went by, Li Du and I spent our free time at school huddled together at the bench near the stand of bamboo, talking about the latest news or the things we'd heard others discussing on the matter of Kuomintang resistance. I told him some of the things I learned from Uncle Yutang. He told me about things his father had discussed with men who visited their home.

No one seemed to pay us any attention and for a time I thought they did not notice that we were together during recess and not with the class. Then one day Torvik called me to his office and offered me a seat across from him at the desk. "I notice you are spending more time with Li Du," he began.

My cheeks felt warm and a sense of embarrassment swept over me, though I did not know any reason I should feel that way. "We are friends," I replied, somewhat defensively.

Torvik seemed not to notice my discomfort. "You used to be friends with Bo Zhongfa. What happened between you and Bo?"

"Nothing."

"He is still your friend?"

"Yes," I said. "Of course."

"And what is it that makes you such good friends with Li Du?"

I looked away. "We enjoy each other's company."

"I see you sitting together on the bench," Torvik continued. "It seems as though you don't want to be interrupted by the others."

"Not everyone enjoys the things we do."

Torvik raised an eyebrow. "Which are?"

I shifted my position in the chair and leaned against the arm-rest on one side. "Politics, mostly. And Chinese history."

Torvik nodded thoughtfully. "I hear many of you talking about politics."

"Is that wrong?"

"No," Torvik answered with a shake of his head. "It's not wrong, but perhaps there is a better use of your time."

"Such as?"

"Discussing literature. Or Scripture."

"I would be happy to discuss literature with my classmates," I said. "But none of them are interested in the Chinese classics and they do not read English well enough to understand the literature."

"You could help them."

I was not persuaded by the suggestion. "Am I not to be concerned with my country?"

"Well," Torvik mused, "concern for each other is at the heart of Jesus' teaching. But politics has always been a problem for the church."

"How is that?"

"It tends to take over the discussion. Politics becomes the gospel. Persuasion and argument replace evangelism."

"But shouldn't all aspects of life conform to the teachings of Christ? Even the government?"

"Yes," Torvik conceded. "But politics is the domain of this world, concerned with the issues of this world and this kingdom. Jesus came to establish the kingdom of God. Politics always becomes about winning. About us against them. It tends to divide rather than unite."

I did not realize how aware Torvik was of the political climate in which the school operated and how much he wanted to avoid trouble with either side—imperialist or otherwise. A few days later, however, that point was pressed upon us when imperial guards arrived at the missionary compound.

As they entered the building, Li Du and I went around the outside to a place beneath the window in Torvik's office. As we listened, the guards questioned him about political activities at the school.

"We have reports that revolutionary agitators are active in the compound," one charged.

"That is incorrect," Torvik replied. "We have only schoolchildren here."

"You have people who espouse the teachings of the Kuomintang."

"No one on our staff is involved in that sort of thing."

"We have reason to believe some of them are."

"What reason could you have?"

"We hear reports of revolutionary ideas circulating among your students."

"Our students are children," Torvik said.

"Precisely."

"I don't understand," Torvik countered.

"Children reflect the values of their parents. And of their teachers."

"You are accusing us?"

"No. We are warning you."

"Warning me?" Torvik's voice sounded tense. "Of what?"

"Revolutionary activities bring the penalty of death."

"Even for children?"

"Even children," one of the guards said resolutely.

As I listened at the window, I was reminded of the conversation I had with Torvik a few days earlier. That's when I realized the importance of what he had been saying and why he had taken me aside to his office. Political discussions of the students could have consequences. He knew this and was attempting to convey the gravity of the matter to me, just as Uncle Yutang had tried to tell me earlier. No one was immune from the political issues of the day or the political repercussions that followed—not even young boys were exempted, although they were only repeating things they heard from their parents or other adults.

Sounds from inside the office where Torvik and the imperial guards were talking indicated the guards were leaving. Li Du and I turned away from the window to leave, too, before we were seen. As we did we saw Bo Zhongfa standing nearby, watching us. Our eyes met his and instantly he turned away and hurried off in the opposite direction. Li Du did not like it.

"Bo will cause trouble," he commented.

Still remembering my conversation with Torvik about the repercussions of our schoolboy antics, I shook my head. "Bo will not cause trouble." It was more a statement of faith than of fact. Bo was my friend. I was certain he was only jealous of the time I spent with Li Du instead of with him. "Besides," I added, as if to reassure myself, "we have done nothing wrong."

Li Du still was angry. "We should—"

I cut him off. "Let's leave Bo alone and not bring unnecessary trouble on ourselves."

For the remainder of the day, I continued to think of the conversation I had with Torvik about politics and the trouble it caused, the discussion I heard between Torvik and the imperial guards, and the anger I observed on Li Du's face when he realized Bo Zhongfa had been watching us. *"Politics divides,"* Torvik had warned. *"It does not unite."* And that afternoon those words seemed truer than ever.

But why?

Why does politics divide? Does it have to be that way? Can we not discuss civic matters and disagree without becoming enemies of those who did not accept our ideas? I, being quite young at the time, perhaps lacked the maturity to formulate my thoughts in those precise terms, but that is what I was thinking.

That evening when Uncle Yutang came for a visit, as he now regularly did, I was prepared to raise my questions with him, certain he could give me answers that made sense. When he arrived, though, I never got the chance to question him. He had his own questions for me.

"Imperial guards came to your school today?"

"Yes," I replied. "How did you know about them?"

Uncle Yutang ignored my question. "Do you know why the guards were there?"

"They came to meet with Torvik."

"What did they meet about?"

"Accusations that our teachers and some of the students are spreading revolutionary teachings."

Uncle Yutang frowned. "You heard them?"

"We were . . ." I looked down at the floor. "We were listening outside the window to Torvik's office." I glanced up at Uncle Yutang and saw him smile with approval.

"They accused Torvik of this conduct?"

"They said they had come to warn him; that spreading revolutionary thought carried the penalty of death."

"They were threatening Torvik," he said.

"They mentioned all of us."

Uncle Yutang's eyes opened wider. "You and your friends have been discussing the things we talk about at night."

"Yes."

Uncle Yutang shook his head. "That is not good."

"Why not?"

"Much talk can only lead to trouble," he muttered.

"That is what Torvik said."

"To them?"

"To me."

"When did that happen?"

"A few days ago. He tried to explain to me that political talk causes problems. He said it only divides us and does nothing to unite us."

"Torvik is correct."

"But why?" I implored. "Why is it wrong for us to discuss the things that matter? The things we hear adults talking about?"

Uncle Yutang looked me in the eye. "This is precisely the trouble I told you we would face."

"I do not understand," I sighed.

"When the imperial guards hear of your talk," he explained, "they know that you are too young to have those ideas on your own. They conclude from the things you say that you are only repeating things you have heard from your parents. They will use that information to determine the identity of people who oppose the imperial government."

"Our parents."

Uncle Yutang had a knowing look. "And your uncles."

This was an inescapable quandary. The things we heard from our parents intrigued us. It intrigued *me* and it certainly excited Bo Zhongfa and Li Du. But the things we talked about only served to implicate people we revered. It did nothing to advance the causes to which we were so devoted. And yet we could not avoid discussing them.

After a moment I said, "Will the guards come to our house?"

"I do not think so." Uncle Yutang rested his hand on my shoulder. "I cannot guarantee it, but I don't think so."

I looked up at him. "Is trouble coming?"

"Yes," he said slowly. "I think it will."

"If trouble is coming, shouldn't we prepare?"

Uncle Yutang looked away. "Many are. But you and I should

talk no more of this for now. And tell your friends they should not continue to discuss this at school. If you must talk, do so at home. Talking about it at school will only implicate the missionaries and bring trouble on those with no stake in the future of our country."

CHAPTER

5

IN SPITE OF our heightened fears, nothing extraordinary happened for the next few months. My life fell back to a rhythm of school, home, study, school. Later that year, however, a small cadre of officers from units of the imperial army garrisoned at Wuhan—a city not too far from where we lived—led the foot soldiers in a revolt. Fighting broke out between army factions, and several generals who supported the emperor were killed along with soldiers who were loyal to those generals. Some of the loyalists escaped, but when the fighting ended on the grounds of the post, the revolutionaries controlled the facility and the area immediately surrounding it.

In the days that followed, students at Wuhan University, emboldened by the army unit's success, protested against the imperial government. Revolutionary soldiers from the Wuhan garrison left their post and entered Wuhan proper to show support for the students. More soldiers followed and soon the revolutionary army took control of the entire city.

A few weeks later, General Yuan Shikai, the imperial government's most important military leader, arrived in Wuhan with units from the imperial army in Beijing to put down the army uprising. General Yuan's men attacked the garrison post in an attempt to retake it but were unable to break the control of the revolutionaries. Fighting was severe and many from both sides were killed.

One evening, while the unrest at Wuhan continued, I was visiting Uncle Yutang at his house when several men came to see him. One of the men, who seemed to be an important figure, took Uncle Yutang aside and they talked privately. I could see them talking but was unable to hear what they said, though from the expressions on their faces the conversation seemed quite serious.

Others in the room, however, were not so careful or circumspect in their remarks and I overheard their conversations clearly. From them I learned that they had come to see Uncle Yutang to discuss plans for assisting the revolutionaries of Wuhan, perhaps even spreading the revolution to Changsha as a means of seizing control of the entire province. Changsha, after all, was the capital of Hunan.

Upon hearing their plans and aspirations, I was at once proud that my uncle was among the leaders of the movement but I was equally fearful that something might happen to him. Uncle Yutang was Mother's brother, and not from Father's family, but he was the most prominent male in my family and a person I trusted for guidance in learning the way to manhood. The thought of losing him was something I dared not consider.

Later that evening, after the men departed from Uncle Yutang's house, I asked him about them. He explained, "The man I was talking with was Chan Siu-bak. He is a leader of the Kuomintang in Hunan and a close personal friend of Sun Yat-sen."

"And Sun Yat-sen is the leader of the entire Kuomintang?"

"Yes."

"Chan Siu-bak was talking to you about obtaining support for the revolutionaries in Wuhan."

Uncle Yutang shook his head. "They are not revolutionaries. They are fighters for freedom."

"And we are going to help them?"

Once again, my uncle gave me the smile adults give to children who ask simple questions about complex issues they do not fully understand. "Some things you do not need to know."

"I will help you," I said offered earnestly.

"No," he quickly replied. "You must concentrate on schoolwork. That is your contribution to the effort."

"But how does that help?"

"This will be a long-term struggle," Uncle Yutang explained. "It will not end in a day or even a week. But one day it will end and we will control the government for the benefit of the people. When that day comes and the imperialists have been removed, we will need capable people to lead. You will be one of those capable leaders."

A sense of pride and affirmation welled up inside me. To learn that I—right then, as a young boy—was someone with gifts and talents that singled me out as a potential leader seemed like the most wonderful news I could ever receive. But I also felt a sense of frustration. I wanted to participate in whatever was happening. To actually do something, not merely talk about it. Yet Uncle Yutang held the key to my involvement, or so I thought. Without his help, I could do nothing, so I kept my feelings and thoughts to myself and, instead, reached out with both arms and gave Uncle Yutang a hug.

While fighting between imperial troops and revolutionaries continued around Wuhan, imperial guards and agents spread throughout the entire Hunan province, searching for those who were actively supporting the revolutionary effort. Word of their presence traveled quickly. Everyone was tense and alert, even at the missionary school.

With everyone anticipating the worst, I worried that imperial agents might come to Uncle Yutang's house and arrest him. Many of our neighbors knew people who had been arrested and sent to prison. Some had been shot on sight, their bodies left to decay in the dust. Because of Yutang's involvement with the Kuomintang, I feared imperial agents might come for him, too. One day after school I tried to go to his house, but Mother saw me and prevented me from doing so. "You must remain here," she ordered. "With me."

"But Uncle Yutang might be in trouble," I argued.

"If he is in trouble, and you are there, you will be in trouble, too. And for what purpose?"

I had no answer for her and so, reluctantly, retreated to Father's room and sat on the stool by his bed, reading. As I did so, I remembered Uncle Yutang's words to me about how studying was my contribution to the revolution. I smiled at the thought of reading as a revolutionary activity. Imperial guards and agents might hinder me from physically taking part in the struggle, but they could not prohibit me from reading or thinking. They could not win the battle for my mind. In fact, they already had lost in that regard, and so I opened one of the books Torvik gave me—a devotional written in German—and began to read.

The following day at school, I noticed Li Du was absent. I asked about him among my classmates and learned from Bo Zhongfa that imperial agents had come to Li Du's house the night before. "They arrested Li Du's father," Bo Zhongfa said, "and accused him of giving aid to the revolutionaries."

"Where did they take him?" I asked, eager to learn more.

"Before the guards could take him away, men from Hunan appeared and rescued Li Du's father. Several imperial guards were killed in the fighting. Now the imperial guards are searching for the men who rescued Li Du."

As Bo Zhongfa spoke, I remembered the men who came to Uncle Yutang's house when I last visited him. Yutang must have been involved in whatever happened. Suddenly I was concerned for his safety, this time more so than before when Mother refused to let me go to his house.

That afternoon when we finished with school, I avoided Mother at the compound and, instead of walking home with her as usual, I departed the schoolyard alone and went to Uncle Yutang's house. As I approached, though, I noticed two men seated on the steps out front. Rather than boldly ignoring them by and entering through the front door, as was my privilege as Yutang's nephew, I made my way through a neighboring siheyuan, passing between the houses and crossing the courtyard, then approached Uncle Yutang's house from the side.

Through a window I saw three men seated inside. Two of them were men I had seen before; they had come to the house on previous occasions. The other one was a stranger. Across the room from them was Li Du's father, seated on a chair beside my uncle. They were huddled close together, their heads almost touching, talking quietly and sipping tea. This confirmed for me that Uncle Yutang really was involved in rescuing Li Du's father. Only, now he was in even more danger for continuing to harbor him. I wanted to enter the house and confront Uncle Yutang but I remembered the words Mother had said to me, warning me that close association with him placed me in danger. And if I was in danger, she was, too.

After a moment longer at the window I slipped away and returned home. On the way, I thought of all I had seen and heard at the house and in the past few weeks. Remembering it made me even more fearful for my uncle than before, but then I remembered the story of David from the Bible that Torvik had given me. David was a brave soldier and many times faced overwhelming odds, even as a young shepherd boy, but more so as an adult. Each time, his bravery led him to danger and each time his bravery delivered him from it. Bravery was a desirable quality and one that Uncle Yutang had in abundance.

As I meditated on the story of David, the fear that had gripped me as I departed Uncle Yutang's house began to ease and before I was home it had left me altogether. In its place I was filled with a deep sense of pride that my uncle—and through him, my family— was a participant in the revolution and bravely facing overwhelming opposition. I prayed that his bravery would be the means of his delivery, too, and that I might become as brave as he. But I told no one about the things I had seen at his house. Not even Mother.

Late that night, I was awakened by the arrival of someone at the door to our home. Mother's footsteps trailed across the floor of the front room as she went to check on the visitor. A moment later I heard them talking. Their voices were firm and serious but not excited.

Though they spoke in hushed tones, I heard the visitor tell Mother that Uncle Yutang had been injured. Fear struck me as it had earlier that day and for a moment I gave it a place in my heart, then I remembered a passage from the Bible and one from Torvik's devotional about how believers did not have a spirit of fear but of power. I repeated that thought in my mind as I strained to hear every word Mother and the visitor spoke.

As best I could hear from my bed, Uncle Yutang wanted Mother to know of his injury and asked if she might come to him to help tend to his wounds. I listened to them talking but remained in bed, my eyes closed, feigning sleep in case Mother should look in on me. A moment later, she did just that, but I lay motionless on the bed with the blanket pulled past my chin.

Apparently convinced I was asleep, Mother left with the messenger. I remained in bed until I heard them depart by the front door, then rose, dressed quickly, and followed after them.

As I approached Uncle Yutang's house I once again slipped through the neighboring siheyuan and came to his house from the side, then made my way to the window where I'd stood earlier that day. Through it I could see nothing so I slipped around to a window along the rear wall. There, I listened intently for the sounds of conversation coming from inside. At first I heard only the voices of men and listened for news of what might have happened to Uncle Yutang.

From the nature of the discussion, I learned that imperial agents came to my uncle's house and demanded that he produce Li Du's father. Uncle Yutang did as they instructed but as the agents were carrying Li Du's father away, men who'd been hiding outside Yutang's house sprang forward, attacked the agents, and freed Li Du's father. Outnumbered and overmatched, the guards fled.

Later, when Uncle Yutang and the others were taking Li Du's father to a new place, the imperial agents returned and surprised Yutang and his men. A fight ensued and in that confrontation, Li Du's father was killed. My uncle was injured, along with several of the men who were with him.

The male voices from inside the house faded away and a moment later I heard Mother speaking. "Are they returning to capture you?" she asked.

"I do not think so," Uncle Yutang replied. "Our forceful confrontation has persuaded them not to try again."

"You should see a doctor," Mother continued.

"I cannot."

"And why?"

"They will report me."

"A doctor would report you for seeking medical attention?"

"They have reported many of our people and caused them to be arrested." Then I heard him add, "I must tell you, Feng Shan came to see me earlier."

"When?" Mother's voice had a stern tone.

"This afternoon. After school."

"I told him to stay away. What did he want?"

"I do not know. He didn't come inside. He was listening by the window."

"You saw him?"

"I heard him." Uncle Yutang chuckled. "And the men who were guarding the house told me, too."

Mother finished treating Yutang's wounds, and they talked a moment longer, then I heard her footsteps as she departed through the front door.

Initially, I was filled with fear at the realization that I had not been as cautious as I thought in approaching Uncle Yutang's house earlier that day. If he knew I was there, perhaps the imperial guards and agents did, too. Once again, however, I remembered reading from the devotionals that Torvik gave me and from reading about the life of Jesus in the Scripture that fear was our worst enemy. This was no time for fear but for action and so I pushed my feelings aside, slipped away from the window, and started confidently toward home.

From Uncle Yutang's house I took a shorter route than Mother normally followed and was back in bed by the time she arrived. As I lay there, pretending to sleep, Mother came to the doorway. "I know you were there tonight," she announced.

I rolled over to look at her, doing my best to appear sleepy. "What?" I asked in a muddled voice.

"I know you were there," she repeated. "At Yutang's house. Stop pretending to be asleep."

I smiled at her. "How could you possibly know I was there?"

"I heard you breathing," she replied.

"You heard me breathing from where you were inside the house?"

She was not happy with me for going over there but she had an amused look in responding to me. "I carried you for nine months, and gave birth to you. Suckled you at my breast. Cared for you all these years. Do you think I do not know the sound of your breathing when you are at the window outside the room where I am talking with your uncle?"

"We heard today about what happened to Li Du's father. When the man came for you tonight I was worried for Uncle Yutang's safety."

Mother sighed heavily. "Things are happening that you must not be a part of," she said in a serious voice. "Yutang is involved with powerful people. They are good men, but they are not safe and the people against whom they struggle are very dangerous. You must keep yourself away from them."

"But Yutang is my uncle," I protested. "I want to—"

Mother interrupted me before I could finish. "You love him very much and want to help him. And he loves you. But these are dangerous times and we must be careful."

CHAPTER

∞ 6 ∞

THE NEXT DAY after we learned what happened to Li Du's father, his son did not come to school. Once again, I asked among my classmates but no one seemed to know where Li Du was, though they had heard rumors about his father, the imperial agents, and the fight that ensued.

Later in the week, Bo Zhongfa took me aside at school during recess. "I have been asking in the neighborhood about Li Du."

"What did you learn?"

"Li Du has moved."

"Only Li Du?"

"He and his entire family. The neighbors told me this." Bo Zhongfa glanced around as if checking to see if we were being watched, then added, "I saw his house for myself."

I was taken aback by his statement. "You went to Li Du's house?"

"Yes."

"What did you see?"

"The house is empty."

"You are sure of this?"

"Actually, I went there first. To see him. To find out for myself why he was not at school. And I saw then that they had moved."

The timing of his visits and discussion with the neighbors left me confused and doubtful of his story, so I said, "I want to see it for myself."

"Good," he replied. "I will take you there this afternoon."

After school was over for the day, I went with Bo Zhongfa to Li Du's house. Through a window in front I saw that the house was empty, just as Bo Zhongfa had said. Still, I wanted to know the reason the family had moved and went inside in search of a clue.

Inside, I found nothing to indicate a reason for their move and after a moment I said, "They really are gone."

"Yes," Bo Zhongfa replied. "They are gone."

Just then, the sound of footsteps came from behind us. Bo Zhongfa and I turned to see four men standing at the doorway. They were dressed in the garb of imperial agents and were armed with pistols and swords. Before we could move, the two men in front grabbed us.

"We knew you would come," one of them said with a sinister grin. "You are one of them."

"One of who?" I asked.

"The Kuomintang. And now we will take you for interrogation to find the truth of all that you have done against the emperor."

They were strong men and we were unable to resist, but as they dragged us from the house a group of neighbors appeared. Looking angry and determined, they formed in a group as one before us, blocking our path.

"Disband at once!" one of the imperial agents shouted. "Disband at once or join these two in prison."

As we watched and waited to see what would happen, an elderly woman elbowed her way through the crowd and stood before the agent who had addressed them. "These are young boys," the woman said in a stern voice. "Would you disgrace yourself by disrespecting their mothers?"

The agent who spoke looked indignant. "I am not—"

The woman cut him off. "They are but children. The fruit of their mother's womb. As were you."

The two agents who stood beside me glanced at each other with a sense of bewilderment and I heard them murmuring about the karma of pushing her aside. I no longer trusted in the notion of karma or believed it to be real, but they did and it seemed to bother them that they might reap some negative impetus in their lives by opposing the woman. I knew from the books Torvik had given me and from my conversations with him that what the agents really faced was the wrath of the Holy Spirit, but I did not warn them and thought it right if they incurred His response on their own, unaware.

After a moment, however, the agent who addressed the crowd turned to those who were holding us and said something. I could not understand the words he used, and was not certain the language he spoke was Chinese, but the men who were with him seemed to know what he meant. They released us at once, smiled politely to us, and turned to leave.

The crowd that had gathered parted as the imperial agents approached and watched while they marched through. As the agents passed, several of the older men bowed their heads politely in a show of respect.

When the imperial agents were gone, the elderly woman turned to us and with the same stern voice she'd used when addressing the agents said to us, "You should not be here." Her eyes gazed into mine and she pointed to me with a jab of her finger. "Especially you."

I wondered what she meant and whether she knew me, or Mother. . . our Uncle Yutang, but as I glanced around at the others, still staring straight at us, I realized they *all* knew Yutang. And they all knew *me.*

"You are young and eager and that is to be commended, but nothing good can come to you here," the woman continued. "Go home where you belong. There's nothing you can do for your friend now."

And then I realized the neighbors not only knew who I was, they knew that Li Du and I were friends. At the same time, it was inescapable to me that those who gathered to help us paid no attention to Bo Zhongfa. Not only did they pay him no attention, they seemed to make a point of ignoring him. And that caused me to think that perhaps more was happening right then than I realized.

With nothing further to say on the matter, and certainly nothing further to do, we left Li Du's house and started toward home. As we walked, Bo Zhongfa asked, "What did she mean by that?"

"By what?"

"What did she mean by those things she said to you? She spoke as if she knew you."

"She spoke as if she knew *me,* but she acted as if she knew *you.*"

Bo Zhongfa looked surprised. "Knew *me?*"

"They all did. They all acted as if they knew you."

"Why do you say that?"

"They went to great lengths to avoid addressing you at all."

"Well . . . I . . ." he stammered.

"This is what I mean," I added. "They were as obvious in their avoidance of you as you are in avoiding my point just now." I looked over at him. "How do you know them?" Bo Zhongfa did not reply and we continued toward home in silence, but my mind raced through all that had happened.

It seemed as though we'd fallen into a strange and mysterious tale. People whom I did not know nevertheless knew me—even though I was certain I'd gone unnoticed in previous trips to that area. Not only that, they knew my friends and my family. And the imperial agents—why were they watching Li Du's house? Were they watching the house, or watching me?

And why did no one address Bo Zhongfa? He already had been over there, or so he said. If he really had been over there, wouldn't they know him, too? Or was it all just a ruse? A plot to lure me to the house in order to make it easy to affect my capture. But why would they want to do that? The imperial agents already knew that Yutang was my uncle and that he had been involved with the Kuomintang. They did not need me. Or did they?

"The intrigue of it is too much for me," I mumbled.

"What do you mean?"

"It is nothing," I answered, unwilling to share more with him until I knew the true nature of his involvement. "Come on. Let's get home quickly." And we picked up the pace of our walking.

⚜ ⚜

At an intersection not far from the missionary compound, Bo Zhongfa left me to follow the road that led to his home. I turned toward my home and continued alone. When I arrived, Mother confronted me. "What were you doing at the home of Li Du?"

I was astounded that she knew where we had been, as we had told no one where we were going, but I recovered enough to say, "We heard he had moved. We wanted to know for certain."

Mother glared at me. "Bo Zhongfa put you up to this."

A sinking feeling came over me as Mother's words seemed to confirm the suspicions I'd had earlier about Bo Zhongfa and how we came to be at Li Du's house. "No," I said, unwilling to concede that I might have been duped by him. "He did not convince me to go. I wanted to go for myself. It was my idea. Bo Zhongfa merely came with me."

Mother placed her hands on her hips in a pose that indicated she was not convinced by my explanation. "And for what purpose did you go there?" she asked.

"Li Du has been absent from school. We have been talking about it, and today Bo Zhongfa said he had been to their house to see about them and learned that they were no longer living there."

"And you suggested you wanted to see it for yourself."

"Yes."

Mother still did not seem satisfied with my answer but I sensed she was unable to think of anything more to ask, so she said, "I told you before, you must have nothing to do with the things that are happening."

"But *what* is happening?" I asked in an insistent tone.

"Terrible things. Things that will get men killed. Things that have already gotten some of them killed."

"Is that what why Li Du's father is dead?"

Mother turned away, just as Uncle Yutang had on several occasions before when I asked questions he did not wish to answer. "We must talk of these things no more. And," she added sharply, "stay away from Yutang, too."

"But why?" I implored. "He is my—"

"Imperial agents are watching his house. If you go there, they will see you and think that you are involved with Yutang."

"But you went to his house," I argued. "Will they not already think we support him?"

"Listen," Mother snapped. "They know that I am his sister. They know that you are his nephew. They will not suspect me of anything for merely treating his wounds. He is my brother. I am *supposed* to look after him." She stepped close to me and looked me in the eye. "But you, they will suspect. You are nearly a man and these things that are happening are the business of men." She lowered her voice and ran her hand over my head. "They will suspect you," she beamed, unable to disguise her pride in me. "You must not go there now."

The intensity of her concern struck me in an unexpected way.

CHAPTER

7

MEANWHILE, fighting between imperial soldiers and revolutionary warriors in Hunan province continued with both sides inflicting heavy casualties in a running series of intense battles. At the same time, the Kuomintang enjoyed great success in organizing civilian volunteers to serve as support groups and to exert further influence over provincial affairs. The broad sense of enthusiasm that effort created led to widespread protests against the imperial government.

Though the struggle proved intense and continued for several months, eventually the revolutionary forces in Hunan joined with members of the Kuomintang and dominated the province. As a result, imperial agents were forced to either secret themselves under deep cover or withdraw entirely.

In any event, the threat they posed to our safety was greatly reduced. Mother became less worried about my contact with

Uncle Yutang and permitted me to visit him on a regular basis, for which I was very glad. Every day after school I went to his house. Sometimes we talked in long, rambling discussions of politics and the implications of current events. At other times, he was occupied with visitors who came to him for counsel and consultation regarding revolutionary strategy. During those times, I sat in the corner and read a book, pretending not to hear but following every word that was said and relishing each comment.

As the revolution progressed I became aware of a struggle not only between the Kuomintang and the imperial government but also an internal dispute between those, like Uncle Yutang, who favored a more democratic approach to government and the Communists whom Li Du had mentioned to me earlier. I reread the booklet he gave me and borrowed a book from Torvik on the topic, but I longed for an opportunity to discuss the matter with my peers. None of my current classmates understood the concepts enough for a healthy, lively debate. Most of the time, I could easily best them and they quickly grew weary of the simplest discussions. Bo Zhongfa understood the issues and was always ready for a lively debate, but I didn't raise crucial topics with him because of the things I'd learned from Li Du about his father.

Bo Zhongfa's father worked in a coal mine not far from Changsha. All but a few of the miners in his unit were opposed to the imperial government and, indeed, felt victimized by them more intensely than many, but they were under the influence of organizers who wanted to collectivize them and use them as a unit to force the government to improve working conditions. Those who favored the collective approach were members of a Communist organization and I was certain Bo Zhongfa's father was among them, though I had no proof of it at the time.

Because I thought the topic would be a sensitive one for Bo Zhongfa, I chose to enjoy his company rather than his debating skills and kept political discussion at arm's length from him. He was a friend, and though I was not certain of his own personal leanings (such as they were for any of us at that young age), I did not want to risk losing him or disclosing sensitive information I'd learned from my visits with Uncle Yutang. Consequently, when he spoke of political matters or recent events, I participated on the terms of his assumptions and did not challenge the accuracy of his comments.

News of the Kuomintang's activities in Hunan and the success we had obtained soon spread to other provinces. This energized additional protests and uprisings against the imperial government in several regions outside Hunan, particularly in the southern portion of the country. Sun Yat-sen, who was from Guangzhou in Guangdong Province—one of the largest provinces in the south—used the growing sense of unrest and displeasure to cobble together the disparate Kuomintang organizations from that area into a single unified political party—the Kuomintang Party, transforming it from a revolutionary cabal to a genuine political force. Sun Yat-sen quickly emerged as a leader of what had become a national revolution.

In the weeks that followed, the Kuomintang solidified its control of Guangdong Province and added to its cadre, forming its own army. Several imperial officers from the province renounced their credentials and brought soldiers from their units into the Kuomintang army's ranks. With expert leadership and disciplined training, the army made territorial gains quickly, subsuming neighboring provinces with little difficulty. The party, however, lacked the resources necessary to extend its authority over the entire country, particularly in the north where loyalty to the emperor was more entrenched and the Kuomintang ranks more sparse.

At the same time, Communists also saw the advantages afforded by the general unrest present among ordinary citizens. They, too, were active in the country and developed their own organization under the leadership of Zhu De, an intellectual from Beijing University. Though much smaller in scope than the Kuomintang, the Communists had an organized presence throughout the country and were strongest in the north, where the Kuomintang was weakest.

On an individual basis, Communists participated in Kuomintang-led revolutionary activities but the organization as a whole remained officially uncommitted to the revolution. Sun Yat-sen viewed the Communist policy with skepticism. Privately, he thought their noncommittal posture was part of a broader and more cunning strategy to seize control of the revolution for themselves. In his view, the Communists were lying in wait, hoping the Kuomintang would fight the imperial forces, deplete their resources, and become weakened by the struggle. Thus in a disadvantageous position, the Kuomintang would be unable to resist a change in power; a change the Communists hoped to exploit in their favor.

Uncle Yutang discussed this situation with friends and associates on numerous occasions, receiving reports and updates on events from throughout the country. I was present for some of those conversations and found the topic very intriguing. The interplay of people and issues captivated my attention.

Often after a visit to Uncle Yutang's house, I lay awake at night remembering the conversations I had heard and imagining the things that must take place to resolve the issues presented. I plotted them in my mind like a map with lines and dots connecting the groups and subjects until, exhausted, I would fall asleep. Then, with my eyes closed, I dreamed of the same things all over again. It was a wonderful time in my life and a formative experience that remained with me long afterward.

In order to counter the potential threat posed by the Communists, Sun Yat-sen decided it was better to incorporate them into the Kuomintang Party than leave them on the outside. I disagreed with the decision, but Uncle Yutang thought it was the best strategy. "If they are part of us," he suggested, "they will be equally responsible for the result and unable to dispute their involvement in the decision-making process."

Aside from that, the Kuomintang needed the Communists simply for the number of fighters they controlled and the resources they offered. Though weakened by corruption, the imperial government still had vast resources at its disposal. It also benefitted from centuries of historic Chinese culture, which promoted worshipful obedience to those in power, a practice that remained a central element of daily life even after all that had happened in the attempt to change it. In order to wage a successful campaign against the imperial government and its forces, the Kuomintang needed more than it could offer on its own.

Having spread Kuomintang control as far as its resources and reserves allowed, Sun Yat-sen approached Zhu De and raised the question of the two forces working together under the Kuomintang banner. "Why not work together as a unified Communist Party," Zhu De suggested. "We are not without friends who would come to our aid." He, of course, was referring to operatives within the Soviet Union who sponsored Zhu De and other Communist operatives.

Sun Yat-sen knew better than to agree to such a counter-offer. "Our people will never accept such an arrangement," Sun replied. "They are devoted to the notion of a democratic government, which they expect the party to model as we work to implement it in a national government."

"And you think we would not support free and open elections?"

Sun nodded. "You might, but Communist doctrine dictates policy from the top and disseminates it to those below. The legislative wing of a Communist government addresses only the implementation of policy, not the creation of it. And in that regard, a Communist government is merely a form of imperialism."

Zhu De did not like that argument. "Surely you did not bring me here to insult me."

"No, merely to explore the matter in a full and frank discussion. A democratic government," he continued, "can make room for Communist ideas and ideals—there are many who advocate for a socialist democracy and make excellent arguments in its favor. But a Communist model has no room for the democratic. At least, not a democracy where the people have the power to create policy."

Talks between the two leaders dragged on for several weeks but finally the Communist Party agreed to join the Kuomintang. Following the announcement of that decision, Sun Yat-sen and Zhu De became co-leaders of the party. The Communists instantly became the party's largest faction.

With relative ease, Sun and Zhu folded the smaller Communist groups into the more extensive Kuomintang organization and developed a concerted effort to overthrow the imperial government. The arrangement worked, at least at first, but their collaboration had been fraught with tension from the beginning.

All this time, Pu Yi still was very young and under the control of the imperial staff. Using a strategy of deception, they kept him occupied with increasing levels of indulgence and entertainment. This permitted them to exert undue influence over the government, but it fostered in the young emperor an unnatural and unhealthy appetite for sensational activities. As a result, he grew increasingly obstinate and sadistic, often ordering the beatings of staff for seemingly inconsequential offenses—beatings the executioners were bound by law and custom to fulfill, which they did with greater and greater zeal. Thus the corruption foisted upon Pu Yi was multiplied and reinforced through the lower ranks.

Lacking competent executive leadership from the emperor, government operations fell to Pu Yi's father, Prince Chub, and one of the imperial concubines who obtained the title Empress Dowager Longyu. Chub's focus was external—foreign policy, military policy, and policing of the civilian population. The empress handled internal matters—treatment of the royals, running of the imperial household, support for the thousands of concubines and servants, and maintenance of her own extravagant lifestyle.

When revolution broke out in Hunan, Prince Chub wanted to crush it immediately, which is why General Yuan Shikai was sent to the province with the imperial troops. In spite of the imperial army's inability to put down that revolt, Prince Chub still had great faith in the imperial government's supremacy and as revolution spread to other provinces, he sought to press the fight against the rebelling forces with brutal force.

The imperial government, however, existed in a constant state of confusion. One group of advisers and ministers favored one policy or plan, another group favored something else. All of them, however, held one point in common: They all blamed General Yuan Shikai for the army's ineffectiveness. Prince Chub favored yet another plan—his own plan—and viewed General Yuan Shikai as the best hope of leading a military effort to effectuate that plan.

Informants in the military told Prince Chub that Yuan was personally reeling from his inability to suppress the rebellion in Hunan. According to them, he was embarrassed and frustrated by the unacceptable result he'd produced regarding the revolutionaries and searching for a way to reestablish himself as the ruthless defender of the empire that he saw himself to be.

To Chub, this seemed like the perfect situation to implement his plan for suppressing the revolutionary Kuomintang—a general in need of redemption and a barbaric plan through which to vent that need. Annihilation of the Kuomintang seemed within Chub's grasp.

During the Spring Festival that year, Prince Chub invited General Yuan to a meeting in the imperial palace—the Zijin Cheng, the Forbidden City—a walled facility covering 180 acres in the center of Beijing. They met in a small cottage on the far side of the palace grounds in order to talk in private.

"Revolution is spreading from Hunan," Prince Chub began.

"That is my fault," Yuan admitted. "We should have been more effective but with the state of our intelligence apparatus, I was unaware the rebels had such strong local support."

"We must do something about that."

"Yes," Yuan agreed. "I have taken steps to address the integrity of our informants but it will require additional time."

"Unfortunately," Prince Chub said, "time is not something we possess."

"You wish for me to resign?"

"No," Prince Chub soothed. "Quite to the contrary. I want you to conduct a military operation that will utterly eliminate the Kuomintang."

"You had something specific in mind?"

For the next two hours Chub and Yuan discussed Chub's plan to counter the revolution: A ruthless obliteration of civilian and military strongholds across the southern provinces.

"Thus destroyed," Chub added finally, "the remainder of the nation will refuse to participate. Control will once again be ours."

Yuan readily agreed and Prince Chub appointed him to the task of executing the strategy. "But will the empress agree?"

"Strictly speaking, we do not need her consent."

"But we should obtain it nevertheless. With her in agreement, we would have no need of guarding our internal position."

The following day, Chub and Yuan invited the empress to the cottage for talks. Away from her usual advisers, they explained the details of their plan, stressing the benefit of success to the imperial family. This delighted the empress and she indicated her complete agreement. "So long as the lifestyle enjoyed by the imperial family and staff remains unaffected," she added.

"I assure you," Chub averred, "military operations against the revolutionaries will produce no untoward effect on your lifestyle."

"To the contrary," Yuan added, "suppressing the Kuomintang will add a level of stability that has not been known since the height of the Qing dynasty."

The empress looked at him coldly. "*This* is the height of the dynasty."

When the empress was gone, General Yuan and Prince Chub discussed the need for additional troops. "We haven't nearly enough for a strategy of this proportion," Yuan warned.

"And how would you propose to acquire them?" Chub asked.

"We would need to consolidate the imperial troops with the provincial guards in provinces where we have unqualified support. Then conscript prisoners for added numbers and gather vagabonds and vagrants to fill the ranks."

"And this would give you enough strength to crush the rebellion with an all-out assault?"

"Yes," Yuan assured. "We will eliminate the Kuomintang entirely."

By engaging General Yuan in such an aggressive campaign, Prince Chub was, in effect, entrusting the future of the empire to General Yuan. If the military plan succeeded, the imperial family would continue its grip on power. But if the strategy failed, the empire and the entire Qing dynasty would come to an end in complete elimination and utter ruin.

As a result of Chub's decisions, General Yuan emerged from the Forbidden City meetings with near-total influence and power over the government, able to bend the imperial strength, purpose, and favor, even if it meant turning that favor toward himself. In the weeks that followed, Yuan increased the size of the imperial army and seized all things necessary to support the growing ranks—including people, crops, livestock, houses and buildings—thereby increasing his own personal holdings in the process.

While amassing an army of unassailable strength, Yuan worked to strengthen defenses and control in those areas where the empire had the greatest civilian support. Places which happened to be the location of his greatest personal assets. With his interests sufficiently protected, and with the imperial army adequately provisioned, Yuan moved his troops south to attack the Kuomintang's entrenched positions.

As fighting with the revolutionaries intensified, Sun Yat-sen and Zhu De convinced the southern provinces to declare their independence from the empire. With little effort, they melded the provinces together to form the Republic of China. Determining the republic's leadership, however, proved difficult and portended future problems.

The Kuomintang, of course, wanted Sun Yat-sen as president; the Communists wanted Zhu De. When approached about the matter, Sun Yat-sen was cautious. "We have the votes to force the matter. But we do not want the Communists to feel they are not a part of what we are doing. We need them as genuine participants."

When Zhu De was approached, he demurred, but not for altruistic reasons. "We must bide our time," he cautioned. "Sun Yat-sen is adept at building an organization but too soft to succeed as a revolutionary leader. He will succeed at the former but fail at the latter. Then we will take control and be in a more powerful position than if we challenge now. If we wait, the organization we require will be built with their help but used by us to take control."

With Sun Yat-sen as president, the republic worked to strengthen the army, adding to its ranks, consolidating arms from imperial armories in the southern provinces and arranging the purchase of modern equipment from foreign suppliers.

British merchants favored the empire but American suppliers were inclined toward the republic's democratic principles. Although the US government was hesitant to show its support, private US businessmen came to the republic's aid early in the revolutionary effort. With their help, and the support of the Communists, Sun Yat-sen was successful in preparing an army that permitted the republic not only to survive but also to advance against the provinces of the north.

や

With relative ease, Sun Yat-sen and the republic acquired control of the southern half of the country. Still, the republic's army remained weaker than the imperial army, which held the northern provinces. Faced with that situation, Sun Yat-sen sought to negotiate an agreement for a peaceful resolution of the struggle, rather than wage a war he knew would be destructive for everyone. To accomplish this and set up a means of negotiation, Sun Yat-sen dispatched emissaries of unquestionable loyalty to discuss the matter with General Yuan.

Zhu De and most of the Communists within the Kuomintang were opposed to Sun Yat-sen's negotiation strategy. They favored fighting to the end or, in the alternative, negotiating a resolution of the struggle that gave the republic the territory it already held, even if the result meant only controlling a portion of China. Once again, however, they decided not protest their opposition forcefully but chose to follow the path already taken of waiting for the republic to collapse. "You will see," Zhu De answered. "The arrangement with imperial forces which Sun Yat-sen seeks will not work."

In accord with his chosen strategy, Sun Yat-sen established contact with imperial entities that were sympathetic to his proposal. Negotiations were first held with key northern provincial leaders, then directly with the imperial government, working through General Yuan as the imperial government representative. Later, Sun Yat-sen and Yuan met in private at a cottage in Shanxi and negotiated through intermediaries.

Both sides were rife with intrigue, much of it promoted by people who wanted to take advantage of the situation and maneuver themselves into a more favorable position. Bringing them under control took a concerted effort but eventually Sun Yat-sen and Yuan Shikai reached a tentative agreement to resolve the conflict.

Convincing the imperial government—namely, Prince Chub and the Empress Dowager Longyu—to accept the proposed arrangement seemed to Sun Yat-sen a difficult task. "I assure you," Yuan replied. "That will not be a problem."

Yuan had the ear of a British intellectual, Gregory Kimble, who served as Pu Yi's tutor and whom the young monarch respected. Yuan convinced Kimble that negotiating for certain favorable concessions were the only way to keep Pu Yi, the imperial concubines, and the empress safe. "Pu Yi certainly can't function in an open society," Yuan argued.

"Yes," Kimble acknowledged. "This is quite true. Our most important task now is to insure the emperor's survival and, if possible, a continuation of his current lifestyle."

Together, Yuan and Kimble conferred first with Prince Chub. He heard their arguments in support of the agreement but initially was reluctant to accept. "The war against the revolutionaries is not winnable?" he asked.

Yuan shook his head. "I am afraid it is only a matter of time before the revolutionaries take control of the entire country."

Yuan outlined the military situation in detail, suggesting, in a convoluted bit of logic, that the imperial army's strength in certain areas actually worked against the possibility of ultimate victory. "They will lay siege to us in these key areas," as he pointed to a map produced for purposes of the meeting. "Over the long term, the area will be devastated."

"You must think of your son's safety now," Kimble noted. "And of his future. Not merely preserving the dynasty. Or even national dignity. Pu Yi must be your primary concern."

"I understand," Chub agreed. "And that being the case, we should work to ensure the emperor is protected."

"Yes."

"Only, who will lead the country when the emperor is gone?" Chub asked, hinting he might still have reservations. "We cannot leave that determination to the revolutionaries."

"Sun Yat-sen is a good man," Kimble suggested. "I think he would do the right thing."

"I don't know," Chub sighed. "It is a lot to leave in his hands, especially if the emperor's future is our primary concern."

"There's always Yuan," Kimble conceded. This was the moment Yuan had hoped would arrive and he summoned all of his strength to keep silent while Chub responded.

Slowly, Chub nodded. "I like the suggestion." Then he looked over at Yuan. "You were my choice for this strategy from the very beginning. I assumed you would win a victory on the battlefield, but if it is to be this way, then may it be so."

Yuan, of course, did not argue.

CHAPTER

∞ 8 ∞

AT THE URGING of General Yuan Shikai and Prince Chub, Gregory Kimble helped convince the Empress Dowager Longyu and other key members of the palace that the imperial government could not prevail militarily against the Kuomintang revolutionaries. Yuan even went so far as to assert that the imperial army would not support the emperor in the kind of severe conflict deemed necessary to ultimately end the revolution. "Our only hope is to negotiate an end to the hostilities and reach favorable terms with our adversaries," Yuan explained.

"And you have a plan for doing this?"

"Yes, we have established a negotiating link with the rebelling forces and have outlined our terms to them."

"What are those terms?" the empress asked.

Yuan provided her with the essential points of the plan and

she, like Prince Chub, came to the most essential points quickly. "Will they guarantee that our life and the emperor's life will go on as always, seamlessly and unbroken?"

"Yes. Most certainly."

"And they will not attempt to assassinate us once we reach an agreement?"

"No."

"Sun Yat-sen would lead the government?"

"General Yuan will be president. And," Kimble added, "I must say, I think we stand at one of the great transitional moments in Chinese history. A moment that will turn the Chinese people either toward greatness and accomplishment or toward complete destruction."

The empress cared little for superfluous words, language, or ideas. Her only interest was in maintaining the extravagant lifestyle that she and special staff members enjoyed. When that was assured—a guarantee made evident in the inclusion of Yuan as president—she readily consented to the negotiated settlement.

Convinced of the plan's efficacy, the empress joined Yuan, Chub, and Kimble in presenting it to Pu Yi. "You would abdicate the imperial throne," she explained, "in exchange for which you would receive certain guarantees regarding the imperial family's fortune, lifestyle, support, and safety."

"What would this mean?" Pu Yi asked. "What would we do?"

In order to answer his question, Prince Chub and Gregory Kimble entered the conversation, supplying details about the specific steps necessary to attain the desired result. Pu Yi listened attentively but seemed strangely detached and rather aloof. When they finished explaining the matter to him, the emperor huffed, "It is no great matter to me. Do with the plan as you wish," and with a disinterested wave of his hand he departed the room.

General Yuan Shikai transmitted the proposal for Pu Yi's abdication to Sun Yat-sen through an intermediary. Sun Yat-sen and the Kuomintang executive committee greeted it with interest. Sun Yat-sen had been apprised of the contents before the proposal was transmitted and already knew about it in great detail when it was offered to the executive council. However, members of the executive council were not privy to the details until the day the transmission arrived. Most were agreeable to the guarantees regarding Pu Yi and his family, but the issue of Yuan Shikai becoming president was cause for great debate.

In the days that followed, the council discussed the proposal at length, often in conversation that devolved into angry shouts and fits of rage. Some favored accepting the proposed agreement as it was offered; others did not. And for a while they struggled among themselves over who should have leadership over the republic—Yuan Shikai, Sun Yat-sen, or someone else.

Zhu De and the Communist faction within the party still did not want to accept any agreement with Yuan Shikai. "They didn't trust him, and felt that this was merely a play for power by Yuan, that once he was in office he would never leave."

"He is an imperialist through and through some say. Now he sees an opportunity to make himself the emperor and he is attempting to use us to accomplish that."

Others felt that if they approved the measure, Yuan Shikai would be the most powerful man in China. Sun Yat-sen will be second. And that they would be eliminated."

And finally, from a minor part of the faction came the blatant plea: "We should abandon Zhu De and the Kuomintang alliance at once and reestablish the revolution we began before. A revolution against all parties!"

In the end, however, Sun Yat-sen prevailed and the republic's parliament accepted the proposal offered by Yuan Shikai on behalf of the emperor. A few days later, Pu Yi abdicated the throne, ending the Qing Dynasty. In his place, Yuan became president.

After resolution of the conflict, the capital of the unified country remained in Beijing, but with an elected parliament. The parliament was duly seated and immediately began work on creating a constitution that would restructure the government along democratic principles and ideals. The American Constitution provided the core model, though the Communists worked to centralize much of the government function, particularly those areas that dealt with economic matters.

At first, Yuan Shikai acted as though he supported the Kuomintang's democratic goals and outwardly embraced parliament's work. Secretly, however, he remained sympathetic to the emperor and to the imperial form of government. Not long after taking office, he began establishing relationships with key parliament members in an attempt to frustrate plans to form a constitution that would limit his power or his term in office.

While he worked behind the scenes, Yuan made great strides to enlarge the reach of his office. He expanded the size of his staff and located his residence inside the Forbidden City—moves designed to reshape his presidency in the form of the monarchy, this time with himself as emperor.

Parliament quickly recognized his objective and attempted to exert control over Yuan by limiting the expenditure of money. It also appropriated for itself the power to approve future presidential appointments, a stricture that infuriated Yuan.

As the struggle between Yuan and parliament continued, the masses became frustrated with the direction the government was taking. Elements within the Kuomintang, both Communist and democratic, began to agitate among the citizen groups that participated in the original revolution, inciting them to action once again. Before long, student protests reappeared on the streets of major Chinese cities. They were joined by working-class citizens.

In the midst of this situation, Wei Binglin, one of Sun Yat-sen's closest friends and most trusted advisers, came to him at night. They had known each other since childhood and were closer than brothers. When the Communists officially joined the Kuomintang, Wei Binglin had sworn his allegiance to the Communist faction. It was a ruse, however, as he had done this in order to bury himself deep in the Communist apparatus where he could keep an eye on the faction's internal politics and discussions. He visited Sun Yat-sen in the nighttime in order to minimize the possibility of detection.

"The Communists are plotting your downfall," Wei Binglin began in an ominous tone.

"Yes," Sun Yat-sen nodded, dismissing Wei's concern with a wave of his hand. "They always are plotting my downfall."

"This time," Wei countered, "they intend to swiftly bring it to pass."

"And how do they plan to do this? With more student demonstrations?"

"The protests in the streets are at their instigation, but that is merely a cover for their true activity."

"And what activity is that?" There was a hint of frustration in Sun's voice.

"Zhu De is shrewder than you realize. While his operatives work with Kuomintang members in the streets, secretly Zhu De's emissaries are meeting with the warlords, telling them that they will fare much better when both Yuan Shikai and you are gone. Rumors suggest that Zhu De already has met personally with key warlords and that they are in agreement with his intentions to dissolve the government."

"And how do they plan to dissolve the government?"

"By withdrawing from both the Kuomintang and the

government simultaneously. Then they will align themselves with the warlords."

Sun Yat-sen appeared somewhat concerned. "Zhu De and the Communists cannot possibly benefit from an alliance with the warlords. The warlords are more ruthless than Zhu De imagines. Too much so, to come within his control. They are only feigning agreement until the government collapses. Then the warlords will seize control of as much of the country as they like."

"Perhaps," Wei conceded. "But the true aim of the Communists seems to be the instigation of a new revolution rather than obtaining control of the existing government."

"And what do you suggest we should do?"

"You must expose them," Wei insisted. "If you expose them, it will bring this effort to an end."

"No. That might work, but I think a better course is to adopt their strategy."

A frown wrinkled Wei Binglin's brow. "What do you mean?"

"We will collapse the government ourselves, before they can bring it to pass."

"But how?"

"We will withdraw from the government before the Communists have accomplished their goal. Then we will call for a new revolution. A democratic revolution led by the people."

A week later, Sun Yat-sen did as he had discussed with Wei Binglin and convened the Kuomintang Party. After restating the current situation, he outlined the many failings of Yuan's leadership and called for dissolution of the government. "We must instigate a new revolution. One led by the people, for the people." He did not mention the Communist plot to bring him down.

Kuomintang Party members voiced their full support for Sun Yat-sen and his strategy. Two days later, leaders of the southern provinces did as well, and the Kuomintang Party formally withdrew from the agreement that had brought General Yuan Shikai to power. With their support no longer available, and with the southern provinces announcing their allegiance to the Kuomintang, the Chinese government in Beijing appeared to be on the verge of collapse.

Rather than simply accepting the outcome, dissolving the government, and withdrawing to private life, Yuan reverted to his authoritarian nature, finally revealing his true self. He dismissed parliament, published an edict assigning legislative power to himself, and issued orders to mobilize the national army. To his great dismay, however, only a few units of the army responded. The remainder refused to follow his orders and either remained in their barracks or sought a rapprochement with the Kuomintang.

With the army refusing to resolve the matter in favor of the central government, the country fell into chaos. Warlords, an obstacle to Chinese national unification since ancient times, emerged once again, reasserting control over large areas, particularly in the rural provinces.

In the midst of that, Yuan Shikai died, taking with him all hope of a quick resolution to the political impasse. Facing a long and bitter civil struggle, the country fractured with several of the provinces declaring their separate independence. Warlords also expanded their control, and over the next several months regional governments emerged. These were well-intentioned entities but governmental services were nonexistent and they were all but impotent to regain control of society. Food shortages were rampant and crime began to rise. All of which lent a sense of urgency to the street protests that had continued unabated.

Zhu De and the Communists who remained in the Kuomintang Party used the unrest to convince the party that Sun Yat-sen could not properly resolve issues with the warlords. Repeatedly, Zhu portrayed Sun as a weak leader, unable to unite the country or save it from total collapse. Even some of Sun Yat-sen's most ardent supporters became convinced of his ineptitude and forced him to resign his position as leader of the Kuomintang Party.

With Sun Yat-sen no longer a party participant, Zhu De and the Communists took control of key Kuomintang leadership positions. Communists in every province won appointments to influential party positions and began squeezing out Kuomintang regulars, bringing Zhu De's original strategy—of transforming the party from within—to the brink of fulfillment.

CHAPTER

৩০ 9 ৩০

THROUGHOUT THE PERIOD of unrest I continued to attend school at the missionary compound. Each day after class was dismissed I walked home with Mother or visited Uncle Yutang. Formal education at school prepared me for the pursuit of further academic advancement. The things I learned from Uncle Yutang and the men who visited him at his house provided the context of understanding I would need in my advanced academic education.

By then I had been promoted through the lower grades and was a student in high school. It, too, was operated by the Lutheran missionaries from the compound at Yiyang. Older students, however, were separated with one school facility for girls and another for boys. We saw the girls at times throughout the day, mostly on the schoolyard at noon, but did not attend class with them.

Because I read at a level above my grade, I often met with students from the upper-level classes and joined their discussions regarding the subjects they were studying. Through that interaction I became friends with several older students. Among them one of my closest friends was Hu Yi, who was a year older and in the next class above me. He and his family lived in the same neighborhood as Mother and me. We knew the extended family well but I did not come to know Hu Yi as a friend until I entered high school. As we became friends we sometimes walked home together in the afternoons, extending our conversation of the day through that extra time together.

Hu Yi had a younger sister named Hu Gin-lien. One day after school, Hu Gin-lien joined us as we walked home. Until then she had been just another girl in the neighborhood, but that afternoon I was struck by her beauty and as we talked on the way home I was even more impressed by her intelligence. Very quickly I found myself attracted to her in a way I had not known before. My route home kept us together only part of the way, then we separated as I turned up a different street, but all the way home and throughout the evening thoughts of Hu Gin-lien occupied my mind and distracted my attention from my studies. Those same thoughts kept me awake that night until very late.

A few days later, I walked down to Hu Yi's house, ostensibly to visit with him as a friend and to discuss a topic related to school, but in reality I also went to see Gin-lien. Upon my arrival I visited with Hu Yi a short while but soon was drawn into conversation with Gin-lien. Before long we were immersed in a discussion that captivated my attention and I lost all track of time. I did nothing to hide the fact that I was attracted to her. Thankfully, she seemed attracted to me and reciprocated my attention.

Hu Yi noticed the interaction between his sister and me and was amused by it. Their mother, however, did not share Hu Yi's view and in the days that followed I noticed that when I was at their house their mother became tense and irritable toward me.

One day at school I asked Hu Yi about his mother and her attitude toward me. "It is not you," he explained. "It's Hu Gin-lien."

His response caught me by surprise, as I was certain Gin-lien had reciprocated my interest and was not upset with me. The thought that I might have misunderstood her response to me left me troubled but I pushed that emotion aside and asked, "What do you mean?"

"Hu Gin-lien is not well," he explained.

The worry I'd felt before evaporated, instantly replaced by concern. "You mean she is sick?"

"Yes. Very much so."

"But how? She looks fine to me."

Hu Yi glanced down at the floor, and spoke in a somber tone, "We think she has tuberculosis."

Tuberculosis was an infectious disease of the lungs—that much I knew. The details of how the disease might affect someone were another matter. I knew very little about that, but I did not care, either. Not really. If Gin-lien had tuberculosis, then she already was infected with it by the time we began seeing each other and there was nothing I could do about it. I wasn't going to let that stop me from seeing her.

Still, I wanted to know as much about her condition as possible. So I continued, "You think she has it?"

"Yes."

"You do not know for sure?"

"No."

Then I understood what he meant. "She has not been seen by a doctor."

Hu Yi shook his head. "No, we have not taken her to a doctor."

"Why has she not seen a doctor?"

"Our parents fear the stigma of a diagnosis more than the actual disease itself."

The absurdity of avoiding the truth was difficult for me to understand. Father had instilled in me the determination to always face the truth. "It is the only way," he used to tell me. I felt my forehead wrinkle in a frown as I said, "I don't understand."

"They worry that the doctors will diagnose her with tuberculosis," Hu Yi explained. "And then they will take her away from us."

Their concern was understandable and their suspicions of the medical response were not unwarranted. At that time in China, effective treatment for tuberculosis was nonexistent and standard practice mandated the quarantine of those with active cases. We had heard of many who were diagnosed with the disease and forced into sanatoriums. Rather than being offered help, they were forced to exist under deplorable conditions, in places that were little more than prisons where the sick were forced to remain until they died. I knew of no one who had entered a facility like that with active tuberculosis and later returned well and whole.

Not only that, the illness posed a serious health risk to those who were continually exposed to an infected person. Gin-lien's family, and to some extent those of us who attended school with her, were made vulnerable to the disease by her presence, but I was not overly concerned for my own health. Others, it seemed, were not as confident as I about the matter.

Over the next several months, my motivation for visiting the Hu household became unavoidably obvious. I went there to see Hu Gin-lien, not Hu Yi. As the days passed, she and I spent more and more time together in the afternoons after school. And although the school structure separated us by gender, we shared many of the same subjects in our classwork, which afforded us ample reason to study together each day. Most afternoons we sat together at the table in Hu Gin-lien's front room, doing homework, always under the watchful but disapproving eye of Hu Gin-lien's mother.

By then I had observed Gin-lien closely and could see her condition was obvious and serious, but I paid that little regard. I was enamored of her and she was likewise of me. That was all I cared about and we continued to grow closer to each other in our relationship, once in a while slipping away for a moment alone.

∽⟳∽ ⟳∽

A few months later I went to Uncle Yutang's house to talk with him, which I did often when I was not with Gin-lien. Several men were already there when I arrived and I took my usual place in the corner, busying myself with study while they talked. When they were finished and the men had gone, Uncle Yutang came to where I was seated. "I understand you are interested in Hu Gin-lien." A forced smile turned up the corners of his mouth and as he spoke I noticed a hint of tension in his voice.

"You are acquainted with her?"

He nodded. "I have known Gin-lien all of her life. She is a nice girl."

"Yes, she is," I agreed. My cheeks grew warm as I spoke. I was confident in my feelings for Gin-lien but revealing them to Uncle Yutang made me uncomfortable. From the look in his eyes I could see that he shared my lack of comfort with the topic.

Uncle Yutang brought a chair and placed it near my stool, then took a seat beside me. I knew what he was going to say but kept quiet and let him talk.

"You are aware of her condition?"

"Yes, but I find my attraction to her unavoidable and I am certain she feels the same toward me."

"I am sure that is true," he agreed. "Everyone can see how you relate to each other when you are together."

"Everyone?"

"Others have noticed."

Such was the way of life in our community. Everyone knew most of the details of everyone's life. Very little was hidden from view. "Her mother does not like us being together."

"No, she does not. But it is not about you. It is about Gin-lien's condition and about Gin-lien's relationship with you. That is what makes her mother uncomfortable with you. She knows that if you and Gin-lien continue to see each other, you two will only grow even closer than you already are. Your relationship will only intensify."

"Why is that a problem?" There was a hint of irritation in my voice and I recognized it as the note of impatience adults often sense in teenagers. When I spoke that way to Mother she usually responded to me as a disciplinarian responds to a child. Uncle Yutang and I did not have that kind of relationship so I was curious about what his response might be.

Again, the strained smile returned to his face and he looked uncomfortable. "Hu Gin-lien. . . cannot be. . . the wife you want. She will not be able to. . . perform as a man expects a woman to perform." He glanced at me with a nervous look. "You understand?"

"I think so." I knew all too well what he was saying.

"The wife she *would* be would require much from you. You would be tested as her companion because of her condition."

Yutang was doing his best to be a supportive uncle while avoiding a heavy-handed delivery of what I knew were really Mother's concerns, so I listened with that in mind. He and I talked awhile longer, then we were interrupted by the arrival of other men and our conversation came to an end.

Later that evening when I arrived at home, Mother was waiting to talk to me. "Did Yutang speak with you?" she asked.

"We spoke about many things." I knew what she meant but wished to avoid discussing the topic with her. She was not deterred.

"Did he talk to you about Hu Gin-lien?"

"Why is everyone so concerned about that?"

"I have talked to Hu Gin-lien at school." Mother was surprisingly calm at my response. "And I have talked with her parents," she continued. "They are convinced Hu Gin-lien has tuberculosis. I am also."

I nodded. "I am certain she does."

"The school has considered asking her not to attend classes."

This alarmed me. "They would do that?"

"I do not know. Karl Torvik thinks many of the students would test positive."

"If they tested," I added dourly.

"Yes." Mother nodded slowly. "And I think sending the students home would be contrary to the missionary purpose." Mother fell silent for a moment and I tried to look busy to forestall further conversation, but after a time she continued, "Gin-lien will have a challenging future and if you are with her, the future will be challenging for you, too."

"I am not afraid of a challenge," I responded bravely.

Mother lowered her voice. "Feng Shan," she said with genuine concern, "life with her would be challenging for you and then it will end very badly."

She meant, of course, that it would end with Gin-lien's death but that did not seem like a determinative thing to me. "Mother," I replied as kindly as she had spoken to me, "everyone dies."

"Yes, but they do not all die so young."

For adults, the death of a child is a terrible thing, but for the young the thought of something that might occur in the future is offset by the glory of the moment at hand. I was a young man. The current moment, with Gin-lien at the center of my world, was most glorious indeed. I had no concern for the kind of future that might lie before us. Only that we should experience it together.

Mother was determined to change my mind and, I think, must have urged Torvik to address the matter with me because not long after she confronted me, Torvik called me aside to the bench by the stand of bamboo. After explaining Gin-lien's condition he noted, "You do realize there is no cure, don't you?"

"I am aware of that."

"With repeated exposure," he added, "you might contract the disease from her."

"I'm not worried about me. None of her family has taken the disease and they have been with her for many years."

"None of Gin-lien's family members have been tested for it, either." That was a fair point, one to which I did not have an adequate response and so I simply kept quiet. In a moment he added, "She might not be able to bear children."

"I understand," I replied. All of the adults who had spoken to me about her had mentioned this, one way or the other.

"And if she does become pregnant," Torvik continued, "the pregnancy might hasten her demise."

"We have not gotten that far," I said as only a teenager could.

Torvik was a good man and determined to fully explore the issue with me. None of my responses deterred him from that purpose. "Everyone can see how much you care for each other already," he said. "Relationships have a way of developing. One can see the progression of things between you and where it is headed. The effect her condition will have on your future is not something you will be able to avoid."

Torvik was an important person in my life and I liked him very much. Mother liked him, too, though they were not romantically involved, at least not in a physical way, so I listened politely to his comments and suggestions, but I was not persuaded to change my mind or my plans regarding Gin-lien.

❦

In spite of the attempts to separate us, Gin-lien and I continued to see each other and during the last year of high school we were engaged to be married. Shortly after we announced our engagement, Gin-lien became very ill. Her condition was so serious that her family had no choice but to confront the reality of her illness and take her to a hospital in Changsha.

As we all expected, doctors at the hospital diagnosed her with tuberculosis. To my surprise, they did not consign her to a special facility but instead placed her in a special ward of the hospital where visitation was strictly controlled and measures were taken to limit the exposure of others to her and the patients who shared that space.

Gin-lien's condition was tragic for her and for her family. It was tragic for me, too, and I worried she might not survive. However, after a few weeks in the hospital her condition improved. Doctors were amazed by her improvement and I thought perhaps it was a sign that she and I were supposed to be together, that perhaps our future would be better than others tried to persuade us to believe.

Gin-lien returned to Yiyang before the academic year ended, but officials at the missionary school would not permit her to attend classes with her fellow students. They did, however, allow her to continue her education at home. We worked diligently together to catch up her course work in order to allow her to graduate with her class, a task she accomplished admirably.

During our senior year in high school, Li Du returned to the school and began attending classes with us. Many were curious about where he had been and why he had disappeared so mysteriously, but when we asked he gave only circumspect answers.

When I saw Li Du for the first time and realized he had returned for the year, and not merely a visit, I assumed we would resume our friendship as before, but Li Du was distant and dismissive. He was as smart as ever, but his personality was different. Equally as confident as before but in a somewhat more abrasive and arrogant manner. I didn't know why he behaved this way but at the time I was preoccupied with Gin-lien and her condition. Consequently, I let the situation with Li Du pass without further attention.

CHAPTER

ᥫᨀ 10 ᨀᥫ

AFTER HIGH SCHOOL, Torvik presented me with an offer of financial support from the missionaries at the compound in Yiyang would allow me to continue my education at the university level. After reviewing all possibilities I decided to enroll at the Yali College, a relatively new college in Changsha.

The Yali College was the work of an organization known as Yale-in-China, which had been founded in 1901 as an American protestant missionary society by faculty and alumni of Yale University. It was the product of a Christian revival that occurred on college campuses in the United States near the end of the nineteenth century. The name Yali was a transliteration of Yale in Chinese.

China had been chosen as the region for the school because the founders wanted to honor a fellow Yale student who had died during the Boxer Rebellion. They chose Changsha after consulting with other missionaries who told them of our area's excellent academic culture.

The school was intended to prepare Chinese students for Christian ministry but before the first year of operation was concluded the focus had shifted notably toward academics. Edward Hume and Brownell Gage were its principle academics.

After high school, Li Du attended a university in Beijing, but Bo Zhongfa joined me as a student at Yali College. We took class together and one day we found ourselves seated next to each other. When class finished we had a few minutes to spend and he turned our conversation to the time when we were younger. "We were close, then you became friends with Li Du and seemed to pull away. What happened?"

The question was one I expected him to ask. It did not catch me totally unprepared. Still, it presented an awkward moment. "Everyone . . ." I hesitated, "said things. . . about your family."

"You mean about my father."

"Yes," I said, relieved by his openness. "They said your father was a Communist."

"And this is why you withdrew from me?"

"My uncle gave an ambiguous answer but—"

"Li Du was adamant," he said, finishing my thought.

"Yes." A sense of shame came over me for the way I had treated him. "I did not—"

"No," he said, cutting me off. "It is perfectly understandable.

You heard things about him. Someone raised questions. You went searching for answers. And the things you learned did not resolve your dilemma. And so you drew back from me out of a concern for your safety."

"I should have been a friend to you," I replied.

"Well," Bo sighed. "They were correct. My father *was* a Communist."

"He really was?"

"Yes." Bo smiled at me. "But that was him. Not me."

"When I listened to the things you talked about at school, I heard many ideas that would have been consistent with Communism."

"He was my father," Bo added with a sense of irony. "What else was I going to talk about except the things I heard from others? Just as you and everyone else did. We were young. We didn't know any of that on our own."

"This is true," I chuckled.

"Back then," Bo continued, "I repeated much of what my father said, but as I grew older I developed my own ideas."

"You are not a Communist now?"

"No." Bo shook his head with authority.

"And your father?"

Instantly a somber expression came over him. "My father is dead," he said quietly.

Once again, a sense of shame swept over me. Not only had I failed to be his friend when we were in school, I had failed to keep up with him afterward and, as a result, I was not there for him when he lost his father. I knew what it was like to lose a father to death. That experience would have been a help to him and I could have given him that benefit, if only I had remained his friend. "I am sorry," I replied. "What happened to him?"

"He was killed in an uprising at Kunming."

We talked awhile longer as Bo unraveled the details of his father's move from our neighborhood. The frantic trek that followed as he sought safety among friends, then hid in the mountains with others from the province, and finally the terrible end he'd met in Kunming. I knew that his father had disappeared; now I knew what happened to him.

Later that evening, I went to Gin-lien's house and told her about Bo Zhongfa, his father, and the conversation we had earlier in the day. "And you believed him?" she asked when I finished telling her the details.

A puzzled look came over me. "Why wouldn't I believe him?"

"Well, he certainly has no reason to tell you the truth."

"He has no reason to lie, either." Bo Zhongfa was a bit difficult to handle but he was not given to lying merely for amusement.

"You do not know that," she insisted.

No, it was true. I didn't know whether he had a reason to lie to me. But neither did she.

"When we were in high school," Gin-lien continued, "Bo came here to my house."

I felt an eyebrow arch in an expression of the concern I felt.

"Why did he do that?"

Gin-lien had a playful smile, which she quickly suppressed. "He came to talk about schoolwork," she said slowly, "but when we were alone he expressed a romantic interest in me."

A sense of anger rose up inside me. "Did he harm you?"

She shook her head. "It was not like that. But when we talked he said things to me about you."

"Such as?"

"He did not think you were ambitious enough to properly care for me. And he didn't think you were smart enough to succeed in life."

I laughed out loud. "Bo Zhongfa talking about who's smart and who is not?"

"He thought that you and I would never be intellectually compatible."

"And—"

"And," she interrupted. "That is why I say I don't trust what he says."

Obviously, Bo Zhongfa had been willing to say whatever he thought he needed to say in order to obtain the result he wanted. But I was curious about something else, too. "What did you tell him in response?"

"It does not matter what I told him." She had a coy smile. "I am with you, aren't I?" She moved closer and put her arms around my neck. "I have always been with you," she added, then leaned forward and gave me a kiss.

In 1921, Sun Yat-sen returned and regained control of the Kuomintang Party. From his newly recovered seat of power, the party established a government in the southern part of China with a capital at Guangzhou, Guangdong Province, and a reach that brought stability to the surrounding region. However, four years later, before he'd taken control of the entire country, Sun Yat-sen died from a sudden illness. In his place, Chiang Kai-shek, one of the most important party operatives, became leader of the Kuomintang Party.

Under Chiang Kai-shek, the Kuomintang purged the Communists from the Guangdong Provincial Party and suppressed the left wing of the party. After that, Chiang launched a Northern Campaign, something Sun Yat-sen had put off repeatedly. By that effort Chiang sought to expand Kuomintang control over the warlords, defeat the remaining elements of Yuan Shikai's imperial army, and complete the reunification of the country.

With the Northern Campaign underway, Uncle Yutang found his party enthusiasm renewed. The collapse of the agreement with Yuan and the chaos that followed had left Yutang less enamored of politics than before, but Chiang Kai-shek's emergence as party leader and his decision to confront the Communists reinvigorated Uncle Yutang's sense of purpose. As Kuomintang forces neared Hunan Province, he joined their ranks.

In spite of Chiang Kai-shek and the Kuomintang's success in the south, and despite their ability to neutralize many of the warlords, Hunan Province remained a Communist stronghold. Attempts to eliminate them by less than complete warfare proved unsuccessful and necessitated the application of a full military assault, which was brought against the Communists' fortified positions.

A struggle ensued between the two sides, both on the battlefield in a fight for territory and in the schools and neighborhoods in a battle for the hearts and minds of the people. Not unsurprisingly, Yali College came under attack.

As had happened earlier at the missionary school in Yiyang, Communist leaders came to the college campus and accused the faculty of being imperialist tools. I was not present during the questioning but one of my fellow students listened from the hall as the Communists confronted Professor Hume and Professor Gage. "You teach your students capitalist ideas," they said.

"We teach many ideas," Gage replied. "But we do not teach them to prefer one over the other."

"And those ideas involve the rhetoric of American college students."

The statement made no sense to anyone in the room, probably not even to the person who made it, but Gage did his best to respond. "We are obviously American. And America was founded on principles that give place for a certain economic system, but we are not here to promote one view over the other. Merely the pursuit of truth."

Apparently the confrontation lasted quite some time, but

eventually the Communists departed. The next day I went to find Uncle Yutang and reported the event to him. He was not at his home but on the opposite side of the city with a unit of the Kuomintang army. When I told him what had transpired at school he said, "It does not surprise me. The Communists are violently opposed to Western culture and its values."

"But we are not being taught that. At least, not exclusively."

Uncle Yutang steered me away from the others, and lowered his voice, "Listen, I am not unsympathetic to your study, but some in the Kuomintang Party are suspicious of Americans who work in our country."

"But why? They only seek to teach us about academic subjects."

"Yes, but some of what they have heard sounds like the former imperialist agenda."

"To the Kuomintang?"

"Not to everyone," he replied, "but to some of them. We must be careful when we talk not to reflect the old ways. Not now. Perhaps later we can talk more freely, but not now."

The things Uncle Yutang told me that day left me troubled and suspicious of many things, but I knew then what Gin-lien must have felt that day when I told her about my conversation with Bo Zhongfa. Everyone seemed to be on edge and now I joined them in that sentiment.

While attending Yali College, I took a position teaching middle school English. That experience gave me confidence in the field and shortly afterward I established my own middle school.

With a good job and adequate income to provide for our living, Gin-lien and I married. By then she was obviously ill, as her health oscillated between recurring bouts with tuberculosis. But we went through with the wedding anyway.

After we were married, Gin-lien and I rented a house in Changsha and made our home there. The new environment and the stability of our relationship seemed to improve Gin-lein's condition and life seemed to move in a good direction.

A few months later, we learned that Gin-lien was pregnant. We were elated at the prospects of having our own child and starting a family, but the implications for Gin-lien's health were always on our minds. She progressed through the initial months without complications from either condition—the pregnancy or the tuberculosis—and we thought perhaps the doctors were mistaken about the effects of pregnancy on her body. We also wondered if pregnancy had somehow changed her bodily functions to give them new properties against the tuberculosis, but we knew very little about human biology and were only guessing— and hoping.

As the time for Gin-lien's delivery drew near, Mother moved in with us. She did not like living at home alone in Yiyang and we needed help in caring for the new baby. However, only a few weeks later, Mother died. Her passing was stressful for me. I arranged her funeral with the help of Uncle Yutang and invited Torvik to conduct the service. It was a mixture of traditional Chinese observances and Christian liturgy, which some of our family members found to be odd. I knew what they meant to Gin-lien and me, and I knew how Mother would have felt about them, which was all that was important. The others could learn from the experience, but it was a matter for them to decide. No one tried to dissuade me from the plan for the service.

Together with my marriage to Gin-lien, Mother's death marked a season of change from the life of my past to the life of my future. With the present emerging before me, I became quite philosophical about our situation and found quotations from Confucius springing to mind at every moment right alongside quotations from the Bible: The quotes from Confucius that Father had insisted I memorize. The ones from the Bible that Torvik had instructed me to learn.

Later that year, Gin-lien gave birth to a healthy baby boy. He was big and strong right from the beginning. We called him Monto, a name that was prevalent in Mother's family. I felt that she would have thought it an honor that we chose that name.

⁓⌀⌀⁓

In the fall of my senior year at Yali College I was elected president of the student body. New students enrolled that year, students who were not from Hunan Province. I suspected something might be amiss with their presence and by winter it had become clear that I was correct in my assessment. They were Communists and they were not silent about their beliefs.

Later we learned that they had enrolled at Yali College for the specific purpose of disrupting classes. They worked through the fall organizing students and winning them to their cause. In the spring, they began openly agitating for their position. Groups of them gathered at strategic locations on campus and held public rallies. Once they had attracted a crowd, they upped the level of their rhetoric and called for a shutdown of the school. "If the leadership will not follow the peoples' mandate, the people will rise up and stop them themselves," they shouted.

Professor Hume was head of the college that year and, as president of the student body, I approached him about the need for an official response to the Communists. "If we do not speak against them," I said, "others will think we are weak or that we agree with their position."

Hume disagreed. "If we speak against them, we give their position a dignity it does not deserve. Let them have their say and then they will go away. This will pass."

Having seen these kinds of situations through my uncle and his associates, I was convinced the trouble with the Communists would not simply go away. Ignoring them seemed the worst possible response, and so I did my best to resist their attacks and accusations. With the help of my fellow students who were loyal to the Kuomintang perspective, we organized seminars that offered a reasoned consideration of the Communist tenets. That effort was well attended but had little effect on many of the students' enthusiasm for the Communist cause.

To be fair, economic conditions in the country were deplorable, perhaps even nonexistent. Poverty and disease were rampant and neither the quasi-imperial government of Yuan Shikai nor the well-intentioned efforts of the Kuomintang had done anything to alleviate those conditions. The Communists offered a third alternative. One that, unlike the imperialist or democratic approach, suggested that ordinary citizens—working people who suffered the most—could solve their own problems if they simply realized they had the power within them to do so. It was a winsome message. I did not accept it, but I recognized the merits of its appeal.

Near the middle of the spring term, a strong group of Yali College students was on the verge of going on strike. Most of them were avowed Communists, though some were merely disruptive and searching for a cause. Their intent was to bring all college activities to a halt except for their own.

Seeing the dire circumstances we faced, Professor Hume finally came to my aid and together we renewed our efforts to convince the students that striking was a bad decision. The students, however, refused to listen to our views and were not persuaded by our opinions. A few days after our last meeting with them, many walked out of class and refused to attend.

Not all of the students at the school were members of the Communist student organization, but many who had originally voiced opposition to the protests refused to ignore those who walked out. These additional students were merely sympathetic to their fellow classmates. They joined the Communists in refusing to attend class.

With the number of students attending classes reduced to only a handful, Yali College struggled to maintain its academic integrity. Faculty and staff did not desert those of us who did attend, but by the end of that academic term it was obvious to all that the school faced difficult financial decisions regarding the future. I and others who completed the required course work graduated at the end of the spring term. By the end of 1927, though, educational activities at the school came to an end and it was forced to close.

CHAPTER

ᥦ 44 ᥭ

AFTER GRADUATING from Yali College, I took a position at Nan Hua University in Changsha, but with Communist-inspired unrest becoming more widespread, teaching proved difficult and very soon impossible to accomplish. Frustrated in that regard, I turned my attention to promoting the interests of the Kuomintang Party. I had an office at the school and a female assistant named Peng Daosheng, who also worked with three other teachers. She was quite intelligent and also a Kuomintang member. We worked together organizing party meetings and rallies in an attempt to counter the efforts of the Communists, both those who were inside the party and those working outside its structure.

Before the end of my first year on the Nan Hua faculty, I was named the Kuomintang Party's regional leader for the city of Changsha. Communists, still working within the party and bitterly angry over Chiang Kai-shek's rise to power, opposed our efforts to promote a democratic form of government and began working behind the scenes to oust me. Eventually they accomplished that goal by deceptively placing their members in key party positions. I realized too late what they were doing. Using those key officials, the Communist faction took control of the Kuomintang Party apparatus in Hunan and moved me out.

Once in power, Communist operatives instigated a series of purges to remove the remaining members who supported democratic ideals. Their efforts were not limited merely to those in leadership positions but encompassed the lower ranks as well.

Those party members who were viewed as favoring the traditional Kuomintang Party doctrine were labeled capitalist imperialist traitors—a clever moniker, actually, and one that served several purposes: On the one hand, it aroused common sentiment—particularly prevalent among the working class—against the former Qing dynasty and the yet lingering notion of its reinstatement. At the same time, it reminded the intelligentsia that the primary proponents of capitalism—the United Kingdom and the United States—wished to extend their influence to us in a colonial manner. And it suggested that the people being accused of suspicious activity were in collusion with those outside forces. Quite a lot to accomplish with only three words, yet it did so very effectively.

The Communist effort was led by Chen Biwu, an activist from Hunan province who had been educated in Paris and trained in Moscow where he learned the Soviet version of Communism. Intelligent and decisive, he moved the party quickly toward his goal of dominating the provincial government, then extending his control to neighboring regions. His method of doing that grew increasingly intense and increasingly brutal.

During one of the purges, a public meeting was held at a location near the Liuyang River on the east side of the city. The meeting attracted much attention and an unruly crowd assembled, filling the entire space. Chen Biwu was present and spoke to the gathering from the bed of a large truck that had been parked there for use as a speaker's platform. At first, Chen Biwu spoke calmly of events that had recently transpired. As he continued, however, his rhetoric became more forceful and shifted from facts to Communist interpretation. Before long, those gathered to listen were in a state of frenzied agitation with many calling for mass riots and other acts of vandalism.

At the height of his presentation, someone handed a chair up to Chen Biwu, which he placed in the center of the truckbed. "We have among us one of the capitalist imperialist traitors," he said in a dire tone. "I want you to see what he looks like."

As the crowd watched, Cai Liting, a faithful Kuomintang Party member who was loyal to Chiang, was dragged to the back of the truck. His hands were bound behind his back, his feet were tied together. The men who held him hoisted him onto the truck bed and dropped him beside Chen Biwu. He landed with a thud and the crowd cheered wildly.

Chen Biwu kicked Liting with his foot and shouted, "This is what a traitor looks like!" He kicked Liting again, then nodded to the men who had brought him there. The men climbed aboard the truck, lifted Liting to the chair, then bound him in place with a rope.

"But don't take my word," Chen Biwu continued. "We have witnesses."

A young woman appeared from the crowd, and the men standing near the truck helped her up to Chen Biwu's side. "The capitalist imperialist traitor before you today is Cai Liting," she shouted to the crowd. "And standing here next to me is his daughter, Cai Danyan. She will tell you who her father really is."

For the next twenty minutes, Cai Danyan shouted to the audience about things she contended her father had done that were against the interests of the people. None of them were specific and I spoke to no one who was at the meeting who could remember a single specific charge against him.

When Cai Danyan concluded her remarks, Chen Biwu spoke up. "Today we must decide. You must decide. Will we tolerate traitors among us? Or will we rid them from the earth and from our lives?"

Someone in front began to shout, "Cai must die! Cai must die!" I suspect that person was a plant, placed there for the very purpose of leading the crowd in repeating those words, which they did. Before long, the audience became a mob, shouting over and over at the top of their voices, "Cai must die!"

Chen Biwu allowed the mob to chant the slogan for a few moments and smiled as he listened to the sound of it reverberating through the neighborhood where they were gathered. After a time, he raised his hands to calm them, and the mob grew quiet. "You have spoken today. The *people* have spoken today! Cai must die!"

The crowd began to chant once more, this time at deafening levels. As they chanted, Chen Biwu drew a pistol from the waistband of his trousers, placed the end of the barrel against Cai Liting's head, and pulled the trigger.

At the report of the gunshot, bone, blood, and brain matter sprayed from the side of Cai Liting's head where the gun had been placed. The crowd gave a collective gasp, then instantly fell silent. Seeing her father now dead, Cai Danyan clasped her hands over her mouth and screamed. Two men took her by the arms, moved her to the end of the truck bed, and lowered her to the ground. Others standing there took hold of her and hustled her away.

Cai Liting's body was slumped forward in the chair, his weight pressed against the rope that bound him to the chair. Chen Biwu took hold of Cai Liting's hair and lifted his head rudely. "The traitor is gone!" he shouted, but the crowd remained silent.

As the threat of more executions loomed, Colonel Xu Ke-xiang, one of Chiang Kai-shek's most trusted military officers, led Kuomintang troops into Hunan and took charge of Changsha. Uncle Yutang was assigned as an adviser to Colonel Xu and came with the troops when they arrived.

With the province under military control, Chiang Kai-shek installed Ho Chien as governor. At Governor Ho's direction, Colonel Xu and Kuomintang troops arrested most of the Communists operating in Hunan—those from the Kuomintang Party and otherwise. Uncle Yutang coordinated those arrests and supervised the detention of key Communist leaders. Chen Biwu was the key person sought by everyone, but in spite of the government's best effort he escaped and authorities were unable to locate him.

With order restored, Kuomintang Party members were installed in key positions in the provincial government. Yutang received an appointment to the governor's civilian staff.

In the days that followed, rumors circulated that Chen Biwu was alive and well and reorganizing the Communists. Communists remained in Hunan Province, even after Colonel Xu restored public order—not all were arrested—but several weeks went by and no one had reported actually seeing Chen Biwu. Life remained unsettled, but with no confirmed reports about him I began to doubt the rumors of Chen Biwu having escaped. I convinced myself he had either been arrested or killed.

My assistant was not so confident. "No one has reported finding Chen Biwu's body," Daosheng said, reminding me of the things

I'd already noted. "And there has been no indication that he was arrested."

Not long after that, Peng arrived at the office and instead of beginning her work as usual she took me aside to a private room. "My brother has heard rumors that Chen Biwu is indeed alive."

"Everyone has heard that rumor."

"But my brother has heard that Chen Biwu is telling some of the Communists that you were responsible for the arrests Colonel Xu was able to make."

"I had nothing to do with that."

"Yes. I know."

"Why would they think I did?"

"They think that because you and Governor Ho have the same family name you are related."

"They think I am informing on them and having them arrested?"

"Yes."

"And they think I am using the government to purge them for political reasons."

"Exactly. They are waiting for a chance to move you out."

"What will they accuse me of?"

Daosheng had a grave expression. "I don't think they mean to merely accuse you."

At that moment, I understood the threat by the Communists was not to humiliate me, or imprison me, or publicly disgrace me. They intended to find me wherever I might be and murder me.

Whether Chen Biwu was alive or not, the rumor Daosheng reported to me was not a rumor. It was a message and I was immediately suspicious, first of her and then of her brother. But as I thought about it I realized that Daosheng was not a Communist. I knew her, had worked with her, and had seen her in the presence of others. She was not a communist. Her brother, however, was another matter and I worried not for myself but for my family. But I was resolved to continue the work and not allow the Communists to intimidate me with fear.

Not long after that, Bo Zhongfa came to our house in Changsha. He arrived at night and had a worried look. "I came to tell you there is a plot by the Communists to seize you."

"To seize me?" It all sounded preposterous. "And how do they propose to do this?"

"They know that you walk to the corner each morning to take the trolley and you return that same way in the evening. They plan to grab you there, along the way."

"And they would do this, even though they think I am related to the governor?"

Bo looked surprised. "How do you know they think that?"

"I hear rumors."

"It's true," he said. "They do think you are related to the governor, but they plan to be gone from Hunan by the time your body is found and thus out of the governor's reach."

"And how do you know this?"

Bo had a coy smile. "I hear rumors, too."

Gin-lien and I were unsettled by the news from Bo, as it confirmed what we'd already heard from Peng Daosheng—that the Communists intended to capture and kill me. I was troubled by the substance of the warnings but also from the fact that Bo was the one who delivered this latest news. The plan Bo outlined seemed crude and not very clever—grab me as I travel to the office or as I return home in the evening. Many people would be present at both of those times. They would see such a thing and might even intervene in an attempt to free me. That reinforced my suspicions of Bo.

Gin-lien, however, did not share my suspicious view of Bo Zhongfa. She believed him and was worried. When Bo was gone she looked over at me. "You must leave Hunan and stay away until things calm down."

I immediately dismissed the idea. "I am not leaving without you and Monto."

"I am too ill to travel and Monto is too young. We will be safe here. I have my brothers for protection. You have no one except your uncle, and he is busy. Fleeing to him would only make matters worse. You are brilliant and have a great future before you. I am sick and we both know I will die."

"No," I snapped, cutting her off. "We will not speak of death. Only of life. And we will speak of it together, as a family."

That night I sat alone in the front room and prayed.

In spite of the warning from Peng Daosheng and Bo Zhongfa, nothing more occurred immediately and the mood in the province seemed to grow calmer. As the days passed I once again tried to convince myself that there was no real threat to my life, but I remained conflicted on the matter and worried about Gin-lien and Monto. Then, a few weeks after Bo's visit, Peng Daosheng failed to report for work at the office, as was her normal routine. When she still had not arrived by afternoon, I contacted school authorities and someone was sent to her home. Daosheng was not there but a neighbor reported seeing her with two men late in the previous afternoon. One of those men proved to be her brother.

Under questioning, the brother admitted that he had been with Peng, but that they had visited a café with a friend. He left early and she had remained with the friend. "She was fine the last time I saw her," he reported.

Someone visited the friend's home and found it was empty. A woman who lived nearby said the friend moved out quickly. "He was there in the morning and gone by nightfall."

The next morning, the crew of a fishing vessel spotted a body floating in the Xiang River. When the body was pulled from the water it was identified as that of Peng Daosheng.

An initial examination revealed that she had been strangled. Witnesses came forward and accused Chen Biwu of killing her, but others claimed to have seen him in person. Still others who had not known him previously identified him from a photograph that purported to be a depiction of him.

Once again, suspicions rose up inside me and I wondered if it wasn't all part of a cruel and vicious plot by the Communists. A plot to remove me and intimidate the people by stoking rumors of Chen Biwu. It seemed like something they would concoct, as I already knew from my previous experience that they possessed very little imagination.

As I walked home that day, after Daosheng's body had been found, I debated with myself about whether to tell Gin-lien what had happened. When I arrived, I found that was no longer an issue. Gin-lien already had heard the news and was busy packing a suitcase.

"What is this?" I asked.

"This is for you," she said. "You must leave at once."

"No, we must wait to see what the investigation reveals."

For the first and only time, she gave me a look that bordered on fear. "Will there even be an investigation?"

"Governor Ho is an honorable man. Surely there will be an official inquiry. We will wait to see what they learn."

"Have you prayed about this?"

"I have." That was mostly true. I had prayed about the situation earlier but not that day. Finding Daosheng's body in the river had been difficult for me. She and I had not been romantically involved. We shared nothing other than work, but we had spent many hours at the office together and at meetings, some of which were with opponents who meant us harm. I found her death quite unsettling.

Gin-lien looked at me. "I have a very bad feeling about this. We must pray for protection." And so we did.

The following day, officials from Governor Ho's office came to the university and met with me. They first wanted to know about Daosheng's activities. I told them what I knew about her daily routine and about what the initial inquires revealed when we went looking for her the day she did not report for work.

"And what of the day before?" one official asked.

"She left early that afternoon."

"Did she say where she was going?"

"She said she needed to meet her boyfriend."

"Do you know his name?"

"His name is Li Jinping."

"We have talked to him already. They were to meet at a shop not far from the school. He waited for her but she never arrived."

"I did not know that," I replied, which was true. I did not know the details of her plans from the day before and was not sure how it could fit with what Daosheng's brother reported to us.

"We understand you are friends with Bo Zhongfa," one of the officials noted.

"Yes."

"Did you know he was one of the Communists?"

"His father was Communist, but Bo insisted to me that he himself was not."

One of the men took a photograph from the pocket of his

jacket and offered it to me. It was a photograph of Bo Zhongfa standing next to Chen Biwu. "This photo was taken before Colonel Xu arrived to reassert control of Changsha," he said.

The sudden awareness that Bo Zhongfa had lied to me struck me almost as hard as Daosheng's death. Bo and I had been friends a long time. Now that friendship was proved a lie. It, too, was the victim of a murderous act. The murderous act of Bo Zhongfa's betrayal.

After the officials left my office, I went home and told Gin-lien what I had learned.

"I knew it," she said. "Bo Zhongfa was never someone who could be trusted."

"I thought he was my friend."

"Because that is what he wanted you to think."

"Yes, I can see that now. But it was difficult to take, seeing him in that picture standing next to Chen Biwu."

"Now you know the threat is real."

"Yes."

"They will not rest until you are dead."

Later that evening, after we had eaten and Monto was asleep once more, Uncle Yutang arrived. He had visited us before but his arrival at night, and so late in the evening, was quite unusual. I knew something was wrong and I could see it from the expression on his face as he entered the front room.

"What is it?" I asked.

"Your friend, Bo Zhongfa—"

I interrupted him. "I know Bo Zhongfa is a Communist. I learned that today."

"Bo Zhongfa is dead."

My mouth dropped open. "He is dead?"

"They found his body in an alley not far from the place where the woman, Peng Daosheng, was found." I sank onto a chair. Uncle Yutang continued. "They both were friends of yours."

When I did not respond immediately, Gin-lien spoke up. "Yes. They were his friends."

"I think the Communists are after you," Uncle Yutang warned.

"We have heard rumors," Gin-lien noted.

Uncle Yutang gave me a nudge. "I must insist you leave Hunan immediately. Tonight if possible."

"I have been telling him that for days," Gin-lien said.

"But you must come with me." I was still seated on the chair with my head bent low, my eyes focused on the floor. "We must go together. You and me with Monto."

"You know it is not possible for me to travel and there is no concern for my safety here. I am not involved in party politics."

That sounded naïve to me. "But where would you stay that is less of a risk than traveling with me?"

"She can stay with me," Uncle Yutang offered. "No one will bother her there."

"No," Gin-lien replied. "You are too involved in the party and political affairs. I will stay with my brother, Hu Yi. He has no political affiliation and no political aspirations."

By then, Hu Yi was married. He and his wife had a small child, too. I knew Gin-lien loved him very much and that they would actually enjoy spending time together. Reluctantly I agreed. "I will travel in the morning. Not tonight."

Uncle Yutang spoke with us awhile longer, then departed for his home. I sat with Gin-lien until she fell asleep in my arms. It was peaceful holding her, feeling the rhythmic motion of her body against me as she breathed softly, and for a moment I considered not leaving Changsha but staying to see what would happen next.

As I sat there with Gin-lien I slowly came to the realization that I must leave. Not merely for my own protection but for the protection of my family. If I stayed, they would be in danger.

All at once, an image flashed through my mind of Cai Liting. He was tied to the chair on the bed of the truck and Chen Biwu stood beside him. I saw the smile on Chen Biwu's face, then heard the report of the pistol. I jumped at the memory of its sound. Instantly I knew how ruthless he could be. And there were many more Communists just like him who would stop at nothing to kill me, too. Even if it meant murdering my family in the process.

CHAPTER

⟨⟩ 12 ⟨⟩

THE NEXT MORNING I went with Gin-lien and Monto to the house of her brother, Hu Yi, where they were to stay until my return. I helped them get settled with their things, then we sat in the room together, my arm around Gin-lien, Monto resting comfortably on her lap.

"I do not know how long this will take," I said.

Gin-lien looked up at me. "You will stay away from Hunan until the trouble has passed."

"What if it takes a long time?"

"Then you will be gone a long time."

"But Monto . . ." My voice trailed away as the words caught in my throat.

"Monto and I will be fine." She leaned over and kissed me on the cheek. "We both will be fine and safe and right here waiting for you when you return." We both knew the real risk that weighed on our minds, though we had not mentioned it. The real risk was that she would die before my return. When I glanced down at her the look in her eye told me she understood what I was thinking, even though I had said nothing of it. "If anything happens to me," she whispered, "Hu Yi will contact you."

Tears streamed down Gin-lien's face as she spoke and I felt them well up in my eyes, too. Leaving her was the most difficult decision I ever faced. Then I glanced down at Monto, asleep in her arms, and as hard as it was to leave Gin-lien, suddenly leaving Monto was equally difficult.

In a few minutes, Uncle Yutang arrived with a car from the governor's office for the ride to the train station. He came inside to get me and, after an emotional good-bye with Gin-lien, I departed with him.

As Yutang and I rode away from the house, he rested his hand on my shoulder and glanced in my direction. "This was the only choice you could make."

"I feel like returning to them right now," I replied.

"No," he said. He wagged his finger for emphasis. "This is best. For yourself and for your family. This is the best."

"It seems horrible."

"I know. It is counter to what feels good, but it is in agreement with what *is* good."

I smiled over at him. "You are becoming a philosopher now?"

"No," he replied. "Just a veteran of a long struggle."

"It *has* been long."

"And believe me, as difficult as this may seem right now, you going away is the best thing for your family. This struggle could become even more difficult before we reach the end."

I nodded. "Yes, I have realized that."

"You will see them again," he said confidently.

I hoped he was right.

The train to Wuchang arrived on time and I departed Changsha without further incident. In Wuchang, I changed trains and boarded one that took me to Hankow, then on to Nanjing, the Kuomintang capital of China. My intention was to find a job as a political officer in the Kuomintang government, hopefully a position with the army that paid enough to permit me to send for Gin-lien and Monto to join me.

The train arrived at Nanjing in the morning and I went straight from the station to the Kuomintang army headquarters where a friend, Tian Ruowang, worked. He already held a position as a political officer and I hoped he would assist me in finding a similar position. Tian and I had known each other since childhood.

Tian and I visited at his office—a desk in the corner of a military warehouse—but he avoided my questions about the availability of a job. His refusal to talk about the topic left me suspicious and I wondered why he was reacting in that way, but eventually I let it drop and restricted my comments to casual conversation.

Late that afternoon, he was free to leave and return home for the night. He kindly offered to let me sleep at his apartment that evening, an invitation I readily accepted. The apartment was typical of that era with a single room for everything and a toilet at the end of the building's main hall, which he shared with the other tenants.

When we were alone in his room and the door was shut I brought up the subject of employment once more. "I came with the intention of working for the government," I began. "Hopefully as a political officer for the Kuomintang army."

"No." He was adamant in his response. "You do not want to work like this."

"Why not?"

"I am a political officer. People like me do that kind of work. You are too smart for this job."

"But it is a job," I insisted with a smile. "I need a job."

Tian sighed heavily. "Look, I get coffee for the officers. I write letters for them to their families. I prepare remarks for the senior staff that they never read, much less deliver. And I place their phone calls."

This did not sound like what I knew the job to be. "That is all?" I asked with a puzzled frown. "Surely the remarks you prepare inform the language they use when they speak publicly. And letters and phone calls must be essential."

Tian looked away. "The phone calls are . . ." He looked downcast. "I contact their concubines on their behalf." This did not sound good. I was hesitant to press the issue and realized it only embarrassed Tian. Then he looked over at me with an incisive glare, "And it gets worse."

I held up my hand in protest. "I do not wish to hear more." The details were painful for him. Besides, I did not need the images his words invoked flooding my mind.

The thought of a thing—imagining what it must be like before you encounter it—is always very different from the reality of it. I knew this much. Father had schooled me on the notion from my earliest days. Learning to dream, then pressing forward to encounter that dream as a reality, without losing the mystery of the dream or the determination to see it through, was a difficult thing. I had come from Changsha with the position of political officer in mind and I was determined to do it, to obtain the position and work hard to do my best at it. But hearing from Tian about the nature of his work led me to reconsider things.

That night as I lay on the floor in Tian's house I realized that the goal I should have in mind was not the goal of finding a particular job, but rather the goal of earning enough money to support Gin-lien and Monto so that we could all be together again as a family. That was really the dream—bringing our family back together. I also realized I would have to find another way to make that dream a reality. Being a political officer for the Kuomintang would not accomplish my goal.

The following day I went in search of other employment and encountered some interesting prospects, but nothing definite. Two days later, however, fighting erupted on the outskirts of the city. Tian already had warned me the battle was coming and as the conflict began he insisted that I leave. "Go now," he urged. "There is nothing here for you and if you stay you will be trapped."

"But where should I go?"

"Shanghai. Go to Shanghai. There is plenty of opportunity for you there." Without awaiting my response, Tian gathered my belongings and stuffed them in my suitcase. "You must go now," he insisted.

Tian went with me to the train station and waited while I purchased a ticket to Shanghai. We sat on a bench near the platform and talked for a moment, then we said our good-byes and he returned to work. As he moved out of sight a heavy sense of loneliness came over me. I was farther from home than I had ever been, surrounded by people I had never seen before, about to depart for a city to which I had never gone. And the dream of being with my family seemed to recede into the darkness of my mind.

To my great relief, the train arrived within the hour and I boarded a car for the trip to Shanghai. As I took a seat with the other passengers, I knew without looking that I had twelve dollars remaining in my pocket. I would have to find a cheap hotel and learn to accept being hungry. And I needed to find employment quickly.

Onboard the train, I was seated with a woman and her husband. The woman was on the bench next to me, which made conversation with her impossible to avoid. In the course of our journey she learned that I was from Hunan Province. Obviously, by my presence on the train, she knew that I was bound for Shanghai.

"Where are you staying in Shanghai?" she asked.

"I do not yet have a place," I replied.

"Oh, then," she responded, "you should take a room at the Pu Yi Kun. It is operated by people from Hunan."

"I have never heard of it." In fact, I had never heard of any hotel in Shanghai. "Is it a good place?"

"Yes. Excellent."

As I did not want to seem forward, I did not ask if she was staying there or, more important to me, whether the Pu Yi Kun offered rooms at a cheap rate. She might not have thought my comment too familiar had I offered it, but her husband was seated on her opposite side and I did not wish to offend either of them. So I refrained from conversation as much as possible and turned away to look out the window. I had never seen that part of China and wanted to enjoy the view.

When we arrived in Shanghai, I did as my traveling companions suggested and made my way to the Pu Yi Kun. The fee for a room was one dollar per day but it included meals, which was a good thing. I was hungry.

On the first night at the hotel I became acquainted with others from Hunan Province who were staying there. The woman on the train had, indeed, told the truth. Many people from Hunan were staying at the hotel. Many of them remembered Yali College and respected it as a noteworthy instruction of learning and study, though most were unaware the school had ceased to offer classes.

As we talked I learned that one of my fellow guests, a man about my age named Yang Ma, was from Yiyang. I did not know him, but his brother was one class below me in the missionary school when we were in the elementary grades. He left before his class reached high school and I had not seen him in a long time. I did not inquire what happened but assumed I would learn of his brother's life when it became necessary for me to know about it.

"I am acquainted with Zhao Heng-ti, the former governor of Hunan Province," Yang offered. "I think he may be in need of a tutor for his children. You could do that?"

"Yes," I replied. "That would be a good position and I would be glad to have it."

He smiled. "Excellent. Shall I make an inquiry on your behalf?"

"Certainly," I answered, but I did not really expect anything to come of it. Nothing good happened that quickly.

A few days later, I was surprised to find a message at the hotel asking me to meet with Zhao Heng-ti to discuss the tutoring position. Not knowing where he lived, I inquired of the hotel manager, who instructed me on where to go. I traveled to Zhao Heng-ti's house by trolley and we had a pleasant visit. At the conclusion of that visit, Zhao Heng-ti offered me a position as tutor for his children.

The following afternoon I began tutoring the governor's children in English and math. The money I received for this work eased my immediate financial situation but was not enough to support myself, Gin-lien, and Monto. As a result, I continued searching for a more permanent position with better pay. I very much wanted to send for them to join me. The tutoring was going very well and I enjoyed refreshing my mind once more in the rudiments of both subjects, even if it was at an elementary level.

Not long after I accepted the tutoring position with Zhao, a Yali classmate, Feng Yuelin, arrived in Shanghai and took a room at the Pu Yi Kun. We saw each other at dinner the evening of his arrival and renewed our acquaintance. We had not been close friends but were always on friendly terms; being away from Hunan heightened that sentiment.

Yuelin was just back from the United States where he had studied for an extended period. He was sent there for extra training before returning to his full-time teaching position at the China College of Wusun, a school located in Wusun, a Shanghai suburb. As we visited he said, "If you have time tomorrow you might go with me to the college. I will introduce you to the faculty and you can see the campus."

Having nothing to do that day I answered, "Yes. I would enjoy that very much."

The next morning, Yuelin and I went to the college and he introduced me to his colleagues. They seemed glad to meet me and for a moment I wondered if I might find a teaching position there, but I did not expect anything to happen from those meetings. The conversations were much too casual to be of use in obtaining a position and I assumed Yuelin and his colleagues merely were being cordial to me.

A few days later, I saw Yuelin again in the hotel lobby. He had a broad grin and looked very happy as he came toward me. "I have good news," he announced as he ushered me aside to a place where we could talk.

"What is that?"

"The college is offering you a teaching position."

"What college?"

"China College of Wusun," he exclaimed. "What college did you think?"

"I'm sorry," I said apologetically. "It's just that your announcement took me by surprise."

"They want you to teach English and math."

As these were two of my best subjects, and I already was teaching them with the governor's children, I was excited. "That is great!" I smiled and slapped him on the shoulder. "That is really great."

Yuelin gave me the details of the offer, which indeed was good news. The position paid much more than the tutoring position but the scheduling allowed me to do both. Three days each week

I would travel from the hotel to the college and to Zhao's house each afternoon.

Through my time at the hotel I made several friendships that had an effect on my future. One of those friendships was with a man named Chen Rong. We first became acquainted one morning at breakfast but our normal routines best afforded time to visit in the evenings, usually two or three times each week. Chen Rong was well educated and our conversations ranged over a variety of topics, including the Kuomintang politics, Chinese history, and the collapse of the imperial government.

At first we talked in the hotel but later we took long walks together, talking as we made our way through the neighborhood. Our usual route took us past a building that I learned was a Jewish synagogue. Shanghai, it seemed, had a thriving Jewish community. I had never met anyone who was Jewish until I took the teaching position at the China College of Wusun. One of my colleagues there was a man named Charles Berman. I did not know much about him other than that his family was from the United States and he was a Jew.

One evening, as Chen Rong and I passed the synagogue, I saw Berman coming from the building. He noticed us, too, and came over to greet us. I introduced him to Chen Rong and he joined us for our walk. As we made our way up the street, I took the opportunity to engage him in conversation about Shanghai's Jewish community. "I was not aware Shanghai had such a thriving Jewish congregation," I said.

"They came here to get away from the atrocities of the Russian pogroms," Berman explained.

"But you do not have a Russian name."

Berman smiled. "My mother was Russian. My father was a businessman from New York. They met while he was here on a business trip. After spending time together they fell in love but she wouldn't go back to New York with him. So he stayed here."

Berman became a regular presence on our evening walks and a month or two later he mentioned that in addition to his duties at China College of Wusun he also taught at Chuan-Qi College. "The college needs someone to teach English Literature," he said. "Are either of you interested in the position?"

"I am not qualified," Rong said, then looked over at me. "It might be a good position for you, though."

"Yes," I replied. "But the schedules must be coordinated. I already have the classes at China College of Wusun and I also tutor in the afternoons."

"They can probably work that out," Berman said. "Would you like for me to suggest your name to them?"

"That would be excellent," I answered.

A week later, Chuan-Qi College offered me a position teaching English Literature. I marveled at how it all came together. I had arrived in Shanghai with only enough money to sustain me for twelve days. Before those first twelve days were over, I had obtained a tutoring position that more than covered my hotel expenses. After that, I acquired the position at China College of Wusun and now I had an additional position at Chuan-Qi College. Together, those three jobs provided more than enough money to pay for Gin-lien and Monto to join me, and I began to make plans for us to be together once more as a family.

CHAPTER

❧ 13 ❧

IN JANUARY 1928, Chiang Kai-shek resolved the Communist–Conservative split in the Kuomintang Party by purging all Communists from the party's leadership coalition. Elimination of the party's dissenting elements, combined with military gains on the ground, meant Chiang Kai-shek ruled the entire country. As a result of those changes, Lu Di-ping became governor of Hunan Province. Chen Rong was named secretary general of the provincial government.

After his appointment as secretary general, Chen Rong prepared to return to Changsha to take up the duties of his office. Before he departed, he visited with me at the hotel and asked me to return with him. "I want you to accept a position in the provincial government," he explained. "The provincial foreign office would be a good place for you and I think you would become an excellent diplomat."

This was still in the time of the Unequal Treaties that were forced upon China by the United Kingdom and France in order to open China to foreign trade. The treaties granted foreign nations access to our ports, including river ports in several of China's major inland cities that were situated along navigable rivers. Changsha, Hunan's provincial capital was one of those inland ports.

Dealing with foreigners at the inland ports was a task reserved for the related provincial governments under their separate provincial authority. The national government was not involved. Hence, the existence of Hunan's provincial foreign office.

Cheng Rong's suggestion that I should accept a position at the foreign office was no mere supposition. As secretary general, he possessed the power to hire me, which meant his suggestion was, in fact, a job offer. I was excited at the prospect of returning to Hunan and being reunited with Gin-lien and Monto. Consequently, I readily accepted Cheng Rong's offer and made plans for my immediate departure at the end of the academic term.

News of my pending departure spread quickly across both college campuses where I taught. Faculty and staff were saddened that I was leaving but glad that I would at last be with my family. However, Zhao Heng-ti was quite a different matter.

Zhao had been governor of Hunan before and secretly sought to reclaim the office. According to rumors, he thought that might be possible under either party—the Communists or the Kuomintang. To me, the rise of Chiang Kai-shek made that difficult, a fact that should have been obvious to Zhao.

For one thing, Chiang Kai-shek and Zhao were not on good terms. Also, Chiang thought the provincial governments had been bound by the traditions of the past and needed a new approach. Consequently, he looked to others to fill the vacant positions at the provincial level. Zhao was not someone he was interested in appointing.

At last, the time for my departure from Shanghai arrived. Hou Shei, an acquaintance from the hotel, assisted me in reaching the Shanghai train station and there I boarded a train that took me back across the Chinese countryside. This time the journey was much more enjoyable, as I knew that my family awaited me at the end.

We arrived in Changsha late in the afternoon, just before sunset. The city always is beautiful at that time of day and it did not disappoint on that occasion. The buildings were outlined in silhouette against the sky, the last rays of sunshine illuminating them from behind in the soft light of dusk. I let my eyes rove across the horizon, trying to capture the images in my mind, to hold them as a memory should I ever be away from there again.

Uncle Yutang met me at the station and drove me to the home of Hu Yi, where Gin-lien and Monto were waiting. They greeted me as I stepped from the car and we embraced right there, the three of us squeezed tightly together in an emotional reunion, holding each other as if by doing so we could prevent our separation from ever recurring.

My sojourn had taken me away from my family for almost a year, and in that time Monto seemed to have grown twice the size I remembered. He was vibrant, healthy, and quite active. Gin-lien, however, had not fared so well. In my absence, her condition had worsened and she was given to moments of violent coughing. She'd lost weight, too, and now appeared gaunt and drawn. When I placed my arm around her I felt her bones lying just beneath a thin layer of skin, sharp and angular against my touch, as if all of the subcutaneous fat had dissipated from her body.

We remained at Hu Yi's home a few days as we became reacquainted and I settled into my new position with the provincial foreign office. Monto and I spent time each evening playing on the floor and after he was asleep in bed, Gin-lien and I sat together and talked until late at night.

In spite of her weakened condition, Gin-lien insisted on returning to our previous routine, even going so far as to insist that we return to the house we had previously rented in Changsha. I inquired of the owner if it was available and he was all too glad to lease it to us. We moved there at once.

Work at the provincial foreign office was challenging at first but my academic training served me well, especially the languages I mastered with Torvik's help. English, French, and German were the languages of foreign trade during that era. I knew them well and found my initial place in the office translating documents and interpreting conversations for others.

Not long after I returned to Changsha, Lu Di-ping was replaced as governor of Hunan by Ho Chien. I was acquainted with Ho Chien from his previous term as governor and respected him very much. He was a man of personal integrity and I had every confidence that under his leadership the future would afford me many opportunities for success.

As part of the reordering of the provincial government, Chen Rong resigned as secretary general and took a position with the national government's Foreign Service office. I was sad to see him go, as he was the one who provided a means for my return to Changsha, but he seemed excited at the prospect of a new position so I wished him well in his future endeavors.

A few months later, Gin-lien greeted me with news that she was pregnant. I was delighted at the prospect of having another child but worried about the effects a pregnancy might have on her tenuous health. She dismissed my concerns but I could see from the look in her eyes that she, too, was worried.

Early the following year, Gin-lien went into labor and we called for a midwife. I wanted to take her to the hospital where she could be properly supervised, but she insisted on giving birth the traditional way. Not long after labor began she gave birth to a beautiful girl, whom we named Man-Shia.

At first all seemed well with Gin-lien. She was up and moving around the house within days. Three or four weeks later, however, she began having tremendously violent coughing attacks. Her illness progressed with fever, sweats, and occasionally episodes of delirium. I waited only a short while before transporting her to the hospital.

Doctors at the hospital confirmed what I already knew. The pregnancy had overly stressed Gin-lien's body and exacted a great toll on her health. They treated her a few days to get the fever down, then transferred her to the sanatorium at Xiangya Hospital.

The sanatorium was located in Changsha, which meant I was able to visit with Gin-lien on a regular basis. However, with her no longer present at home, care for our children rested solely on me. But in order for us to survive, I had to work. That meant someone had to be present to care for Monto and Man-Shia. Consequently, I was forced to hire a caretaker to look after them. The woman I chose for the position was Bai Zongying, an older woman with much experience in rearing children.

⌘ ⌘

When Man-Shia was two years old she became ill with diarrhea. Zongying did her best to address the issue but insisted Man-Shia needed medical attention. "She is sick," Zongying insisted.

"And she is just a baby. She cannot tolerate this sort of problem very long."

After another day went by and Man-Shia did not improve, I took her to a doctor who diagnosed her with dysentery, but there was little he could do to help, either. At that time in China, not many medicines were available to address her condition. "Give her clean boiled water," the doctor directed. "And lots of rice. Make sure she drinks as much as possible. Already she has lost too much fluid and you must replace it promptly."

Zongying and I followed the doctor's instructions carefully but Man-Shia's condition still did not improve. In fact, she grew worse by the day. I continued to report for work during normal hours—we needed the money to survive—but it was difficult to leave home with her so ill. When I returned home at night I sat with Man-Shia, talking to her, singing to her, and praying for her, but it was painful for both of us; she from the illness in her body and me from watching her in such torment.

A few weeks later, Uncle Yutang came to my office while I was at work. Yutang was older now and many of his facial features had changed, but I could see from the look in his eyes that something serious had happened. Fear struck my heart.

"It's Man-Shia," Yutang said. "You must come quickly." I returned home with Yutang and found Man-Shia lying on the bed, looking very weak. Zongying sat next to her, speaking to her softly, but Man-Shia did not respond and stared listlessly, her eyes still and not blinking.

As I approached the bed, Zongying rose and moved away. Very gently I took a seat beside Man-Shia, slipped my arms beneath her frail body, and lifted her to my chest. Tears filled my eyes and I whispered a prayer for her, that she would live and enjoy a long life. That she would grow up to know the love of a husband and bear him many children. And if that was not to be, that she would pass quietly, peacefully, and bravely from this life into the next. With her tiny body pressed against me, I could feel her labored breathing and I knew at once which of my prayers would be answered.

From another room the sound of Monto laughing and playing with Yutang filtered through the house. I was glad for their presence, as well as that of Zongying, but at that moment I felt very much alone and longed with all my heart for Gin-lien to come and tell us what to do.

A few minutes later, the doctor appeared in the doorway and crossed the room to where I sat holding Man-Shia. He examined her without taking her from my arms, then stepped back and shook his head. "There isn't anything else we can do for her," he said in a resolute voice. He lingered a moment longer, then departed.

When he was gone, I pulled Man-Shia even closer than before and prayed again that she would survive. I found myself unable to think beyond that thought, so I began to sing the songs we learned when I attended the missionary school. Simple songs, but songs with words that reminded me of the presence of God. I felt encouraged at first but when I looked down at Man-Shia and saw how pale and emaciated she was, the feeling of helplessness returned. Her life was slipping away—that much was obvious even to me—and tears filled my eyes once again.

Holding her in my arms, I thought back over my own life. My childhood had been difficult. There are no words adequate to convey the sense one has when going to bed hungry, rising from a restless sleep even hungrier, and walking to school in the hope of finding something there for nourishment—actual nourishment—a scrap left over from the day before or a crumb that might have fallen to the floor.

When Gin-lien and I were married I vowed that, as much as possible within me, I would make the life of our family different. They would never face the extreme poverty that I had faced. And we had done that. We had avoided poverty. But now we faced an even worse kind of agony than physical poverty. The agony that comes with the poverty brought by the death of one's own child. A poverty of the soul. It was more than I could bear.

Man-Shia lived only a few more days, then died peacefully in her sleep. I lay on the bed that night beside her and noticed not a single whimper as she expired.

When the sun rose the following morning I summoned the doctor to examine Man-Shia once more, just to make certain she was gone. When it was confirmed that she was, in fact, dead, I prepared to travel to the sanatorium to deliver the news to Gin-lien.

The thought of doing that was very difficult for me but going to see her was something I knew I had to do.

On the way there, I stopped at the missionary compound to see Torvik. He was out in the schoolyard when I arrived and as we talked he steered us toward the bench by the stand of bamboo. "This is a difficult thing to bear," he said. "A parent's worst fear."

I nodded. "Almost inexpressible." I glanced in Torvik's direction and saw a pained expression on his face, but his eyes were the eyes of one who was focused on something much deeper. A memory, perhaps, but I did not feel at liberty to ask.

After a moment he said, "Gin-lien will know what to say. You should not be afraid to tell her."

"I am not afraid. Though I would rather do anything else but tell her."

"I know how you feel." And something about the tone of his voice seemed to indicate he really did.

After talking to Torvik, I continued on my way to the sanatorium and made my way to Gin-lien's room. My heart was heavy with loss but no longer burdened by the task that lay before me. I was certain Torvik was correct. Gin-lien would know what to do and say to put things right.

As I entered her room, Gin-lien looked up at me and at once a serious expression came over her. "What has happened?"

I moved a chair beside the bed where she lay and sat down, then took her by the hand. "It is Man-Shia," I whispered.

Gin-lien tried to have a brave face. "She has died?"

"Yes," I replied, choking back the sobs that seemed to catch in my throat.

From the day we learned of Man-Shia's diagnosis I had kept Gin-lien informed of our daughter's condition. In spite of her physical condition and inability to be with us, I thought it only right for her to know the latest information about her children. Now I was glad I had done that. It made telling her the news of Man-Shia's death easier this way. At least it was not a surprise.

We cried together for a long while and did our best to console each other, then I looked over at her. "I wanted things to turn out differently."

"I know, but we must not fight against the way life opens up to us. It is the way for us. Our way. And we must follow it to the end. We did our best with Man-Shia. And we must continue to do our best for Monto. We must find peace with that and trust the direction of our path to God."

Because of Gin-lien's medical condition, I was left alone to plan Man-Shia's funeral. It seemed all too morbid a task at first but ultimately proved to be cathartic and liberating. She was my daughter. I loved her very much. Monto and I honored her with the funeral service.

Following Man-Shia's funeral, I took several days away from work in order to spend time with Monto and recover myself. Zon-gying was still employed to care for Monto, but I wanted to stay with him to make sure he handled the loss of his sister properly.

While I was at home, I reorganized our belongings and helped Zongying clean the house. After a few days, though, I was ready to return to work. One can only grieve officially for a limited time, then one has to re-engage life in order to move on. I was ready for that.

CHAPTER

∾ 14 ∾

HUNAN PROVINCE had a large community of German nationals that primarily resided in Changsha. Most were associated with several German businesses operating there, the largest of which was the international chemical company IG Farben.

In conjunction with the German presence, and in order to facilitate harmonious relations with the Chinese people, the Deutsche Akademie of Munich—a German institute established during the Weimar Republic—sent Walter and Eva Frederick to teach German at Hunan University. The Fredericks were well-credentialed intellects with skills that far outpaced anyone at Hunan University. They could have taught anywhere they wished in the world. But they seemed quite content in our city and did much to help us understand German culture and the German people.

As a representative of the provincial foreign office, I encountered the Fredericks often through various official functions we attended together. Over time, we became good friends and they invited me to their home often.

Not long after Man-Shia died, the Fredericks invited me to their home for coffee. I went there one afternoon after completing my duties at the foreign office. They expressed their sympathy at the loss of our daughter, then asked about Gin-lien and Monto. They were genuine in their concern and we talked about our respective families for quite some time.

The Fredericks were excellent company and I enjoyed spending time with them, but finally the time for me to leave arrived. I had to get home in order to allow Zongying to leave for the evening. She stayed with Monto only during the day and did not remain with us at night. However, as I prepared to leave, Walter asked me to wait while he retrieved something from his desk in the study. He was gone only a minute or two and returned with an envelope.

"The Deutsche Akademie wants to give two scholarships to the Hunan government to allow two students from Hunan to study in Germany." He handed me the envelope and I noticed it bore the address of Governor Chien. Walter gestured to the envelope. "It contains a note that will explain the details."

"That is a wonderful blessing," I replied as I tucked the envelope into the pocket of my jacket. "I am sure he will be delighted to receive the news."

The following day, I went to Governor Chien's office and handed him the envelope from the Fredericks. Chien read the letter, then looked over at me. "You know what this is about?"

"They told me two scholarships had been established for Chinese students to study in Germany and that they were giving those scholarships to the provincial government to award. I assume the letter is in regard to that matter."

"Yes," Chien nodded approvingly. "It is indeed about the scholarships. And I think you should have one of them."

News of the award left me elated and I could only stammer a response. Governor Chien seemed not to notice my awkward response and continued. "But who should receive the other one?"

We talked awhile longer about awarding the second scholarship, but I did not hear much of what we said. I was too excited about the prospect of studying in Germany to worry about whom else might join me there.

A while later I returned to my office and tried to work on the numerous tasks awaiting me there. At the same time, reality began to set in and I slowly put the scholarship in its rightful place in my mind. If the offer was indeed real, accepting it posed several obstacles for me. Chief among those obstacles was the care of Ginlien and Monto. They would be unable to come with me. I would have to go to Germany alone.

Also, I knew the governor too well to let myself be completely carried away by his initial response. He had a habit of saying one thing in the intensity of the moment, then retreating from it later after sober minds intervened. I decided the better wisdom was to say nothing about the scholarship just yet and wait to see how events unfolded.

A few days later, Tong Wei, the head of the Hunan Department of Education, learned about the scholarships. He notified the governor's office that the scholarships came within the jurisdiction of *his* office and insisted that an official examination be conducted to determine the scholarship recipients. Because I was the original contact on the matter with the Fredericks, and to forestall any intervention by the foreign office in the matter, Tong Wei sent me a copy of his notification. A meeting was scheduled for the following day to discuss the matter with Governor Chien. The governor made certain I would be present.

Tong Wei made a compelling argument, but I expected Governor Chien to assert his authority and honor his previous commitment of one scholarship to me. However, when Tong Wei concluded his remarks, Governor Chien agreed with him as to both scholarships, even though it meant taking away the scholarship he already had awarded to me. I was saddened and also angered by this result and wanted to leave the room immediately. However, circumstances and a profound sense of decorum did not permit that kind of response and I was forced to remain in the meeting as we discussed the creation of an examination to determine who would receive the scholarship awards.

As our meeting concluded, Governor Chien asked me to remain a moment and I waited while Tong Wei departed. When he was gone, Chien looked at me sheepishly. "I know I promised you one of those scholarships, but as you can see, Tong Wei is correct. I overstepped the boundaries in the matter. We must do it the way he suggested."

"Yes," I replied, doing my best to hide my sense of disappoint both by the loss of the scholarship and by the governor's failure to stand up for me.

"Just win the competition," he added with a forced smile. "That should not be a problem for you."

"Thank you." I then bowed politely and left the room.

❧ ❧

A few weeks later, the provincial department of education advertised for the scholarship examination and I applied to take it. The examination was three days in length, and on the first day twenty-four applicants appeared. To my surprise, Li Du was among them. I had not seen Li Du in a long time. We talked briefly, but he was as distant as he had been when we were last in school together. As arrogant and conceited, too.

"I have been watching the others," Li Du announced. "And I know that I am the smartest person here today."

"Some of them might surprise you," I suggested. "Intelligence is a matter of the mind. Not appearance."

Li Du shook his head. "None of these people are worthy of

such an honor as the scholarship they are offering. Clearly, I will win one of the scholarships."

Those standing nearby who overheard Li Du's remarks were offended. His remarks were offensive to me, too, and for the remaining days of the examination I kept my distance from him. Rather than engage in pointless small talk, with him or anyone else, I focused only on the examination, doing my best to score as high as possible. More than once I thought of Father and the difficulty he encountered with just that sort of examination. I wanted to make no room for a generational issue of that nature to reappear.

At the conclusion of the examination our papers were submitted for review. Several days later when the results were reported, Li Du and I were tied for first place. Apparently, he was not the smartest person at the examination after all. As a result of our scores, he and I were both awarded the scholarships.

⁂

At the time of the scholarship examination, Gin-lien still was a patient in the sanatorium. Monto was under the watchful eye of Zongying. Our lives followed a settled routine that served us well. I went to work each day and on Sundays, my only day of rest, I journeyed across town to visit Gin-lien.

On the Sunday following announcement of the examination results, I made my customary trip to visit Gin-lien. Only this time, I knew I had to tell her about the scholarship. I was nervous about that, as it had the potential to disrupt our routine and I was concerned about the effect that disruption would have on her and Monto.

Somewhat to my surprise, Gin-lien was excited by the scholarship news. Between coughs she insisted that I must accept the award and pursue the opportunity it afforded. "You cannot remain here for me," she insisted. "I am not far from death. You must think of the future. Your future. Monto's future. The future of the country."

"But how can I do that?" I took her gently by the hand. "Monto is very young. He needs much support and there is the question of his education."

"Monto is brave and smart. He will learn and grow. My brother can keep him while you are away." Tears trickled down my cheeks at the sound of her voice and I could only respond with a nod. "Do not worry," she continued. "Monto will still be here when you return. He will not forget you."

I sobbed. "It is not Monto I fear will not be here when I return."

Gin-lien grabbed hold of my arm with both hands and pulled herself closer to me. "We knew this would happen when we married," she whispered. "We knew even before then. From the day we first met and you learned how sick I really was, we knew how the end would come."

"Yes," I responded. "But I kept thinking there would be another way."

She leaned even closer, her lips brushing lightly against my ear. "This is the way things have opened up for us. We must accept it and do our best. God will honor our obedience. We must trust Him with the result."

After visiting with Gin-lien for as long as the nurses permitted, I departed the sanatorium and went for a walk to have time alone and pray before returning home. I hoped to find resolution for my sorrow over being separated from Gin-lien during that time but found none. In spite of my sadness, however, I realized that she was correct in her advice. The offer of a scholarship of such magnitude was the opportunity of a lifetime. Many of my colleagues longed for such a moment and found none. I had no choice but to accept the scholarship and study in Germany.

The following day, however, I was once again conflicted in my choice. After brooding over it for the morning, I went to the missionary compound to find Torvik. He was seated in his office when I arrived but he escorted me outside and we sat together on the bench near the stand of bamboo.

"Life presents these decisions," he commented after hearing of my dilemma. "Thankfully, they come only a few times." He glanced over at me with a kindly smile. "They aren't an everyday occurrence. But they are sometimes painful when they come."

As he looked at me I noticed the wrinkles at the corners of his eyes were deeper than before. He had dark circles around his eyes, too, and tiny bags had formed beneath them. His cheeks were drawn also and his face seemed much thinner. There was a sense of tiredness about him and I realized also how little I actually knew of him, his life, and the experiences he had encountered. So I asked, "You have faced similar circumstances?"

Torvik nodded. "When I was twenty-three, I had an opportunity to study at a school in Switzerland. My wife was pregnant at the time and did not want to travel before the baby was born, but I had already applied and was accepted." He looked at me again. "I had been awarded a scholarship that would pay for everything."

"But you would have to go there without your wife."

"And without the baby she was due to deliver later that year," he added.

"What did you do?"

"We prayed about it. And we talked about it. All of which I'm sure you've already done."

"Yes," I said. "And then what?"

"And then I went."

"You left them?"

"Yes," Torvik said.

"Did they join you later?"

Tears filled Torvik's eyes. "They both died during the delivery."

"Oh, my," I said softly. At once I realized that this was the memory I had seen in his eyes when we talked the day of Man-Shia's death, before I went to tell Gin-lien what had happened. Even after all the years that had passed, the sorrow remained deep in his soul. So deep that merely telling me about it brought it to the surface anew and painful in a way that left him unable to respond immediately. So I reached out and touched him on the arm. "I am so sorry."

"Thank you," he whispered.

Tears streamed down Torvik's cheeks and he did little to stop them. A drop formed at the point of his chin and hung there a moment, then dribbled onto the front of his shirt. As that happened, he took a handkerchief from his pocket and dried his eyes.

After a moment, he said, "I returned home in time for the funeral and considered abandoning the notion of attending school altogether, but my father-in-law took me aside and told me that one of the last things my wife said was, 'If anything happens to me, make sure Karl finishes school.'"

"So you went back?"

He nodded. "I went back."

After talking to Torvik, I was more convinced than ever that I should accept the scholarship award and travel to Germany to study. In order to confirm my decision, I resolved to place it before Gin-lien's brother, Hu Yi, as he would be the one to care for Monto until my return. If he was agreeable, I would go. If he was not, I would decline the scholarship and remain in the employ of the provincial government's foreign office.

A few days later, I visited Hu Yi at his home and told him about the opportunity to study in Germany. "I have already discussed this matter with Gin-lien," he grinned from ear to ear as he spoke. "Everything will be taken care of. This is a great honor.

You must accept it and go to Germany."

"But I am not sure I can leave Monto. He is young and needs me."

"My wife and I can look after Monto," Hu Yi countered. "We already treat him as our own son. He will live with us and we will care for him until you return."

"There is another issue, though."

"Gin-lien?"

"She is the love of my life and my most important relationship. Monto, of course, but Gin-lien most of all." I looked over at Hu Yi. "She will not survive until I return."

"I understand that," he said with sadness. "Gin-lien understands it, too. But the country needs you to do this. We don't have many who can think like you. We cannot afford to waste even a single mind. And those minds we do have cannot afford to waste an opportunity of this nature. It is a great honor."

"But what about Gin-lien?" I asked once more. "If she dies while I am away . . ." The matter of her death was no small issue. Her death would require a funeral that honored her memory. If I were away in Germany, I would be unable to return to Changsha in time to see to her details. Doing that would fall to Hu Yi. By the look on his face I knew he understood the issue I was attempting to raise.

"We have known about her condition for a long time. She has known about it, too. We did not keep it a secret from her even when she was a young girl. We will face the issues presented by her death when the time comes. You need not concern your-self with that as a limitation. Only as a matter of sadness and memory." He smiled at me in a brotherly way. "We will handle the arrangements."

Nothing else remained for us to discuss, so with a heavy heart I accepted Hu Yi's offer regarding Monto's care and matters related to Gin-lien. He visited Gin-lien each week and I knew he would continue to do so whether I was present or not.

As I departed Hu Yi's home I expected to struggle with the decision further, and to be overcome with sadness, but as I started home a strange sense of peace came over me and I felt released to pursue the scholarship opportunity. From that moment my prayers changed from supplication to giving thanks for all that God had provided for me—family, friends, and academic study.

That evening, I explained the situation to Monto. "You will live with your uncle Hu Yi and his family while I am away."

At first, Monto responded with the kind of excitement only a child can express. "That will be fun! I like playing with Uncle Yi."

Later that evening, though, Monto realized I would not be with him and he became very sad at the thought of my prolonged absence. We continued to discuss the matter and I allowed him to ask as many questions as he wished. He did just that and late that night drifted off to sleep lying beside me on the bed.

Over the next few weeks Monto and I revisited the subject of my departure as I enlisted his help in preparing for my trip. He asked many of the same questions he had before and I dutifully answered them, interpreting his repeated questions as a request for additional information. I expanded my previous answers as much as possible, being careful not to minimize his worries by giving him childish answers but answering him truthfully and honestly, as one adult to another, then explaining the parts he did not comprehend.

CHAPTER

∾ 15 ∾

FINALLY THE TIME CAME for me to depart for the trip to Germany. I visited Gin-lien one last time. In spite of her illness I kissed her as I did when we were younger. She bravely promised to be waiting for me at the train station when I returned again but I knew she would be gone before I finished the course of study in Munich.

The night before I was to leave, Monto and I went to Hu Yi's house and spent the night there. I thought doing that would make my leaving easier for him to handle. The following morning, I awakened Monto early and we spent time alone, reviewing the things that were about to happen. An hour later, we said a teary good-bye at the house and Hu Yi drove me to the train station in Changsha. I did not like leaving Monto behind but by then I had little choice.

We arrived at the station to find Walter and Eva Frederick waiting for us. Li Du was there, also. I introduced Hu Yi to them, as he had never met either of them, then we stood near the tracks and talked.

After exchanging pleasantries, Walter explained, "We have a friend in Germany named Karl Breker. He will be available to help you when you arrive."

"He was our assistant when we lived in Munich," Eva added.

"That would be most helpful," I said. "Thank you."

"He will meet you at the train station in Munich," Walter continued. "And he will see that you get settled at the college and that you know what to do next."

News of Breker's availability was a great relief to me. In all of our discussion and planning for the trip, we had failed to address the issue of transition—what to do when we arrived and how to get started on our first day there. I had never been to Germany and I was certain Li Du had not, either. The uncertainty of that situation left me apprehensive. Walter and Eva's words to us that morning on the train platform brought clarity to the moment.

A few minutes later, the train arrived. I said one more good-bye to Hu Yi, bid the Fredericks a fond farewell, then Li Du and I boarded the train for Shanghai. The conductor led us to a special car, one that had individual compartments rather than the traditional plain benches on which common passengers sat. Li Du and I occupied the same compartment, sitting opposite each other the entire journey, but through all that time we rarely spoke. I spent most of the day staring out the window, watching the countryside of my beloved China slip past and wondering where this opportunity would lead.

In Shanghai, Li Du suggested we should take time to see some of the sights. "Perhaps we could have a meal at a restaurant. Or take in a play or a movie. Our ship does not sail until tomorrow."

"I would rather not," I replied.

"Why?" Li Du had a condescending tone in his voice. "Clearly, we have the time in our schedule."

"We can board the ship a day in advance," I noted. "Which means we can board today. I suggest we do that and spend the evening familiarizing ourselves with that environment."

Li Du was not satisfied with my answer but when we discussed what our accommodations on the ship might be like, he realized we would most probably share a room with bunk beds, as we were both assigned to the same compartment. Li Du made it known that he did not wish for me to have first choice of beds. However, in order to ensure that did not happen, he had to board early with me, as I was resolved not to spend the time sight-seeing and risk an unwanted confrontation on our trip. Reluctantly, Li Du boarded the ship with me on the day we arrived in Shanghai.

When we reached our ship's compartment, we found it was as we suspected—very small. Just room enough for beds and a place for one suitcase each. And, as we expected, our room had bunk beds, one upper and one lower. Li Du sought to have first choice but I rejected that idea.

"We will toss a coin," I said. Li Du did not like that idea. He was used to having things his own way and was not averse to bullying others to get it. But I would not permit him to bully me and so we decided the issue by tossing a coin.

Li Du won the coin toss and chose the bottom bunk, thinking it the better of the two. He also chose it because he thought I wanted that bunk also. I did not mind sleeping up top as it afforded me sleeping space without interruption. Being on top, I was not forced to endure someone climbing over me in the night on their way to the floor—a fact Li Du realized quite soon after that and found very much to his irritation.

As with our journey on board the train, Li Du and I rarely spoke the entire time we were on board the ship. We slept in the same room, one above the other, only a few feet apart, took our meals together, and even went for walks together on the upper decks, but almost never exchanged more than the perfunctory, utilitarian comments necessary to navigate the rudimentary details of our daily schedule.

Ten days after leaving Shanghai, we arrived at the port in Hamburg, Germany. Once again, Li Du wanted to interrupt our schedule and spend a day seeing the sights of the city, but I insisted on continuing our journey as planned. We were scheduled to take a train to Munich that same day and I did not want to deviate from the itinerary. Part of my concern was we did not know the country or the culture and would be vulnerable to the vagaries of our ignorance, which posed a risk to our ultimate goal of extended time for study. The scholarship we'd been given was a great honor; one that imposed a condition of duty upon us. We could not disrespect our superiors, or the Fredericks, by treating our mission with anything less than the dignity and commitment it deserved.

We arrived in Munich late in the afternoon, just before sundown. As planned, Karl Breker was waiting for us at the station when we stepped off the train. He assisted us in collecting our luggage and then accompanied us to the school.

Ludwig Maximilian University had been established in 1472 by Duke Ludwig IX of Bavaria. By European standards, it was quite old and prestigious. Its faculty and alumni were among the top academics in their fields, many of them Nobel Prize recipients. The faculty was particularly strong in economics, which was the field I had chosen to study.

Breker gave us a tour of the school's facilities, then took us to our rooms. Li Du and I had separate private rooms. Although we shared a bathroom with others on our hall, living alone was a luxury rarely available to someone my age in China.

Having completed the details of our initial arrival, Breker took us to dinner. On the way back to our accommodations, he showed us the building to which we would report the following day and gave us the name of our contacts in the admissions office. "They are expecting you," he said. "They will see that you are properly enrolled and show you what to do after that."

The year we arrived in Germany was 1929, just as Adolf Hitler was beginning his push to take control of the German government. Posters and placards hung around the city and even on campus that displayed his likeness. He seemed unusually stern and angry to me and I was repelled by to them immediately.

What I saw made me suspicious of Hitler's goals and I was deeply concerned for the future of the German people. As a result, I spent considerable time learning about the details of his political career, both through conversations with German students and patrons at a coffee shop near the university as well as through articles that appeared in the Munich newspapers.

From those sources I learned that Adolf Hitler was born and reared in Austria. As a teenager he was a high school dropout and a loafer. Living aimlessly and without ambition, he drifted into art but refused schooling and produced works as a self-taught artist, most of it apparently mediocre at best. For a time, he survived by selling his art, but that failed to provide much of a living.

At the same time, Hitler became fascinated by the German people and all things pertaining to German life. When the Great War broke out, he voluntarily joined the German Army as a foot soldier. Entirely consumed by the German cause, Hitler risked his life in combat and received many prestigious awards for his actions.

When Germany later surrendered to the Allied Powers, Hitler was crushed and felt he had been personally betrayed by the

German leadership. Disgusted by what he viewed as cowardice, and determined to do something about that situation, he joined a political league known as the Free Workers' Committee for a Good Peace. The league was led by Anton Drexler and became active in German elections as the German Workers' Party (DAP). With the party, Hitler, it seems, found something that deeply interested him and he steadily rose through the ranks, exerting more and more influence over party policy.

In 1920, the German Worker's Party changed its name to the National Socialist German Workers' Party and became known by the acronym NAZI. The following year, Hitler replaced Drexler as party chairman.

After taking office as party chairman, the Nazi Party Congress—the organization's legislative body comprised of members from a broad range of backgrounds—was dissolved and Hitler became the sole figure of authority. It was a pattern of conduct that would be repeated later, though we did not realize it as a mere rehearsal at the time.

Fighting during the Great War and the resulting peace left Germany very unsettled and soon the country was beset with unrest; some of it spontaneous and some of it highly organized. In that climate, Hitler saw the Nazi Party as a revolutionary organization and sought to use it as a means of overthrowing the Weimar Republic. Hitler had two chief aims: to promote German nationalism and to advance a particularly virulent form of anti-Semitic policy. To that end, he spoke often about eugenics and his ideas of an Aryan race, which he thought of as the perfect form of humanity.

Hitler's ideas drew on Darwin's theories of biological evolution and formed a radical blend of scientific determinism and political authoritarianism. I was immediately put off by his ideas but did not realize their full potential until I read about his view of Christianity and the church. Both of those entities stood for principles that were diametrically opposed to Hitler's rhetoric and posed a serious challenge to his goal of seizing control of Germany, then remaking it into a master race. Consequently, under Hitler's leadership, the Nazi Party took steps to subvert the role of faith and the church in the life of everyday believers.

The first steps were subtle. One I noted was that the party adopted the swastika as its symbol and demanded that all members wear a likeness of it on their clothing and position it in a place of honor in their homes, replacing the cross. The party also demanded allegiance of its members to the as-yet-unformed National Socialist State, promoted as an entity to replace the church, which party members viewed as weak and no longer useful to German society. In effect, Hitler sought to promote worship of state and its leader. I realized then that if he should succeed, Germany would become a nation-cult, at once both political and religious, but a religion nonetheless with him at the center.

In 1923, before my arrival, Germany had failed to make war reparations payments required under the Treaty of Versailles. In response, France sent its army to occupy the Ruhr industrial district. Economic chaos ensued and the German government collapsed. In that resulting power vacuum, Communists who were organized and active in the country attempted to lead a revolt while Hitler and the Nazis attempted to launch a coup. Neither of the groups was successful and many were arrested, including Hitler. After that, the Nazi Party was banned from German politics.

While in prison, Hitler wrote a book entitled *Mein Kompf*— meaning "My Struggle"—a political autobiography in which he stated his political views. I read a copy of it not long after I arrived in Munich and found it to be a compilation of many different ideas, some of which were contradictory to others he stated. In that book, Hitler blamed Germany's troubles on three groups: the Triple Entente—the Allies of the Great War; the Communist Party; and the Jews. The book became an immediate bestseller, propelling Hitler to national fame and notoriety.

After the book became popular, Hitler was released from prison. With seemingly little difficulty, he convinced German authorities to reauthorize the Nazi Party. In the process, the party disavowed its revolutionary past and reassured officials it no longer intended to take control of the government by force.

Shortly after the party was reauthorized, Hitler was once again chosen as its leader. Rudolf Hess, Hermann Göring, Joseph Goebbels, and Heinrich Himmler were installed in positions as leading party functionaries. All authority, however, rested with Hitler.

The Nazi Party was intensely organized with levels of accountability that reached from the upper echelons of power all the way down to the local level. For all its structure, however, the Nazi Party found only meager success and continued to poll around three percent of the electorate. But the year I arrived in Germany brought the worldwide Great Depression, which introduced unemployment on a massive scale. Almost overnight, the German political landscape was transformed before my very eyes. From the safety of our university campus, I watched as the Nazi message, taken straight from the pages of *Mein Kompf,* found a readily receptive audience.

In a matter of weeks, Jewish financiers and the Communists, once the object of only radical hatred, became the focus of national blame for Germany's economic and political situation. It was a message reflected not merely in the political opinions of a few, but in widespread public belief. I knew it was only a matter of time, perhaps a very short time, before Hitler would become the leader of the German government and his racist political views would quickly emerge as the gospel of ordinary German citizens. Waiting to see that happen proved to be even shorter than I first thought.

The year after I arrived, elections were held. Hitler stood as the Nazi Party's candidate for president. He was opposed by Paul von Hindenburg, a hero of the German Army and of the Great War.

In the weeks before the election, violence and unrest erupted on the streets of many German cities. Much of that disruption was instigated by Goebbels, who served as the Nazi Party propaganda director. Hitler, campaigning as a law-and-order candidate, singled out Jews and Communists as the source of the country's trouble and promised to restore order.

On Election Day, Hitler lost the presidential bid to Hindenburg. However, the Nazi Party received more than eighteen percent of the vote, making it the second largest party in the German parliament and Adolf Hitler became a very real force with which to be reckoned.

CHAPTER

16

ONE SATURDAY in the autumn of my third year in Germany, I was studying in the library when an administrative assistant from the dean's office came to me with an envelope. "This arrived for you," he said and he handed me the note. I opened it and my heart sank.

Inside the envelope was a telegram from Hu Yi informing me that Gin-lien had died. I read it, then leaned back in the chair, too overcome with emotion to cry. I knew this would happen but now that it had occurred it seemed too real to be true. I was there, in Germany. Gin-lien was far away in China. And Monto now was without either of his parents.

Deep sadness swept over me as I thought of these things and of the impossibility of my situation. Returning for Gin-lien's funeral was not possible, as I had no money for travel except for the return trip at the end of the scholarship period.

Still, I had to share the news with someone, to unburden my heart enough to consider fully how Gin-lien's death affected my life. Speaking with Li Du on a matter of that nature was out of the question, so I went to see Karl Breker—the Fredericks' assistant.

Breker was sympathetic for my loss and for my situation, but was unable to offer a solution, as we both realized the distance and expense of travel posed an untenable difficulty.

"We could contact the Fredericks," he offered. "They have a telephone at the university in Changsha and I have one that is accessible here."

"No," I replied. "That will not be necessary. Calling them would only shift the sadness to them." I thought of using the phone to contact Hu Yi but decided against it. He had no telephone and getting to one would be very difficult for him, along with the added encumbrance of being present at the phone when I called. The logistics would be as impossible to address as the travel.

"There is no solution for me except to study until the end of the term and complete the work I came to do," I explained. "I could not make it back to Hunan before the funeral anyway. And Hu Gin-lien must be buried promptly. They cannot await my return."

Breker nodded. "I understand, but you cannot let this news pass unacknowledged. It is too important, especially for your son. You should respond to the telegram."

"Indeed," I said. "You are correct. But I am not certain I have enough money for the fee. Is it expensive to send a telegram in reply?"

"I will pay for it," Breker offered. He rose from his chair as he spoke and started across the room to collect his jacket. "Come. This much I can take care of with very little difficulty."

Without further delay, we departed Breker's house and drove over to a telegraph station located just off the university campus. I wrote out a message to Hu Yi, Breker paid the agent, and we left.

Later that evening, after Breker dropped me at school, I walked to a church located a block or two from our building. The doors were open so I went inside. The sanctuary was empty but a light at the altar illuminated the table near the pulpit. I took a seat in a pew about halfway up, bowed my head, and wept.

༄ ༄

The following day, a second telegram arrived from Hu Yi. Once again, an administrative assistant from the dean's office brought it to me, this time in the later afternoon while I was in my room. The message acknowledged my reply of the day before and told me that they did not expect me to return. "Have explained to Monto," the message read. "Will arrange funeral and continue care for Monto."

As I read the telegram I heard a knock at the door. I opened it to find Li Du standing in the hallway. "I heard from Breker about Gin-lien. I am very sorry she has died."

Li Du entered my room and took a seat at the desk near the window. I sat on the bed. For the next hour we talked much the same as we had when we were younger and students at the missionary school. Small talk, recalling pleasant memories and the silly things we did as young boys. Talking about everything and nothing.

Finally I raised the question that had been on my mind since the day we sat for the scholarship examination. "What happened before, when we were younger, in Hunan?" I asked. "You simply disappeared."

"Yes," Li Du acknowledged. "We departed after my father was killed in the Communist uprisings."

"But even since your return you have been distant and not interested in friendship."

"I find it difficult to be friends with you because of your uncle," Li Du replied.

"What is it about my uncle that presents a difficulty between you and me?"

"Our family was told that Yutang turned traitor on my father," Li Du explained. "Informing on him to the men who killed him."

"The information you were told was not correct."

Li Du seemed not to accept the truth of what I said. "You are supportive of your uncle and I recognize that, but this is what we were told."

"I was present one night and saw your father at Yutang's home."

Li Du was taken aback. "You saw him?"

"Yes. Other men were there, too," I explained, "and they were all committed to defending your father. The following night, Yutang was wounded in the effort to protect him."

Li Du had a questioning expression. "He told you this?"

"And I saw it, also."

"You are certain of these things?"

"One of the men came to our house the night of the attack. He told my mother what had happened to Yutang and instructed her to return with him. When they left, I followed them and watched through the window. She dressed Yutang's wounds and I heard them talking about what had happened. Yutang was injured defending your father."

As I talked, the expression on Li Du's face softened, and for the next hour we talked from our hearts, renewing our friendship.

Through the remainder of our time in Germany, Li Du and I were together each day in the same spirit we shared as children. We visited many of the tourist sites in Germany and several to which they were not permitted. Our status as visiting students and our friendship with the Fredericks had many other benefits as well.

In 1932, I completed my studies in Munich and graduated from the Deutsche Akademie with a PhD in Political Economics. Li Du finished then as well and we returned together to China.

On our trip home, Li Du made a stop in Nanjing, but I continued on to Changsha. Monto was waiting for me and I was anxious to see him again.

When I arrived at the train station in Changsha, Hu Yi and Monto were there to greet me. We hugged each other warmly but I could sense the distance between us had grown. He was older now and on the cusp of adolescence. Much of his personality had been influence by Hu Yi, rather than by me. I realized that in our first few minutes together. When Monto was born, I had wanted our futures to unfold together but that did not seem to be possible, though I hoped it would be more so in the years ahead than it had been to that point.

After a few days at Hu Yi's home, Monto and I rented a house in the neighborhood where we'd lived before. We spent the following week settling into our new home with efforts to get reacquainted.

A week or so after we moved into the house, I went to the missionary compound to see Torvik and thank him for his telegram regarding Gin-lien's death. When I arrived I noticed the place seemed calmer than I remembered and soon learned that the school's student body had been reduced in size by about half what it had been when I was a student there. I also shocked to learn that Torvik was dead.

"We found him in his office," one of the teachers told me. "He was slumped over his desk."

"What happened to him?"

"The authorities told us it was his heart."

"I always thought he was in good condition," I offered.

"We did, too," the teacher agreed. "One of his sisters came from Europe to collect the body. We learned from her that their family had a history of heart ailments."

A frown wrinkled my forehead. "He had a sister?"

The teacher smiled. "That was our reaction as well."

We talked awhile longer, then I excused myself and turned to leave. As I did, I caught sight of the bench that sat on the opposite side of the schoolyard near the stand of bamboo. "May I sit there a moment?" I asked.

"Certainly," she replied.

The teacher went inside the building and I made my way to the bench, where I sat alone and thought of Torvik, remembering the sound of his voice and the many things we'd discussed there. I had shared most of my deepest thoughts with him and he had guided me through many of my life's most important moments. A sense of sadness came over me at the realization that he was no longer present, and never would be again, but I was glad to have had his friendship.

Later that month, I accepted a position on the faculty at Hunan University as an economics professor. Because of faculty limitations, I also was assigned to teach a course in English Literature.

Between teaching and advising the provincial government on economic matters, I spent as much time as possible with Monto to rekindle our relationship. During my absence he had not only grown like Hu Yi in his personality but also had become quite fond of him. This did not trouble me—it was as it should be; a boy left in the care of his uncle for an extended time would naturally come to see the uncle as more than merely an uncle—but adjusting to each other took Monto and me more time than I thought would be necessary. We both learned a great deal about each other during those days. As I learned very quickly, however, more had changed in China during my absence than merely my relationship with my son.

While in my final year in Germany, military forces from Japan invaded northern China. In just a few months those troops seized control of the Chinese region known as Manchuria. As if to add insult to the injury inflicted on our national pride, the Japanese installed former Chinese emperor Pu Yi as emperor of a puppet government that ruled over the region. A region they renamed Manchukuo. The Japanese attack on our sovereign homeland was a travesty, but Pu Yi's service to them as their servant to do their bidding was both disgusting and treasonous.

Although we were in a state of war with Japan, the Chinese government of the Kuomintang had few resources to devote to the fight against our invaders and little hope of expelling them without foreign assistance. Chiang Kai-shek thought that Germany would be our best hope of assistance and a concerted diplomatic effort was made to secure their support. Favorable terms were reached for the purchase of arms and ammunition, but there was no commitment from Germany for direct assistance.

As always, I remained suspicious of the German government and of Adolf Hitler's growing influence over it. Most of my news about events in Germany came from the Fredericks, who kept me supplied with German newspapers. They also offered information gleaned from their own sources—government officials and members of the German royal family, all of whom were deeply distrusting of the Nazis. What they reported was ominous and portended a deeply troubled future for the German people.

In the 1932 German elections, held the year I returned to China, the Nazi Party won the largest block of seats in the German parliament. As a result, Hitler was appointed chancellor and took office in January 1933. In February of that year, a fire in the parliament building gave him the pretext for suppressing his political opponents, which he did in a ruthless manner. Not long after, the Nazis coerced parliament into passing a law known as the Enabling Act, which granted Hitler's cabinet the authority to enact laws without parliament's approval. That authority in the hands of a few people, all of whom were more loyal to Hitler than to the state, made Hitler a de facto dictator.

Members of the faculty at Hunan University kept a watchful eye on events unfolding in Europe and discussed those events with regularity. Some favored Hitler and the Nazi approach. Guo Fenglu, a history professor, was his most outspoken advocate.

"Hitler is a brilliant leader," Guo argued one day over lunch. "There is no one like him anywhere."

"Not even here?" I asked with a raised eyebrow.

Immediately I recognized that in his enthusiasm for the topic, Guo had rushed ahead with a comment that carried serious implications. Chinese culture instilled its citizens with deep respect for their leaders. Politically, the country had moved beyond an imperial government but not so far that it had shed itself of its ancient cultural priorities. Everyone in the room noted Guo's overreach and the potential affront to Chiang Kai-shek that was implicit in his remark.

"I did not mean to imply disrespect," Guo quickly added with a troubled frown. His cheeks glowed with a look of embarrassment. "You all know that," he continued, attempting to redress his error. "I just mean—"

"I know nothing of what you mean except by what you say," I responded, unwilling to let the moment pass.

Hitler posed a serious threat to governments everywhere, especially all forms of democracy, the most serious of which was the insipid banality of his statements. Most of his ideas were ludicrous to the point of bewilderment. All of which made them easier to ignore than to resist. But I felt the consequences of not responding were grave, even though we were far away from Germany and other parts of Europe where the consequences of Nazi policy would most likely fall.

"You obviously have a different assessment," Guo stated, his voice transformed from embarrassment to arrogance. "I assume you feel your time in Germany gives you superior knowledge in this regard."

"I did observe political matters there firsthand," I replied.

"Then please, by all means, share your wisdom with us. What do you think of Hitler?"

"Hitler will lead Germany into war again," I replied. "A war that might well consume all of Europe. Perhaps far more. Perhaps the entire world."

"That is ridiculous," Guo scoffed. "You know nothing of world events except what you have read in books."

Tsiang Shen from the mathematics department spoke up. "The central problem for Germany is the issue of the Jews."

"How so?" someone asked.

"The Jews are a group of people foreign to the German race and culture. They share little with the German people in the matter of background, religion, or custom. Yet they occupy a central position in the economy."

Mention of the Jews reminded me of Charles Berman, whom I met while living in Shanghai when I fled Changsha to avoid the Communist uprising. At the memory of him and of his friendship I became quite defensive, but I kept those thoughts to myself for the moment and listened to see how others would react.

"You're saying they pose a threat?" Tsiang asked.

"I'm saying the German people view them that way."

"And that's why the Jews should be expelled," Guo offered.

"They have lived in Europe for almost two thousand years,"
I noted.

"Yet they have never been accepted," Tsiang added.

"They have never *sought* acceptance," Guo argued. "Instead,
they have devoted themselves to maintaining their own identity."

"A distinct identity," Tsiang pointed out. "They have never
assimilated."

Wang Shih, an instructor in art, spoke up. "Should *we*
assimilate?"

Guo frowned at him with a look of disdain. "What does that
mean?"

"The Japanese have occupied parts of our territory," Wang
explained. "Should we assimilate into them or them into us?" Most
of us grinned at that response. It was simple, yet concise.

"That is different," Guo answered with a dismissive gesture.

"Oh?" I asked, taking up the point. "How so?"

"They invaded us."

"And you are suggesting the Jews invaded Europe?"

Guo nodded. "After a fashion."

"They invaded yet they have been there almost as long as
anyone. Meaning, they invaded Europe but not Germany?" Needling him was fun, as well as necessary.

"That is correct," Guo conceded. "There was no Germany at
the time they arrived." The nature of his argument forced him
to assert that the Jews had invaded Europe, but he knew that
not to be true and thus his concession on the matter of historic

fact—Germany only formed as a nation in the nineteenth century—an issue which I and others in the room thought telling of the entire discussion.

"As I said," Tsiang reiterated. "The Jews did not assimilate into European culture. Nor did they found a political state. They simply existed among the people who already were there."

"The Jews have their own place," I responded.

Tsiang looked puzzled. "Their own place?"

"Palestine," I said. "But no one seems to want them to return there."

"Yes." Shih nodded in agreement. "No one wants them to stay. And no one wants them to go."

"Which is why I said the Jews were the central problem," Tsiang added. He looked over at me. "Do you not agree?"

"The situation for them is dire. And it will only get worse."

We talked awhile longer, but none of us realized that day just how bad things would become in Germany, for the Jews and for others.

◦◦◦ ◦◦◦

Later that year, I was offered an opportunity to represent Hunan Province as a member of the Chinese delegation to the World's Fair, which was being held in Chicago. This was a great honor and opportunity in and of itself but also would mark my initial visit to the United States. I had heard of life in the United States and had met Americans while studying in

Germany, all of which heightened my interest in seeing that country.

However, Monto and I were only beginning to get reacquainted with each other. Serving as a member of the World's Fair delegation would require me to leave him once more, presumably in the care of Hu Yi. I did not like the prospect of that.

While living in Germany I had found peace with Gin-Lien's death but that was within the context of my life there. Back in China, I was confronted with her absence anew, which was difficult and I felt plagued by a deep sense of loneliness. A trip to the United States seemed to be a great way to avoid all of that and something I found difficult to resist. Once again, I turned to Hu Yi for advice.

The day after I was offered a place in the delegation I left the university campus and went to see my brother-in-law. On my way to his house, I stopped by Uncle Yutang's home to talk with him. He was elderly then and not in good health, but his mind was sharp and he was fully possessed of his faculties.

When I explained the offer for service in the World's Fair delegation, Yutang smiled at me. "This is difficult for you, isn't it?"

"It would mean leaving Monto behind once more."

He shook his head. "Not the trip, but living here."

The question seemed odd. "I don't understand."

"You find living here without Gin-lien difficult," Yutang said. "I see it in your eyes every time you visit me."

The realization that my sadness was obvious left me unsettled and I looked away. I sighed softly. "It is worse than I imagined."

"That is to be expected."

"Do you really think that?"

Yutang nodded slowly. "When you were in Germany and you heard the news, you knew with your mind that Gin-lien was dead. Now that you are here, in the place where she lived, where all the memories of her live even though she is gone, you are experiencing the sorrow of her loss more deeply."

"I cannot stand the thought of living here without her."

We sat in silence a moment, then Yutang looked over at me. "Your mother would tell you to face the difficulty, defeat it, and do your duty to Monto."

"I have heard her voice saying those words many times in my mind. And you agree with her?"

Yutang shook his head. "That is the answer of a mother. You must seek an answer in your own terms."

"And what is that?"

"You studied in Germany for the purpose of serving our country. This delegation is the kind of service for which you have prepared." He patted me reassuringly on the knee. "And it is the way in which your life is opening."

His words were a great relief to me. "So, I should go?"

"You have no choice but to move in the direction that opens to you. It is the way."

Later that day, buoyed by my conversation with Uncle Yutang, I visited with Hu Yi and he told me much the same thing as

Yutang, only in a different way.

"Monto and I get along very well," Hu Yi said. "He will be fine staying with us."

"Yes," I replied. "I am sure he will enjoy his time with you."

"I think that is good," Hu Yi continued. "But it is difficult, too."

I was not sure where the conversation was headed. "How is that?"

"He likes me and it leads to a conflict between you and him."

"Getting reacquainted has been difficult."

"And that," Hu Yi said, "is the real basis of your problem, isn't it?"

"Yes," I admitted. "It is."

"But that is a price your life requires," Hu Yi pointed out. "That is not an easy word to accept from me. After all, perhaps I enjoy having Monto with me and would easily agree that you should take the trip. But I know that we do not have many in our country who can serve in the manner you can offer. You have been trained for the service being offered to you. And so you and Monto must serve in that manner."

I was puzzled by his statement. "Me and Monto? You understand, I cannot take Monto with me? That is what we are discussing." I was concerned that perhaps he had misunderstood my situation.

"Yet," Hu Yi replied, "Monto must pay a price for your service by enduring your absence. And so you both serve."

Hu Yi and I had become friends while attending school because, even though he was older than I, we both were interested in the same things. He often thought of me as the smarter one and said so many times, but I knew in my heart that was not the case. Talking to him that day I reaffirmed my earlier conviction. Each time we engaged in conversation he told me something I had never considered, as he had that day. Indeed, Monto and I were servants of the state. Until then, I had not thought of my son as my fellow servant. I did not make that mistake again after that.

⚬⚬⚬

For the trip to the United States, we took a ship that sailed from Guangzhou. I shared a room with Fu Taihua, an official from the central government. Fu enjoyed reading at night and kept the light burning near his bed until well past midnight. Otherwise, the trip was uneventful.

Our ship arrived late in the afternoon at the port of Los Angeles. We spent the night at a hotel, then took the train to Chicago the next morning. Traveling across the continent by rail was an enlightening experience. The first thing I noticed was the vast wide-open spaces of the North American continent. The second was its size—our journey required almost three days to complete.

The Chicago World's Fair was a yearlong exposition conducted to celebrate the centennial of the city's founding. The fair's theme was technological innovation with an official slogan: "Science Finds, Genius Invents, Industry Applies, Man Adapts."

The centerpiece of the event was the Sky Ride, an aerial tramway suspended two hundred feet above the crowd that ferried people across the harbor in downtown Chicago. I had never seen anything like it before and neither had anyone else in our delegation.

While in the United States I had the honor of accompanying Shi Zhao-ji, China's minister to the U.S., on a visit to the White House for a meeting with President Franklin Delano Roosevelt. We traveled to Washington, D.C., by train from Chicago. On board the train and at stops along the way, I heard talk of an expected war in Europe. Articles about it were broadcast on the radio and published in almost every newspaper. It seemed as though everyone expected war to begin soon, but no one expected it to involve the United States. Few knew much about our situation with the Japanese, and those who did failed to recognize it as an American concern.

When we arrived at the White House, even the president seemed to feel that war was inevitable. He, however, thought war in Europe was a threat to the entire world, as it had been only a few decades earlier. And he was well aware of the dangers posed by the Japanese.

"Japan is an immediate threat to China," he told us, "even greater than what they've already exhibited. Unless they are stopped, they could subject the entire continent to their controlling influence, if not to their direct control."

When he learned that I had been in Germany recently, he

turned the conversation toward me. "What do you think of the German situation?"

"Most certainly war is coming," I replied. "But Hitler is not merely interested in restoring Germany to her former glory. I think he intends to take control of as much of Europe as possible."

"Yes," the president agreed. "And I think he wants more than Europe. I think he wants to rule the world."

Our time in the United States had been rewarding in many respects. Culturally, we had seen a lifestyle most Chinese citizens could not even imagine. Technologically, we were afforded a glimpse of human innovation with the potential to transform our Chinese lifestyle. And in spite of our rigorous and demanding schedule, the trip had been a pleasurable one with none of the responsibilities associated with our daily jobs back home. However, as we neared the end of our stay, most in our group were ready to return home. Several were eager to get to work making China as much like America as possible. I, however, was not ready to leave.

In America, I was once again far from China, which meant far from the sadness that confronted me there. When I walked the streets of Chicago, I saw nothing associated with Gin-lien. In Changsha, everything reminded me of her and I found myself looking for her appearance at every turn. Returning home seemed like returning to a funeral. A funeral for the love of my life.

A funeral with no end.

One of the places I visited often during our stay was the campus of the University of Chicago. Most of the buildings were constructed of heavy stone blocks and when I walked down the hallways I heard the faint echo of my footsteps. In my mind, it was the perfect place of learning. And as I spent time there I was overwhelmed by the warm, inviting sense I received while sitting in Father's room on the stool beside his cot.

Not long before we were to return, I stopped by the registrar's office at the university and inquired about classes for the coming academic term. The university had a world-renowned program in international law and I was curious about the courses of instruction it offered. As I read through the brochures and catalog I received that day, my mind came alive with the thought of studying at the school.

A few days later, I located a telegraph office and sent a wire to Sha Qing, the president of Hunan University, asking if it would be possible for me to remain in the United States awhile longer in order to study at the University of Chicago. After due consideration, Sha Qing agreed that I could remain in Chicago after the delegation departed for a period of one year in order to study international law. He also indicated that if I studied English Literature, one of the subjects I taught, Hunan University would pay for all of my courses.

Shortly after enrolling for class, I met members of the Chinese community in Chicago. They invited me to a party that was held at the Drake Hotel, which was located near the center of the city close to the shore of Lake Michigan. Our ballroom afforded a magnificent view of both the lake and the city and I was enthralled with all of it.

As I stood at a window, gazing out at the lights that evening, James Chong, one of my newfound American friends, approached. He was accompanied by a woman whom he introduced as Grace Lee. She appeared to be about my age and I was immediately struck by her beauty.

After introducing us, James drifted off with other guests of the party, leaving Grace and me to talk among ourselves. I learned later that she had noticed me and asked James to introduce us. As we stood at the window that evening, I knew none of that. Only her name and her beauty.

Even more mystifying than the images I had seen outside the window, Grace evoked sensations in me that were similar to those I felt years before when I saw Gin-lien that day walking home from school with her brother. Immediately, however, my heart was torn between that desire for Grace and a sense of abandonment that arose inside me at the notion of feeling that way about anyone other than Gin-lien. Still, thoughts of Grace seemed unavoidable at the moment and we talked the remainder of the evening, ignoring the other guests and focusing only on each other.

The next day, I invited Grace to dinner. She readily accepted and we enjoyed an evening together, talking and dancing. But mostly talking.

In our conversations I learned that Grace was Chinese American—a fact I had deduced from her appearance and her lack of accent. Her mother was Chinese. Her father was a descendant of early Protestant immigrants, and the family had lived in the United States almost as long as any Europeans, which made them quite American. An executive with a Chicago corporation, her father's position afforded Grace an above-average lifestyle, free from want. I wasn't sure I could ever meet her expectations, but the attraction I felt for her demanded my attention. She seemed to reciprocate those feelings.

Over the weeks that followed, Grace and I spent more and more time together. The sense of loneliness I had felt before and the preoccupation I'd had with the death of Gin-lien receded into the background of my memory. The sense of guilt over being with someone else evaporated, too.

As the end of my year of study approached, I found I could not bear returning to China on my own and being separated from Grace. Consequently, I proposed that we marry and that she return with me to live in Changsha. Despite the misgivings of her family—the difference between life in the United States and life in China was their primary concern—Grace readily agreed to marry me. Rather than celebrating our marriage with a traditional large American wedding, a few weeks after my proposal we slipped away to a place on Lake Michigan and were married in a private ceremony.

CHAPTER

❦ 17 ❦

AFTER MARRYING in the private ceremony, Grace and I spent a few days in Wisconsin at a cottage owned by a family member. When we returned to Chicago, we began preparations for our trip to China. Packing Grace's belongings and saying good-bye to her family took longer than I expected but I did my best to have patience with her. After all, she was leaving the only life she had ever known and heading off with me to a world unlike anything she'd ever experienced.

As Grace prepared to leave, I came to realize just how different our lives had been to that point and the magnitude of the transition we would face upon our arrival in Changsha. She did not speak Chinese, which meant she would be reliant on me and Monto for all of her conversations, either in English or as her translator with others. And then there was the matter of Monto.

They did not know each other, and on top of that, Grace was a woman who had reached adulthood without experience as a mother. Moreover, her life had taken her toward a style that was focused solely on her needs and wants. I knew before we left the United States that this was going to be an interesting but difficult journey.

When everything was packed and the final good-byes had been said, Grace and I took the train from Chicago to Los Angeles, then boarded a ship and sailed for China. We arrived in Changsha during the spring of 1934. In addition to the language difficulties and obvious cultural differences, living conditions in Changsha were considerably more rustic and Spartan than in the United States. Most obvious among those differences was the lack of running water and our non-Western toilets. For Grace, the reality of her choice in marrying me struck with full force and in the simplest but most unsettling areas. Understandably, she was uncomfortable from the moment of our arrival.

After returning to China, I expected to resume my position on the faculty at Hunan University as my primary job. Instead, I was asked to take a position with the Hunan government under Governor Ho Chien. The position offered to me was that of the provisional government secretary, a position second in power only to the governor.

In addition to being governor of Hunan Province, Ho Chien was a friend of mine and on numerous occasions had opened the way for my career development. When he offered me the position of provincial secretary, I readily accepted but still felt an obligation to Hunan University for its support of my extended studies in Chicago. Consequently, I continued to teach English and Economics at the university. I also taught International Relations at Chuen Chi School of Law and Politics.

Working for the provincial government as its secretary was not a standard job with established hours. My workday had no limits and often my duties at the office extended well past the time others had gone home for the evening. Likewise, being at home was no guarantee that work duties would not intrude upon my otherwise private time. The position did, however, come with one benefit we very much enjoyed. Monto, Grace, and I lived in a residence provided by the governor. The house was large and offered amenities more in keeping with those to which Grace was accustomed. Still, the adjustment to new surroundings placed Grace under a great deal of tension, which in turn affected me as well. As a consequence, our relationship was less settled than I had hoped.

Later that year, China established diplomatic relations with the Republic of Turkey. He Yao-zu was named minister of the delegation appointed to establish an embassy there. Not long after his appointment to that position, Yao-zu paid me a visit at my office. "I need someone who speaks German, understands English, and knows economics." He smiled over at me. "You are the only person I know who fits that description."

"And what would you have me do?" I asked.

"Join my staff. Come with us to Turkey."

My thoughts immediately turned to Grace, Monto, and the unsettled nature of our household. "I am newly married. And I have a son," I said in response. "I have been away from my son too long and my wife has not yet adjusted to life in China. I cannot leave them in China, and relocating our family to Turkey would be too much for them."

"I would not think of taking you without them," Yao-zu answered. "But perhaps you underestimate conditions there or the reaction of your family to the change. They might find life better in Turkey."

That evening I discussed the situation with Grace. She had been very dissatisfied with life in China and to my surprise thought Turkey might be a better place to live. I was not convinced of that, as I had heard reports of conditions there and I told her so, but Grace insisted, "Whatever it is, it will be an improvement over what we have here."

"But you do not know Arabic," I persisted. "And you have exhibited neither interest nor aptitude for learning languages."

Grace was offended by my remarks. "You think I am not smart enough?" she retorted.

"I think you are smart enough," I acknowledged, trying not to make matters worse. "But in the months since we arrived from

Chicago, you have only learned a few rudimentary words in Chinese. Instead of learning the language, you rely on Monto and me to translate for you. At the market. On the street. Wherever you are. And as a result, you have made no friends."

Grace realized this was true and she seemed to relax. "Languages other than English are difficult for me," she conceded. "But even so, I think life in Turkey would be better for me than here. If you want to go, I want to also."

The following week I had business to conduct in Nanjing and while I was there I visited with Chen Rong. Since leaving his position as secretary general of Hunan, he had been assigned to a position with the Foreign Service. At the time he made that choice, I thought he was making a mistake. The position of secretary general was second in power only that of the governor and an all but permanent appointment. Chen Rong's decision, however, proved to be the correct one, as he had risen in prestige with the Foreign Service and now was minister for European affairs.

"I understand you are set to join us," he began as we sat together in his office.

"Yes," I replied. "It seems as though I am."

"You have some hesitation?"

"Only my inexperience in working with Yao-zu."

"Ahh," Chen Rong smiled. "You have heard about his reputation."

Indeed I had, and it was not good. Many found him

winsome at first, only to encounter him later as petty, trifling, and frustrating when addressing the mundane issue of agency routine.

"But you should not worry," Chen Rong added quickly. "I suspect you will not be required to work with him in day-to-day operations. That will not be your duty."

"What will be my duty?"

"They are bringing you on staff because of your ability with languages," Chen Rong explained. "That is the skill they want from you."

"Translating documents?"

"And interpreting for them during meetings. Most of the men on Yao-zu's staff are his friends. Or the friends of friends. That is why they were included. They need you in order for their office to function."

"It can't be that bad," I replied.

"It can be. But," he added quickly, "I will do my best to protect you from any injurious consequences that might result."

In spite of what I learned from Chen Rong, I thought joining Yao-zu's staff would be the correct decision. I was interested in foreign affairs and I thought the change of location would benefit Grace. After talking it over further and discussing the matter with Monto, I met with the governor to inform him of Yao-zu's offer. He already knew of it before I arrived and asked, "What is your decision?"

"I would like to accept."

"Good," he replied. "This will be a great opportunity for you and a new opening in your diplomatic career. Now you will represent the entire nation, not just our single province."

A few days later, I formally accepted Yao-zu's offer and joined the Chinese Foreign Service. The following day, the director appointed me to the embassy staff in Turkey.

The region known as Turkey has a long and storied past. Home of many ancient civilizations, Seljuk Turks, who were Sunni Muslims, began migrating to the region in the eleventh century. Originally from different clans, they united in the thirteenth century to form the Ottoman Empire. The empire's defeat at the hands of the Allies during World War I led to the disintegration of the empire into separate states, most of which were occupied by the Allied armies. As one might expect, civil war soon followed, led by Mustafa Kemal Atatürk, and resulted in the creation of an independent Republic of Turkey in 1923, under a form of democratic rule without influence from the Ottoman sultans.

In order to complete the new nation's break with its Ottoman past, Turkey's capital was placed in Ankara, rather than in Istanbul, the traditional seat of power. The city of Ankara and surrounding area was the site of numerous ancient settlements extending back almost to the dawn of civilization. However, it only began the process of becoming a modern city after its designation as the new nation's capital. The Chinese Embassy in Turkey was located in Ankara. When we arrived the streets were still unpaved. Central water and sewer services were under construction. As I expected, accommodations there were at least as Spartan as China, if not worse.

To make matters more difficult, at least for our family, Grace could not speak a word of Arabic and there were fewer people in Ankara who spoke English than in Changsha. Monto and I picked up the language quickly and even when we encountered difficulty in communicating, there usually was someone present who spoke French or German, both of which we spoke well. Grace, however, could speak only English and was relegated to talking only with the wives of other Chinese diplomats. This presented further difficulties, as the wives tended to rank themselves according to the status of the positions held by their husbands. Often Grace was shunned by the wives whose husbands held positions higher in rank than mine. As if that were not bad enough, some of the members of our delegation and their spouses avoided Grace because she was born an American of mixed race and therefore not *really* Chinese.

Unable, or perhaps unwilling, to learn the language, and with limited personal interactions, Grace's situation only grew worse. Often she resorted to communicating with the domestic staff by pointing and shouting, as if raising the volume of her voice could overcome the linguistics barrier. I sensed there was more to our problems than merely language and wondered if she hadn't come to feel that our marriage was a mistake, but I decided not to address those concerns.

We were a long way from the environment either of us had known, surrounded by a culture neither of us had encountered before. Attempting to address the root causes of our marital difficulties, in a remote location, where language and cultural differences complicated our situation, did not seem wise to me. Nevertheless, as Grace's sense of frustration grew more intense, so also did her belligerence. And with things tense at home, Monto and I spent much of our time elsewhere.

During the following year, 1935, reports arrived at the embassy regarding the latest developments in Germany. One of those reports addressed a region known as the Saar Basin, an area between Germany and France that had been administered by France and Great Britain following the end of the Great War. In a plebiscite conducted that year under the auspices of the League of Nations, citizens of the Basin voted to reunite with Germany. The League of Nations certified the vote count and control was handed over to the German government.

Our diplomats in Germany were concerned about this latest development but they were utterly alarmed when, shortly after taking control following the plebiscite, Adolf Hitler, now in office as chancellor and prime minister, deployed German military units into the newly reacquired Basin. Before we, or the world, could digest that news, Germany announced its repudiation of the

Treaty of Versailles, the agreement reached among the warring parties to end the Great War.

As the reports arrived, our embassy staff met to discuss the latest developments. Often those discussions became heated, with members arguing passionately for one view or the other.

Jing Wenjing, our military attaché, was a strong supporter of Germany. I thought he took that position only because the army received weapons from German suppliers. Many of the things he said also left me suspicious that he was sympathetic to the Communist cause, but I kept those thoughts to myself.

One day, as we discussed these latest developments and their implications, Jing looked over at me. "So, as German expert and all-knowing adviser, what do you think of this situation?" He addressed me with an arrogant and condescending tone, which I did not appreciate but I did my best to accept it in the context of his personality. He spoke in that tone to everyone and on every occasion, from a casual greeting in the morning to his formal discussions with He Yao-zu, the ministerial head of our legation.

"These developments serve to reinforce my previous opinion," I replied.

"And what is that opinion?" Jing asked, his arrogant tone continuing.

"That Hitler will bring trouble to all of Europe."

"You still think he has greater plans than he has shown?"

"He is not merely reestablishing Germany or showing his

German pride. Each of his moves is strategic in nature with something more already awaiting implementation. He means to take control of the entire continent."

Xian Sicong from our cultural exchange section spoke up. "The Saar Basin *is* heavily industrialized."

"And it is home to Germany's largest coal deposits," someone else noted.

Jing raised an eyebrow as he glanced around the room. He huffed. "So, you all agree with Feng Shan? You think Hitler has bigger plans?"

We all nodded in unison. "These maneuvers make it plain that he intends to increase the industrialization of the Basin," I continued, "And he will use resources from that region for further industrial development throughout all of Germany."

As we talked, Su Sheng, a member of Yao-zu's office staff, entered the room and overheard our discussion. "The Germans have a coal gasification plant in the Basin as well," he added, joining in our conversation. "And that is very important because they have little in crude oil reserves."

"All of which serves my point," I continued. "For their strategy to succeed, they need control of this region."

"But that doesn't mean they intend to dominate Europe," Jing retorted. "They could simply be—"

"This is the groundwork necessary for a robust German economy," I cut him off. "As well as the establishment of a formidable German Army."

Most members of our legation were also of the opinion that if there was war in Europe, Turkey would enter the conflict on the side of the Germans. After all, their reasoning went, Turkey and Germany were historic allies, as they had been during World War I. But I did not think that would happen. I thought they would remain neutral and I wrote up my opinions in a report for Yao-zu. We met to discuss it.

"Why do you think Turkey will remain neutral?" Yao-zu asked.

"Look around us. The Turks have nothing. At the beginning of the Great War, they were an important part of the Ottoman Empire. Now they are a breakaway nation fleeing the clutches of colonialism and struggling to survive on their own."

"And they have paid the price for that decision," Yao-zu noted. "Out of a vast empire, they are left with only the region of Anatolia."

"Which is why they will do all in their power to avoid being entangled in a war that does not directly involve them."

"Perhaps," Yao-zu mused. "I think it is likely they will follow that strategy until there is some indication of a clear winner."

I smiled. "I suspect that is a strategy many will attempt to follow."

Not long after retaking the Saar Basin, the German cabinet enacted a set of measures known as the Nuremberg Laws, which, among other things, stripped Jews of their German citizenship, making them stateless subjects. In the days immediately following passage of those laws, 450,000 Jews fled Germany, most moving to France or Palestine. The rush of Jews leaving Germany created a refugee problem, not just in the countries of destination but in the transit countries, too, as many who fled did so with little or no preparation. Desperate simply to cross the border wherever possible, they arrived in countries bordering Germany with very little in the way of personal possessions. The sudden influx of new people, most of whom were destitute, caught surrounding governments by surprise, and they scrambled to accommodate the new arrivals.

The movement of displaced people quickly spread, with Jews from Europe arriving even in Turkey. Some settled for a time in Istanbul and their arrival brought to mind Charles Berman, my friend from Shanghai. I wondered how he was doing and whether he might still be living in Shanghai. By then, the Japanese were in control of the entire city and I was certain they shared many of the Nazi anti-Semitic views.

The Saar Basin wasn't the only area within Germany's traditional border that had come under international restriction following World War I. Per the terms of the Treaty of Versailles, the Rhineland—an area along the western side of the Rhine River—had been off-limits to the German military. In 1936, however, Hitler positioned units of the German Army within that area in open violation of the terms of that treaty. Earlier, he had repudiated the treaty, now he gave definition to what that repudiation meant—the renewed exertion of German military authority.

The week German deployments were announced, we spent hours in meetings discussing the meaning of it, attempting as best we could to forecast how other countries in Europe might react, and projecting the consequences that might fall on China.

In my analysis, deployment of German troops in the Rhineland was a cause for war against Germany by the Allies and all parties to the treaty. As obligors, the parties were bound by their signature to enforce its provisions. Failure to do that would send a message to the German government inviting them to assert themselves as they wished against any of their neighbors. I stated my position at every opportunity but no one felt it had merit. At least, not enough to form the basis of a national policy.

"You are correct," Xian Sicong agreed. "This ought to be a cause for war. But it will not. No one in Europe wants a repeat of their experience in the Great War."

"It was a great slaughter," Su Sheng added. "Years of young men marching to their death. And for what? It accomplished nothing."

"Because they had no one who understood total war," Jing Wenjing responded.

"It appeared rather total to me," I said. "Very nearly toppled every regime in Europe."

"Even that of the winners," Sheng noted.

"And might topple them," Jing inserted. "Even after all these years."

"How so?"

"The nations of Europe fought. But no one really defeated anyone, except perhaps the Ottomans. The Allies only ended it by maneuvering Germany into a position from which it could no longer defend itself. But the peace they established was only a cessation of conflict. Not a resolution of the issues."

"It was a bad war. And a bad agreement."

"Yes," I agreed.

"Europe lacks the energy, stamina, or determination to stop Hitler and the Germans," Jing continued.

"But they ought to," I argued. "Otherwise, he will rule them all."

"I think he has bigger plans than simply to rule," Sheng sighed with a dour expression.

"What do you mean?"

"I think he means to remake them as well."

It seemed like an odd comment. "Remake them?" I asked with a quizzical expression.

"I think he means to remake the European people. Have you read *Mein Kompf*?"

My eyes brightened. "You mean about the Jews?"

"Does he not assert that the Jews and the Romani are the only alien people in Europe?"

I nodded my head slowly, trying to remember exactly what Hitler had written in his book. "Yes," I said finally. "I think so."

"I think he means to remove them."

"How?"

"I don't know, but I think he means to remove the Jews, Romani, and everyone else who does not fit into his poorly scienced view of humanity."

"An ethnic cleansing," I noted.

"Of the worst order," Sheng added.

"Poorly scienced," Jing scoffed in his typically condescending tone. "Is that a new word?"

"A new phrase," I said, coming to Sheng's defense.

"And it is absolutely accurate," Xian Sicong nodded. "Hitler is politicizing everything—science, religion. All of it. Every aspect of German life is being restyled after a new political order."

"Remaking it," I interjected.

"Yes." Sheng nodded vigorously. "Remaking everything, and not for the better." I noted the look on his face when he spoke and the way he kept his eyes focused on the floor, as if seeing something none of the rest of us could. And I wondered then if he had been privy to information that came only to the minister's office. Su Sheng's position on He Yao-zu's staff gave him access to every document that reached the ministerial office. Very few reached Yao-zu's desk without first passing through Su Sheng's hands.

Our discussion that day once again brought to mind Charles Berman, my Jewish friend from Shanghai. And once again I wondered where he was and how his life had fared. If anyone at our embassy knew of the conditions facing the Jews in Shanghai,

Su Sheng would be that person and I considered asking him, but that would require a meeting without the others and a location other than the embassy. A difficult meeting to arrange under our circumstances, but I began that day to consider how I might bring it to pass.

CHAPTER

18

EARLY IN 1937, Su Sheng called me to the ministerial section and informed me that the Foreign Service had decided to transfer me to the Chinese Embassy in Vienna, Austria. This was not an offer submitted for my review and approval but a directive authorized by Chen Rong. I had little choice but to prepare for the move and be on my way.

Being ordered to a new location without consultation made the change less palatable than it might otherwise have been, but it was made more acceptable by the additional news that my assignment included an appointment to the position of first secretary. This was a promotion for me and a realignment of my status in the Foreign Service to a level more in keeping with my academic credentials and prior experience. In fact, it was the position He Yao-zu suggested for me when he first recruited me to his delegation but which had been negated by Foreign Service personnel directors. I was being hired for my initial position with the national government, even though I had worked with the provincial government for a number of years.

At the time Su Sheng informed me of my pending relocation, the workday was not yet complete. I still had several hours of duty at the embassy in Ankara before leaving for the evening. During that time I thought about the coming move and how news of it would be received at home. I was glad to get the promotion but moving to Austria did not involve only me; it included Monto and Grace. Monto was still an adolescent and I knew he could accept change more readily than any of us. For him, the move would be merely one more step in a grand adventure. With Grace, though, I was uncertain how things would turn out.

That evening, I came home early and we enjoyed dinner together, all three of us seated at the dining table with the meal served in courses by our staff, something Grace valued from her childhood. Afterward, I asked them to remain while the staff cleared the table, then I carefully told them about our situation.

As I expected, Monto was excited at the prospect of living in a new location and was immediately accepting of the idea. He also was immediately interested in leaving the table, which we readily allowed. When he was gone from the room, I turned to Grace. "What do you think?"

"I think we have no choice," she answered. Her voice sounded restrained but for an instant I was certain I saw a smile flicker at the corners of her mouth.

"No, we do not have much choice." I addressed her in a serious manner so as to be certain not to offend her. "I think if we do not go to Vienna, I would have to resign, which would mean returning to China. But I do not want to force you to go to either place."

Suddenly a broad smile burst over her face. "Living in Austria would be a *dream* compared to Turkey."

Her burst of happy emotion caught me by surprise and left me uncertain of how to respond. "So, you are agreeable to the move?" I wanted to make certain I had not misunderstood.

"I am agreeable." Then she leaned over and kissed me with a warmth that had been missing since we left Chicago. "Can we go tomorrow?" she asked softly.

Of course we could not leave Turkey that quickly. Concluding my pending work and handing off ongoing matters to others took several weeks, as did packing our belongings, but by the following month we were prepared. The embassy staff held a party for us and we spent the evening saying our good-byes. For the first time, and perhaps owing to the formal setting of the event, wives of every level visited with Grace. "We should have done that earlier," she told me later. "They actually talked to me."

The next morning, Su Sheng arranged for delivery of our household goods to Vienna, then scheduled a car to drive us to the train station in Ankara for the first leg of our journey, a short trip that took us only across Turkey to Istanbul. After a day to relax in the city, we boarded the Orient Express for the trip through Europe on a route that took us from Istanbul to Bucharest, then on to Budapest before reaching Vienna three days later.

In Vienna, we resided at Beethoven Place in the city's Third District. Our residence was across the street from the city park. After several days to settle in, we enrolled Monto at a school in the nearby Graben neighborhood. The school was near St. Stephen's Cathedral in the city's First District, which we made our church home, attending services each Sunday that we were in town even though it was a Catholic congregation and we were not.

Vienna was a charming city with a rich history. The people were vibrant as well, both intellectually and personally. I made sure to present myself as a distinguished diplomat with an accomplished academic record and offered them what I hoped was a witty, engaging personality. For the most part, I was well received by the diplomatic community and by the Viennese intelligentsia.

At first, Grace found conditions in Vienna to be an improvement over what she had endured since leaving Chicago. Running water and Western-style toilets made her daily routine much more pleasurable than it had been in Ankara or Changsha. Before long, though, she once again encountered the problem brought on by her difficulty with language—this time with German and French— and was forced to spend her day among people with whom she could not communicate. A few people we met spoke English and she made one or two friends outside the wives of diplomatic staff, but mostly she was left to herself. Before long, the newness of the residence wore away and her sense of frustration began to rise. That frustration simmered into bitterness, and her attitude grew caustic.

In the meantime, my work brought me in contact with several Viennese organizations eager to learn about China and all things Chinese. I was all too eager to tell them. In doing that, they learned of my expertise with English literature and before long I was booked to address the city's literary and theatre clubs. One of those was an English club sponsored by a woman from Australia whose last name was Littlejohn. The club met in the evening and everyone who attended was expected to speak only English the entire time. This was perfectly suited for Grace, and I insisted she accompany me when I spoke. She had a delightful time and, in turn, insisted that we attend the club each time it met, which we did.

At the time, Austria's population included approximately two hundred thousand Jews. A majority of them lived in Vienna. During my first year of duty I met most of the Jewish leaders and quite a number of Jewish professionals and academics. One of those was Karl Meitner. He was fluent in many languages, one of which was English, and often attended Mrs. Littlejohn's English club. Grace and I met him there on our first visit and we all enjoyed each other's company.

Meitner held a PhD in neurology, which he obtained under the guidance of Edward Flatau, a noted Polish neurologist and pioneer in the study of the brain. Ironically, Flatau died from a brain tumor several years earlier, but Meitner understood his research and continued his work at the University of Vienna, where Meitner served as a professor.

Although Meitner was quite different in demeanor and education, he reminded me of Charles Berman, whom I knew when I stayed in Shanghai. Like Berman, though, Meitner was personable and engaging. After our first introduction at the English club we continued to get along very well and met regularly over dinner, where we engaged in wide-ranging discussions on a broad list of topics. Issues and ideas that took us beyond his field of study or my field of expertise.

Often when Meitner and I met he was accompanied by his sister, Anna, and I came with Grace. As with her brother, Anna was fluent in English and the two women easily engaged in conversation as lively and stimulating as any Meitner and I enjoyed. Very quickly, Anna and Grace became good friends, which was a positive development for all of us.

One evening, though, when Anna was out of town, Meitner and I met for dinner alone, just the two of us, at his home in District Four of the city. Afterward, we shared desert followed by coffee. As we sipped coffee, Meitner related, "I would like to share some troubling news."

He looked quite serious and I wondered if something had happened to his sister. "By all means. Tell me what is troubling you."

Meitner took another sip of coffee, then set his cup on the saucer and pushed it aside. "Friends who live in Mannheim—you know where this is located?"

"Mannheim, Germany?"

"Friends who live there tell me that government agents have begun systematically clearing the elderly from nursing homes."

The comment made no sense to me. "Where are they taking them? You mean transferring them to a new facility?"

Meitner gave me a knowing look. "They aren't taking them anywhere. At least, not to a medical facility."

I frowned. "I don't understand."

"According to people who live there, special units accountable only to Hitler are removing the elderly from these homes, placing them in military trucks, and hauling them off to some remote location. No one knows for certain where these sites are located, but information gleaned so far indicates they are places at which these government agents are killing the patients."

My expression switched to one of horror. "Killing them?"

"Rumors suggest the agents in Mannheim are using a former mining pit near Weinheim. They line them up on the edge of a pit—those who can stand—and shoot them from behind. The bodies fall forward into the pit, then a bulldozer pushes dirt in on top of them."

"And the others? The ones who can't walk or stand?"

"They are shot while lying on the ground."

I thought about that a moment, "And then what?"

"The bulldozer rolls them into the pit when it pushes in the dirt to cover the others."

"This can't be correct," I sighed. Certainly, I didn't want it to be true. It was too horrible, too incredible, too inhumane. The thought that a fellow member of humanity could be that cruel, their reasoning that twisted, was more than I wanted to consider. "But how do they explain this?" I asked finally, as if there could be no explanation and therefore surely no one would engage in conduct they couldn't explain. "No one would allow this to happen."

"Thus far government officials have denied all of it, but since coming to power Hitler has been railing against people who consume German resources while producing nothing. We think those speeches were actually the groundwork for this action. Providing the policy rationale."

"I have heard Hitler's speeches," I noted. "We receive copies of them at the embassy. Most people assume he is referring only to racial groups."

Meitner nodded. "As did we. We assumed he was talking about us—the Jews—and the Romani. And several other groups."

"Homosexuals and Africans," I added, identifying other groups that we knew to be included as objects of Hitler's racist rhetoric. "But you think he might have included the elderly?"

"I will show you something," Meitner offered. "But this must be kept strictly confidential."

"Of course."

Meitner rose from his chair at the table and walked over to

a desk near the window, opened a drawer, and took out a piece of paper. He returned with it and handed the paper to me. "This was a memo that circulated among his staff two weeks ago. It is marked Top Secret. We could be shot on sight for having it in our possession."

"We are not in Germany," I quipped.

"It doesn't matter," Meitner said grimly. "They have agents everywhere and they are not interested in following the laws of other countries."

The memo was written by Heinrich Kollmer, staff assistant to Martin Bormann, and in four short paragraphs made the argument that caring for elderly patients in nursing homes—patients who had no hope of returning to productive life—placed an unacceptable drain on Germany's limited resources. Resources, Kollmer argued, that could and should be devoted to other causes having a direct benefit to the national interest. The memo concluded by suggesting that terminating those patients would be both humane and fiscally responsible.

I glanced over the document, then laid it on the table. "And no one opposed this idea?"

Meitner shook his head. "I am told everyone who received that memo signed off on it with approval."

"Including Hitler?"

"That is what I am led to believe. I am awaiting final confirmation of that but we believe this now to be official German policy."

"Surely someone must have opposed it."

"Not a single person." Meitner leaned back in his chair. "We think that what is happening in Mannheim is being repeated all across the Germany." He looked at me and raised an eyebrow. "Even in the areas that they have reoccupied along the border."

We talked awhile longer after Meitner showed me the German memo, then I went home and sat in a chair in our living room, thinking about what I had heard and about the Chinese context into which that information fit. Although I had not mentioned this action in specific, I had discussed the possibility of this kind of thing many times since living in Germany.

My time there afforded me a view of the German people's reaction to Hitler. I felt then, as I have continued to believe in the years that followed, that the situation was moving toward a catastrophic moment, though I did not know the specifics.

That the information Meitner shared with me that evening was deeply troubling on a personal level needed no real explanation. The notion that a human being would think such action acceptable under any condition was utterly unthinkable. And as difficult to accept as that might have been, its implications were equally unsettling politically.

Chiang Kai-shek was on very friendly terms with German officials, both those in China and those in Europe. He was particularly close to Hermann Kriebel, the German consul in Shanghai. German companies were integral to the economic development of our key provinces, among them Hunan Province, and Chiang had gone to great lengths to promote their investment in our economy.

But beyond that, Chiang deeply admired Adolf Hitler and his nationalist interests. Hitler's leadership in effecting his ideas fascinated him. Even more than that, the ingenuity of the German people was a model Chiang wanted to adopt for China. In an effort to implement that desired result, he worked tirelessly to make Germany a Chinese ally. Purchasing arms from the German government for our army—transactions that were coordinated through Kriebel in Shanghai—was but one step in the development of a relationship he hoped would broaden into a much stronger alliance.

So serious were Chiang Kai-shek's intentions toward Germany that he sent his son, Chiang Wei-kuo, to voluntarily join the German Army. After extensive training in mechanical warfare, Wei-kuo became a junior officer in a Panzer division and commanded a tank crew. This seemed to harken back to a time when alliances were made through intermarriages of royal families. When I thought about it, I often wondered if Chiang Kai-shek didn't see himself in that same way.

All of this was on my mind as I sat at home that evening after returning from dinner with Karl Meitner. Grace and Monto were asleep when I arrived and I did not wish to wake them, nor was I ready to retire for the night. So I sat alone in the darkened living room with only the silence and my thoughts for company.

Sometime later, I heard footsteps on the stairs. From the sound of them I knew Grace was coming down to find me. A moment later, she appeared before me and asked, "Are you okay?"

"Yes, I am fine."

"But you are sitting in the dark. Did something happen?"

"Nothing like that."

"Then something like what?"

Speaking in vague terms I told her that Meitner shared my suspicions of Hitler, the Nazi Party, and the German government. She seemed not to accept that as an explanation and took a seat on a footstool near my chair. "Are you sure that's what's on your mind?"

I was somewhat irritated by her question. "What else would it be?"

"Gin-lien, perhaps."

"I was not thinking of her." And indeed, I was not, though I might have been had it occurred to me. Memories of her came to me often, usually in the small things like the way someone smiled or the sound of their laughter. Until that night, however, it did not occur to me that Gin-lien's shadow might linger over my life, perhaps in a way that was obvious to others and yet hidden from me. I reached out and took Grace's hand in mine. "She was an important part of my life, but that was another life and a time long before I met you. I was not thinking of her."

"Then how is it that your discussion with Karl brought you here, in the dark, sitting all alone?"

"We discussed things that cannot be spoken of without endangering others. Matters related to the work we do at the embassy."

"Oh," Grace wrapped her hand around mind and stood. "If that's all it is, come with me." She had a sly expression that was apparent even in the dim light. "Let's see if we can find a way to make you forget about work for a moment."

CHAPTER

❧ 19 ❧

THROUGH THE REMAINDER of the year, events
in Austria moved inexorably toward confrontation, conflict, and
unification with Germany. Sometimes, conflict appeared immi-
nent. At other times, unification appeared unavoidable. But always
there was confrontation in one form or another as the Nazi propaganda machine applied pressure from every direction on the
Austrian government, slowly bending it to Hitler's will.

Since the time of classic antiquity—a period commensurate
with Greco-Roman culture—Germanic tribes had occupied
central Europe. Goth, Burgundian, Lombard, Angle, Saxon,
Jute, Suebi, and Vandal, to name a few. Their ability—or inability—to coexist and later their success—or lack thereof—in defin-
ing themselves collectively as a Germanic state was largely the
history of Europe. Their descendants became the groups we

know of today as English, German, Austrian, Swede, Dutch, and French.

In the sixteenth century, Germanic tribes formed the core of the Holy Roman Empire. During that time, Austria came under the control of a branch of the House of Habsburg and was ruled by a monarchy whose authority territorially overlapped that of the Holy Roman Empire.

Although ethnically one of the great Germanic tribes following the Protestant Reformation, Austria's place in Germanic statehood shifted with the political and military tides of Europe. It was part of the Germanic Confederation but later excluded by Prussia. It was part of the Austro-Hungarian Empire but forced to withdraw when the empire collapsed following World War I. Left to languish as a rump state—a remnant of a once-mighty nation with no governmental or historical context—Austrians briefly sought unification with Germany, but were forbidden by the subsequent Treaty of Versailles.

With the rise of German nationalism under Hitler, the long-held dream of Germanic people uniting to form a Greater Germanic Reich once again came to the fore. Austrians were enticed by the sentiment of finally resolving their national identity—once and for all. Hitler was enticed by the natural resources Austria offered—resources that were sorely lacking within Germany's borders—and by the Austrian factories and mines left idle by the Great Depression. With those resources at his disposal, Hitler could build the Germany of his dreams.

Throughout the remainder of 1937, Hitler placed great pressure on the Austrian government to effect unification with Germany. He hoped to do so peacefully through parliamentary procedure or at least through a plebiscite as he had with other regions along Germany's borders. Peaceful unification meant taking control without destroying the factories, highways, and bridges he deemed necessary for his plans, and without inflicting irreparable damage on the Austrian economy. He wanted the country intact, not in fragments.

Unification through political means moved slowly, though, and in the spring of 1938, Hitler recast the issue of conquest as one of liberating the suppressed German people who lived in countries that bordered Germany. He singled out Austria as one of those countries. The tone of Hitler's rhetoric continued to escalate, applying great pressure to Austria's political leadership as sentiment while among the Austrian population grew in favor of unification.

In response, the Austrian government, desperate to preserve some form of secular Austrian identity, tried to accommodate German demands without totally collapsing. Finally, however, Hitler's patience ran out and in March 1938, German troops crossed the border into Austria, effecting unification by force. Days after German occupation, an election was held to ratify the decision already imposed on the country. Not surprisingly, ninety percent of those who voted expressed approval of unification with Germany.

From our position at the embassy in Vienna, the vote count appeared accurate. However, the electoral process seemed quite manipulative, with Nazis officials prevalent at voting locations throughout the region to oversee every phase of the casting of ballots. Nothing about the process seemed free or un-coerced.

The day German troops arrived in Vienna, I went outside to watch as they paraded past our embassy location. Crowds lined both sides of the street and cheered wildly at their arrival. To my amazement, I saw Chiang Kai-shek's son, Chiang Wei-kuo, riding past as commander of a Panzer unit. He was perched in the turret of the tank, waving as if he were a celebrity.

Not long after the tank went by, Anna Meitner approached me. I had not noticed her in the crowd and was startled by her appearance. She looked quite downcast. "Karl didn't join you?" I knew he wasn't there, but her presence caught me off-guard and I found myself feeling awkward just then.

"He refused to attend."

"Not an unexpected response."

"He thinks we all should be praying the Kadesh."

"He thinks that we are going to die?"

"He thinks this is a funeral procession, not a victory celebration."

The mention of funerals brought Gin-lien to mind and in an instant I saw her face. She was smiling and laughing and then, just as quickly, I imagined what her body must have looked like, lying on the bed at the sanatorium in the moments after her death. Those images, brief and odd though they were, changed my perspective on that day. I had not been in a celebratory mood, but I had not been particularly dour about the moment, either.

Until then, although I was certain that Anschluss—as unification had been termed—was nothing more than a German takeover and that the presence of German troops was an occupation—not a liberation or merely legislated integration of command and control. It was an occupation of Austria, not of China. Whatever happened there would not prevent me from returning to China and a life far removed from the moment when the Germans arrived in Vienna or the consequences thereof. But all of that changed when Anna mentioned praying the Kadesh. Karl was right. This was a celebration of death, not of life.

Just then, Anna nudged me with her elbow and pointed toward the street. "Look, isn't that him?"

As I turned in the direction to which she pointed, I saw a black automobile approaching. It was a convertible and the top was lowered, allowing us to see inside. Several German officers were seated there, all of them wearing dress military uniforms with rows of medals pinned to their chests. Among them, however, was a single man who stood, his body positioned slightly ahead of the rear seat, one hand on the top of the front seat to steady himself. The other hand was raised in a stiff, rather awkward bent-arm gesture that fell somewhere between a wave and a salute.

Once again, my mind was flooded with memories. This time, memories of the morning I had stood in awe as the emperor, Pu Yi, passed us as we walked to school. The crowds. The sedan chair. The people around me kneeling. The images were so powerful that I glanced at once over my shoulder, checking to see if the imperial guards were coming toward me to whack my legs with their canes.

"He is much smaller than I imagined," Anna noted.

The sound of her voice brought me back to the moment. "Yes," I noted. "Hitler is not quite as large as his rhetoric." And immediately I was self-conscious about whether anyone around us heard me, so pervasive was the sense of Nazi intimidation.

After annexing Austria, Germany's Nuremberg Laws were applied to Austrian citizens. Those laws imposed severe restrictions on Jewish occupations, travel, and property ownership. In a matter of days, Jewish doctors, lawyers, and other professionals were no longer allowed to practice their professions.

Many Jews living in Austria wanted to leave the country immediately and settle elsewhere. German authorities were prepared to grant them permission to go, but only for those who held a duly-issued visa from another country granting them the right of entry at their destination. German authorities also required Jews who wished to leave the country to surrender all of their property to the German government and to pay a departure tax.

At the same time, the increased regulation of Jewish life and the harsh treatment imposed on Jews by German officials inspired similar action by private citizens. Not long after the German parade and Hitler's arrival in Vienna, Jews in Vienna were subjected to increasing levels of abuse—both officially sanctioned abuse and the harassment of private citizens, which was not officially promoted, but not discouraged, either.

Early one morning late in spring, Karl Meitner took the bus to the University of Vienna, as was his typical routine. Also as was his custom, he alighted from the bus at the campus entrance and strolled across the grounds to Lorraine Hall, a three-story stone and masonry building near the center of the university. When he arrived, he went upstairs to his office on the third floor.

As Meitner opened the door to his office, he was startled to find the room completely empty. Books, bookcases, files, papers, even the desk was gone, leaving nothing but the bare floor and walls. He checked the room number on the door just to be sure he was in the correct location, then stared again in disbelief.

After a moment to gather himself, Meitner walked up the hall to the office of Werner Eckert, the dean of the school's science department. A German soldier was posted at the office doorway and as Meitner attempted to enter the office, the soldier blocked his way. "No Jews," he commanded tersely.

"I am Karl Meitner. I am a professor at this university."

"No Jews," the soldier repeated and he pushed Meitner a few steps back.

As the two men stood face-to-face, locked in an angry glare, Eckert, the dean, appeared. "What are you doing here?" Eckert asked in a demanding tone.

"I came to my office but I—"

Eckert's voice took on a tone of condescension. "Sorry, your space was needed for someone else. You no longer have a position with us."

"But we have a contract," Meitner protested. "I have tenure. The faculty senate will—"

Eckert curtly cut him off. "All tenure has been reevaluated. It has been aligned with the university's new personnel policies, which the faculty senate unanimously approved. You no longer meet the requirements of our policy."

Meitner frowned. "What requirements?"

"We are no longer permitted to employ Jews in any capacity."

"Where are my research papers?" Meitner asked. "My files? And my books?"

"Everything in your office has been destroyed."

Meitner's jaw dropped. "Destroyed?"

"Burned in the disposal incinerator."

Meitner sagged against the doorpost at the thought of his years of research and study going up in flames and smoke. "What incinerator?" he asked weakly. He had no recollection of a campus incinerator.

Eckert looked away. "I must insist that you leave now. This is a busy day and I have other things to attend to."

Eckert retreated into the office and Meitner moved to follow after him, but the guard who had been standing nearby stepped between them and shoved Meitner back toward the hallway. "Leave at once," he barked.

"I want my—"

Whap! Without warning, the guard struck with the butt of his rifle hard against the side of Meitner's face. Blood trickled down Meitner's cheek and he staggered backward from the force of the blow. He caught himself against the wall to keep from falling, then turned away and staggered up the hall. When he had gone only a few steps, the guard came behind him and gave him a shove. "Leave now!" he shouted. "Jews are not permitted on this campus!"

With the guard close behind, Meitner made his way to the stairs and stumbled down to the first floor. He paused there to reflect and consider what to do next when Hans Hager, a colleague from the biology department, passed by. Meitner looked over at him. "Hans, what has happened?"

"It seems," Hager smirked, "the university has finally come to its senses."

Meitner was puzzled. "What do you mean?"

"They have finally decided to purge you filthy Jews from our faculty and from our campus."

"But my work," Meitner pleaded. "What about my work?"

Hager leaned close, his face in an angry scowl. "Your *theories* were ideas stolen from others and passed off as your own. I've always thought you were a fraud and a plagiarist, but no one else would believe me. Now, thanks to the Germans, they see the truth for themselves. It will take decades to cleanse our thinking from your Semitic corruption, but at least you will be gone."

As Hager talked, another German soldier appeared behind him. He glared at Meitner over Hager's shoulder. "Why are you here?" he demanded.

"I am a professor," Meitner replied.

"He is a *Jew*," Hager added scornfully.

"There can be no Jewish professors," the soldier stated. "It is against the law."

"He is on his way out," Hager responded.

"But, Hans," Meitner said in a desperate tone, "if I can't teach, if I can't work, how shall I live? How will I survive?"

"Relocate," Hager chided. "Find somewhere else to live. Grovel in the street. It's no difference to me. Just leave and never come back here."

"And if I do?"

The soldier stepped around Hager and took Meitner by the arm. "If you do," he said as he dragged Meitner from the building. "You will die."

That evening, Meitner came to my house and told me these things. I was infuriated at the treatment he had received and resolved to raise the matter with government officials.

The next morning, instead of going to the embassy I went from my house to the Ministry of Education, the Austrian agency that provided regulation and oversight to Austria's universities. After a short wait I was ushered into the office of Emil Brunning, an Austrian official whom I had met and with whom I had dealt before. A German Army officer, whom Brunning introduced as Major Otto Vahlen of the Waffen-SS, was with him.

Brunning sat at his desk and did not stand as I entered. "I understand you wish to speak to me about a matter involving the university."

"Yes," I replied.

"This is in regard to your friend Karl Meitner. The Jew?"

"Professor Meitner is a distinguished and highly credentialed neurologist."

"Meitner is a Jew," Brunning scoffed. "By order of the Reich Ministry of Science, Education, and Culture, Jews may no longer teach or work at any school or educational institution, including the university."

"But Meitner is a scholar," I protested as calmly as I knew how. "A foremost expert in his field."

Major Vahlen spoke up. "This policy has been issued by Bernhard Rust, our minister of science, education, and culture. It was approved by the führer himself."

The last sentence was meant to impress me, but I found the führer—Adolf Hitler—quite unimpressive and so I ignored it. Instead, I focused my attention on Brunning. "Professor Meitner's credentials are impeccable. There are few people of any nationality who know as much about the human brain and how it functions."

"It does not matter," Brunning insisted. "Meitner is a Jew."

"But he is—"

"You are from the Chinese Embassy?" Vahlen asked, interrupting me in a curt tone.

"Yes, but I—"

"And is this Meitner a Chinese citizen?" Vahlen asked, cutting me off once more.

"No," I replied. "Obviously he is not."

"Then this is a purely German matter," Vahlen pronounced as he moved toward the door. "And as Meitner is not a Chinese citizen, it is none of your concern." He paused at the doorway and gestured toward the hall. "If you would be so kind as to move along, we have to attend to other matters."

As I left the building and started up the street, I noticed a crowd gathered on the opposite corner. I made my way in that direction, and when I came abreast of them I saw four people on their knees scrubbing the sidewalk. Those gathered around them were jeering and laughing and mocking them with shouts of, "Scrub that sidewalk, Jew!" They shouted similar taunts that they delivered in a demeaning manner, often punctuated with a shove or a kick to the side of a kneeling person.

A German soldier stood close by, nonchalantly smoking a cigarette, and I approached him. I pointed across the street, "Do you not see what they are doing over there?"

"What about it?" He responded in a surly tone as he glanced in the direction to which I pointed.

"Can't you stop them?"

The soldier shrugged. "It's a bunch of Jews scrubbing the sidewalk. What's wrong with that?" That's when I realized Austria was indeed in deep trouble. No government—no people—could treat others with such systemic disdain and prejudice without incurring the wrath of God. He would oppose them, I was certain. Though I did not know when or by what means.

In the weeks that followed, prohibitions against Jewish professionals were expanded to include shopkeepers and businessmen of every variety. Even dealing in junk and secondhand merchandise was forbidden to them.

Not long after that, we heard reports from other members of the diplomatic community who experienced an increase in the number of visa applications submitted to their embassies, all from Jews attempting to flee the country. In response, most countries imposed strict limitations on the number of Jews they would accept. As Jews went from embassy to embassy in Vienna desperately trying to obtain visas only to be turned away, news of the limitations spread quickly and only served to heighten Jewish anxiety.

At the same time, anti-Semitic persecution continued to increase. Jewish shops that were forced to close were ransacked of remaining merchandise, the fixtures vandalized, and in some cases the shops set on fire. Jewish homes were attacked, too.

Those who protested these actions were arrested and taken away.

After that, many Jews who had attempted to follow the diplomatic process to leave the country abandoned the legal system and even without proper documentation simply surged across the border into neighboring countries. The rush of people from Austria created a refugee problem in Hungary, Poland, and Czechoslovakia that soon cascaded across Europe and compounded an already dire situation.

Later that year, Germany seized an area they called the Sudetenland—parts of Czechoslovakia that lay along its northern and eastern border and were occupied by predominantly Sudeten Germans. The area had once been part of the Austrian Empire, and leaders of most European nations were willing to concede German control of the region. For Jews fleeing the advancing German influence, the seizure of those borderlands meant they once again faced the heavy hand of Nazi anti-Semitism. And the refugee crisis that had been dire before suddenly became catastrophic in size and effect.

CHAPTER

❧ 20 ❧

WITH AUSTRIA no longer a separate country but rather a
province within the nation of Germany, most of our staff in Vienna
was reassigned to the Chinese Embassy in Berlin. The former
Vienna Embassy became a consulate. I was appointed as the Viennese consul-general. It was a promotion, and the new position was
well above my initial grade, but the consul staff was drastically
reduced to only one assistant, Wang Kai, and a secretary, Soshana
Schonborn, who was an Austrian citizen.

In the summer I was ordered to attend a conference that was
scheduled to be held at Évian-les-Bains, France, to address the
Jewish refugee crisis. I traveled there alone by train. The setting
for the conference was quite idyllic—southeastern France, on the
shores of Lake Geneva—and stood in stark contrast to the chaos
and disruption that then plagued much of Europe.

Delegates from thirty-two countries and twenty-four organizations assembled for the conference. Charles Cotesworth, the
scion of an American east coast industrial family, was there from
the United States. He and I had met years before during the White
House visit on my earlier trip to the U.S.

Many who attended as representatives from European countries also were those whom I had met in years past. Even Golda
Meir attended, though as an observer on behalf of the Jews of
Mandatory Palestine and not as one entitled to vote on matters
of decision.

The conference had been convened at the request of US
president Franklin Roosevelt. Because of that, I thought we
might actually find a solution to the Jewish refugee problem. As
the conference began, delegates talked openly about the scope
of the problem and the need to find a humane solution. At first it
seemed the discussions were moving in the right direction, but
then Cotesworth spoke on behalf of the United States.

"I am delighted to see so many of you respond to President
Roosevelt's invitation," he began. "As fellow members of the
human race, we face an enormous problem. One that already is
taxing domestic resources in the region and threatens to over-
whelm civilian governments throughout Europe and, indeed, the
world."

For almost an hour, he postured and posed, explaining how
the United States could not possibly accept any more refugees
than was currently allowed by US law. "Even at this level," he

pointed out, "the influx of refugees is straining the fabric of our society. A society that still is recovering from the Great Depression. Convincing Congress to permit an increase in Jewish immigration would be impossible under current conditions."

Cotesworth's remarks were disappointing, to say the least, but I feared they would also send a signal to other delegates that real action was something to be avoided. And that is precisely what happened.

One by one each of the delegates who spoke assumed the American posture on the issue, acknowledging their obligations to humanity, then deftly shirking that responsibility and doing so in a manner and with language that, to the casual observer might have seemed honorable and righteous. To me, it was utterly reprehensible.

During a break in the conference proceedings, I approached Cotesworth in private. "I have visited the United States."

He acknowledged with a nod. "I know. I was with you."

"And I have seen your wide-open western spaces."

"They are lovely, aren't they?"

"Plenty of room out there for the entire refugee population of Europe. They all could be accommodated within the boundaries of only one of your western states."

Cotesworth gave a dismissive chortle. "Jews don't want to live in the west. They want to live in New York City with the rest of their kind."

"Their kind?" I asked, arching an eyebrow for emphasis.

"They are not like the rest of us?"

"They look after themselves and that is all." Cotesworth had adopted a condescendingly nasty tone. "I wouldn't be surprised to find this whole *crisis* has been nothing but a ruse, foisted upon us by a Jewish cabal seeking to manipulate and control the world. Probably part of a well-orchestrated Rothschild plot."

The tone of his voice, the look on his face, and the openly racist nature of his remarks were repulsive. Especially since he was speaking to me, a non-Caucasian, and assuming I shared his views. As if the truth of his lie were somehow confirmed by a supposed universality that simply did not exist except in his delusional mind. But I soon learned that he was not unique in his views.

That evening all of the delegates dined together in a great hall. I sat across the table from the French delegation. They talked about the German threat to their borders but, just as quickly, dismissed it as impossible, as they had a line of forts that had stymied German advances in the recent Great War.

A little farther down the table, I overheard some of the delegates from England and Spain talking quite openly of terrible things. Of German squads eliminating disabled people in Germany. Clearing out the nursing homes and hospitals. Their accounts of events in Germany were similar to what I already had heard from Meitner.

"They are not really part of the refugee problem," someone commented.

"Perhaps a solution to it," another added.

Someone seated across the table groaned in response and the man who made the comment defended himself. "I don't mean to sound harsh, but we are talking about people who will die anyway. The question a government might want to address is whether they should die after consuming its limited resources or before."

"But there is a problem with your suggestion," a man seated nearby interjected.

"And what is that?"

"We all are going to die one day. So, if the government draws the line on who lives and who dies, where do they place it?"

Others spoke of less odious but equally troubling ways to deal with the influx of Jews. One delegate, whom no one seemed to know and I later learned was an Italian operative, spoke up. "I hear German officials and some from Czechoslovakia are considering the construction of a railway that would stretch all the way to central Asia."

"And what would be the purpose?" a man seated to my right asked.

"To transport Jews away from Europe," the Italian replied.

"That would be impossible," a delegate responded. "And much too time consuming to be effective."

The Italian continued. "I hear that several construction companies from France are interested in joining the project."

"We already have rails that reach to Istanbul," a French

delegate commented. "It wouldn't require much to extend that line beyond Turkey."

"And then what?" someone asked. "Simply stop the train and force them out?"

"I could think of worse."

"I hear the Germans already are thinking of worse."

"But just push them out? And let them die?"

"Who cares if they die? At least they would have a chance to live."

"A slim chance."

A delegate from Spain who was seated to my left spoke up. "I understand there are refugee camps being established in remote areas of Germany and eastern Austria. That sounds like a positive development. At least they will have a place to go and have minimal care. We never hear about this sort of thing on the news. Only about the bad things."

"That's because they aren't refugee camps," someone snickered.

The Spanish delegate seemed genuinely puzzled. "Not refugee camps?"

"Those are slave camps," the man next to him whispered.

"Death camps," another added.

"Death camps?"

"The Germans send the Jews there—the ones who are able, the ones who can work—and then they work them."

"They work them, but they don't feed them very much."

"Just enough to give them hope that one day they might feed them more."

"So, what happens to them after that?" the Spanish delegate asked.

"There is no *after that*."

"I don't understand."

"They work them to death," someone explained in a hushed tone. "Work them until they die, then dispose of their bodies."

"At least they get something out of them."

Most everyone laughed at the comment, even the Spanish delegate, but I was more than taken aback by the racist, anti-Semitic vitriol. And this from delegates at a conference that was supposed to solve the refugee problem.

That evening in my room I lay on the bed and tried to sleep, but the images that filled my head kept me awake until long past midnight. Images from the things that had been said at dinner and the way in which the delegates had said them.

Then, just as I was about to fall asleep, Charles Berman appeared to me. And a moment later, he was joined by Karl Meitner. As if in a dream, or vision. Or perhaps simply as the result of my imagination. They spoke to me the remainder of the night about the need to do something, the immorality of ignoring the Jewish situation, the requirement of all humanity—especially those who claimed to be Christian, as was I—to find a solution.

The irony was not lost on me—two Jews arguing in my mind about the demand of Christ upon my conduct—and I argued back, asserting that I was only one person with very limited resources at my disposal. They countered with much the same argument—that I was a man, a member of the human race, with resources at my disposal. And as the images faded from my conscious mind, I heard Meitner say, "You can save us."

The following day the conference continued, but the longer the proceedings went the stronger the racist attitude became. Some of the delegates were more subtle in their remarks than Cotesworth, or the ones I had sat with the night before, but they were equally as biased. I knew then we would never reach a solution.

After three days of speeches but no proposals, the conference adjourned in failure. Of course, no one called it failure but instead termed it progress. They said so in joint communiqués, statements, and memoranda. There was even discussion of a follow-up conference after the delegates had time to meet with officials back home. But everyone knew they had done little more than acknowledge the crisis and were unable or unwilling to offer even the slightest solution.

None of the major powers, not even the United States, whose government convened the meeting, would agree to increase the flow of Jews to their country. Only Costa Rica and the Dominican Republic agreed to accept more. I departed the conference feeling disgusted at the attitudes and rhetoric I had witnessed from the delegates.

On the return train trip to Vienna from the Évian conference, I sat near the window, looked out on the mountainous country-side, and thought more about what I had seen and heard at the gathering. Remarks from the delegates in their speeches and their comments during our informal time together played over and over in my mind.

As we clattered through Switzerland, I began to pray about what the countries of the world might do to resolve the issues that affected the Jews and caused them such pain. As I prayed, the Holy Spirit brought several things to mind but then turned my thoughts from what others might do about the situation to the question of what I might do. Praying in that regard, I suddenly saw an image in my mind of walking along the street in Shanghai with Chen Rong and Charles Berman and found myself overwhelmed with emotions of friendship and comradery with him.

Although our time together had been brief, Rong, Berman, and I got along well together back then and by the time I departed Shanghai for Changsha, we were the best of friends. Letters from them were few, but from what they told me, I knew that we were friends for life. Once again, however, my thoughts turned to others and not to myself.

Why couldn't the Germans get along with the Jews in the same way? The Chinese had no quarrel with the Jews; why did the Germans hold such negative and deeply entrenched opinions? Shanghai was an open city and yet it experienced no trouble from civilian immigrants of any kind. Certainly not the Jews who lived there. The city did not even require a visa for entry and yet—

Suddenly my eyes opened wide. By the terms of earlier treaties with the British, Japanese, and many other countries, no visa was required to enter Shanghai. The Jews from Vienna could go there on their own without a visa. "But the Germans will not permit them to leave without one," I whispered, remembering the current state of the law.

"But I am a diplomat." I smiled, suddenly aware of my own status and ability to affect the situation. I did not need the cooperation of faraway nations to address the conditions the Jews faced. I could to something in my own right!

My voice as I expressed these thoughts was loud enough for the people seated near me to hear and they glanced in my direction with puzzled expressions. I smiled and nodded politely, then turned to look out the window once more.

That's when I decided to take action on my own. I was duly authorized and commissioned by the Chinese government to issue travel visas that would allow Austrian Jews to travel to China. Shanghai was a city in China and whether city officials required a visa or not, I still was empowered to issue one.

Jews might not have needed a visa on the Shanghai end of that trip, but they did need one in order to leave Austria. I could fill that. A Chinese visa, however dubious that might seem to a Chinese official, would be a lifeline to the Jews. A document that would get them past the Germans and on their way. Perhaps they would go to Shanghai and live there. Certainly we could use their presence. Or perhaps they would simply use the visa to leave Austria and go somewhere else. At least they would break free of the Germans and be on their way, and that was more than the mighty nations of the world had offered them thus far.

The train from France arrived in Vienna late in the evening. Grace was waiting for me at the station and we rode home together in a car from the consulate. We spoke very little on the way and when we reached the house I went upstairs to bed without engaging in conversation. I still was thinking of the things I had heard at the conference and did not wish to discuss them further at that moment.

Early the following morning, I went downstairs to read while I waited for Grace and Monto to come down for breakfast. In reality, I wanted time alone to compose my thoughts about what I was going to say to them.

Later, as we were seated at the table and the staff was gone from the room, I looked over at the two. "I think things might be better for us if you two went to New York." I was concerned for Grace's reaction. She did not care to have consequential decisions thrust upon her and I had given her no preparation for what I had just asked. Because of the gravity of the moment, I paused to measure my words before continuing. In the resulting silence, however, Grace spoke up. "How long would we be gone?" Her expression was tense and I could see she was struggling to resist a caustic response.

"Awhile," I replied. "I cannot say how long exactly."

Grace seemed to sense the seriousness of the moment and her expression softened to a quizzical expression. "All of us? We all would go?"

I sighed. "Just the two of you."

"Why do you want us to leave?"

"Things are too unsettled here with the Germans and the Jews in constant confrontation. Other countries are talking every day of war. I would feel better if. . . you were not here right now."

Grace reached for her coffee cup. "Has there been a threat? Something specific?"

"I would just feel better about things that way. With both of you gone, I wouldn't have to weigh diplomatic matters with your safety in mind."

Suddenly Grace had a perturbed look. "You are saying we are in the way?"

"No," I responded, doing my best to remain calm. The last thing I wanted that morning was an argument with her. "The Germans have forbidden Jews from almost all forms of gainful employment. They forbade Karl Meitner to teach. Only a few days ago I saw citizens forcing Jews to scrub the sidewalk. And I—"

"We already knew this has happened," she said, interrupting me. "Why are you—"

"I think things may get worse," I blurted out. "Much worse." Grace did not like it when I cut her off in conversation but I did not want to discuss the matter in detail. I simply wanted to present the issue of them going to New York and leave it at that. "If they make life that unpleasant for the Jews, then life here will soon be unpleasant for us all."

"Well," Grace smiled after a moment. "A trip to the United States will be fun. See old friends, perhaps. Eat familiar food."

"Familiar to you," Monto offered. I could see from his expression that he was not excited about the idea of such a trip.

"You object?" I asked.

"First we lived in Turkey. Then we came here to Austria. Now New York?"

"But you will like America," Grace offered. "You have never experienced such a place as America."

"But that's just it," Monto groused. "It is one more place. One more school." He looked across the table at me and then I saw sadness in his eyes. "And you will not be there." I knew what he meant. When Grace became irritable, Monto relied on me to smooth things over. In the give-and-take of that, he and I had become quite close. Obviously, if he was in New York and I in Vienna, that kind of relationship would not be possible.

"I think this arrangement would be bes.," I gave him a look that suggested he drop the matter and accept my decision. The thought of being separated from him was painful enough. I did not wish to argue with him, too.

When I arrived at the consulate later that morning, I asked Soshana Schonborn to make arrangements for Grace and Monto to travel to New York. The remainder of the morning was spent attending to pending matters that accumulated on my desk during my absence. However, at noon I went to St. Stephen's Cathedral to pray and meditate.

As I entered the sanctuary, the senior priest and dean of the cathedral, Father Heinrich Maier, was talking with a German officer. From the look on Maier's face I sensed the conversation was not a pleasant one but I chose to ignore them and took a seat on a pew to one side of the center aisle. With my head bowed I soon was immersed in prayer.

After a while I heard a door close with a bang. Instinctively, I glanced up and saw Father Maier coming toward me. He slid onto the pew beside me with a sigh and bowed his head. A few minutes later, I glanced over at him. "You are troubled," I said, more as a statement than a question.

"These Nazis," he seethed.

"They are harassing you, too?"

"They try to tell me what I should preach and what I should teach. And then they demand the names of our communicants."

"They wish to invade every aspect of society," I noted.

"And they corrupt everything they touch," he added.

"Did you give them what they want?"

"Not yet." Then Maier gave a wan smile. "Shall I hear your confession?"

"I am not Catholic," I was quick to explain.

"It doesn't matter. Not today. Not now." He stood and gave me a nudge. "Come, follow me to the confessional." And I did.

That evening at dinner I informed Grace and Monto of the details regarding their journey. "A car will be available to us. We will drive to the port at Hamburg and you will leave by ship from there."

Grace was enthusiastic and asked many questions. I could see she was relieved to be leaving Vienna and the life we'd lived there. Monto, however, was silent even though I encouraged him to speak up. I was certain my response that morning had dampened his enthusiasm for engagement with me but I decided to leave that issue for another time.

After dinner, when Grace and I were alone, she turned to me. "Okay. Monto isn't down here now. Tell me truthfully, are we in danger?"

Against my earlier resolve, I described for her some of what I had heard at the conference in France. "The attitude of the delegates is not unique," I said as I concluded my summation. "There is not much sympathy for the Jews here, either. You have already seen what typical Austrians are capable of against them. With only a little more suggestion from the Germans, conditions for the Jews could become far worse."

Grace reached over and took my hand. "We can stay if you need us. I know I haven't accepted our conditions well, but I can do better. And I will do better, if that's what you need."

Her offer was touching and I was struck by her expression of sincerity, but I already had made up my mind about how things should be. "I think it would be best if you and Monto were not here." I gave her hand a squeeze. "You know many people in the United States and you know the language. Monto understands English well enough to survive and it will improve when he has no choice but to use it. Being there will be good for both of you." I hugged her close. "When things are better, I will send for you."

"*If* things get better," Grace corrected.

"Yes," I conceded. "*If* things change for the better."

"Or," she added quickly, "you could come to New York to get us."

"Perhaps, but that does not seem to be the situation we face."

A few days later, I used the consulate car to drive the two of them to Hamburg, Germany. We spent the night in a hotel, then I accompanied them to the dock where they boarded an ocean liner for America. I was sad to see them go but glad they were leaving. Europe was no place for them, or perhaps for anyone at that time.

CHAPTER

❧ 21 ❧

AFTER GRACE AND MONTO set sail for New York, I returned directly to the consulate in Vienna. A check of the office revealed that we had no pending visa applications and no one was waiting to apply. To remedy that situation and implement my plan to help the Jews, I walked a short distance to the nearest consular facility—the consulate of the United Kingdom.

As with us, the British office in Vienna had been an embassy, but with the unification of Austria and Germany it, too, had been relegated to consular status. I was acquainted with most of the people who worked there but I did not wish to speak to them that day. The people I wanted to approach were standing outside the building in a line that stretched up the street and around the corner. I went to the last person in line, a man who looked tired and haggard.

"Tell me your name," I said in Yiddish. The man glanced around, as if checking to see who might be watching. "It is okay." I repeated, "Tell me your name."

"Ludwig Eisler," he replied finally with a heavy accent.

"You are here to apply for a visa?" I asked. Once again, Eisler did not respond immediately but looked this way and that with a nervous expression. "I assure you. No harm shall come to you as long as you are with me," I urged. "You are here to apply for a visa?"

"Yes."

"Where do you wish to go?"

"America," Eisler replied.

"That would be a good choice," I said.

"But really," he offered, seeming to warm to me, "we will go anywhere that is away from here."

"We?" I asked.

"Me and my family."

"How many in total?"

"Twenty."

"Perfect," I nodded. "Come with me."

The worried expression returned to Eisler's face and he did not move. "Where are we going?"

"The Chinese Consulate," I answered.

His eyes brightened. "They will help us?"

"Yes."

Eisler still had not moved. "But how do you know this?"

A smile came to me. "Because I am the consul general."

Eisler thought a moment, then nodded. "Very well."

As we turned to leave, I leaned over to the next person, an older gentleman who had been standing ahead of Eisler in line, "Wait twenty minutes, then come to the Chinese Consulate. Tell the guard at the gate that you have an appointment with me." Then I handed him my business card and walked away.

When we reached the consulate I took Eisler upstairs to my office where he waited while I issued twenty visas authorizing him and his family to travel to Shanghai. By the time I finished with him, the person who had been next ahead of him in line was waiting outside my door. I escorted him into my office and he took a seat across the desk from me. His name was Fritz Altenburg, a shopkeeper from the opposite side of town.

"You are really the consul general?" Altenburg asked with a suspicious tone.

"Yes," I replied. "I am the consul general for the Republic of China."

His eyes opened wide in a look of concern. "You are issuing visas for travel to China?"

"Yes," I replied. "Shanghai."

"But we do not want to go to Shanghai." He had a troubled frown and shook his head from side to side. "That isn't where we want to go."

I smiled over at him. "You wish to stay here in Austria?"

"No," Altenburg replied sharply.

"I did not think so," and turned my attention to the papers that lay on my desk. As I finished preparing his documents, I continued to talk. "A visa from our consulate will permit you to leave the country. Where you go after you leave Austria is up to you."

"You would do this for *me*? For my family?"

"I would do it for anyone who wishes to flee the Nazi occupation." I lowered my voice a little. "Please tell your neighbors and friends."

"I will," he assured.

Later that day, two more Jewish families came to our offices, both of them referred to us by Altenburg. I issued visas for them and the following day a dozen more arrived. At first, I processed the documents myself. No one else in our office had done this kind of thing before and did not understand the proper manner in which travel documents were assembled. For me, the work was a form of ministry and I felt as if I were in the sanctuary of a church, rather than the building of a diplomatic facility.

From those first attempts to offer the Jews our help, the volume of work in our office gradually increased. In order to accommodate the growing number of applicants and those I thought were yet to come, and to process the requests quickly, I brought Wang Kai into my office to observe and learn how to prepare visas himself. Wang was a quick study and soon he was interviewing applicants and preparing documents on his own.

News of our helpfulness spread through the city, though not as quickly as I expected. Nevertheless, I knew that word was gradually spreading because of the increase in the number of visa applications filed with our office. Jews were surprised by our acceptance of them. They also were surprised by our friendliness and prompt service, which I insisted we continue to provide even as the volume steadily increased.

Wang Kai was glad to help and seemed to enjoy the work. However, he did not understand the need for urgency or why I insisted on such personalized attention. "They are Jews, not Chinese citizens. Why are we devoting our time to them?"

"Have you not seen how they are treated?"

"I have seen the way the German soldiers treat them. Germans think of the Jews as the Japanese think of us."

"Precisely my point," I replied. "Without a visa Jews will be consigned to a life of misery and persecution. Perhaps worse. We have the capacity to help. The capacity to offer them freedom."

Wang had a puzzled expression. "All of that from a visa?"

"Unless they have a visa, the Germans will not allow them to depart the country. A visa from our office gives them the opportunity to leave Austria and find a better life elsewhere."

"I guess you're right," Wang conceded. "I just don't see why we have to—"

"Our ability to help imposes a moral obligation on us that requires us to act." Wang was a good worker, but he seemed to lack personal morality. I was not certain he understood Confucius, either. At least, not as Father taught Confucian philosophy. Wang's understanding was at a level no deeper than the popular platitudes every Chinese person seemed to repeat, though never gave them serious consideration.

"We must help them escape," I continued. "And we must help them retain their dignity."

Wang looked over at me. "You sound like a philosopher."

"A Christian. I am a follower of Christ. And even if I were not, we still must help them escape and help them remember that they are of great individual worth. Even Confucius would tell you that."

Wang smiled. "My mother tried to convince me I should read Confucius."

"You did not?"

"It was not of any interest to me." And then I knew I was right in my earlier assessment of him.

As Wang and I continued to discuss our work, memories of Father came to mind and I remembered the time we were together in his room during those painful days before he died. Thinking of him in that context brought to mind the four essential pillars of Confucian philosophy he insisted I recite—morality, respect, justice, sincerity.

In that same moment I recalled passages from the Gospels, too. Scriptures in which Jesus taught about helping those in need. That mandate to help others was not a mere suggestion but became the basis for His teaching about the final judgment and as such, gave a glimpse into the essence of what it meant to follow Him. Care for the poor, sick, dying, and imprisoned was not an optional morality only for those who aspired to a higher level of belief in Christ. Those elements were the foundational bedrock upon which all of Jesus' teaching was built. Care for others, regardless of race or condition—or perhaps *because* of their race and condition—was the basic conduct, the minimal conduct, acceptable to the kingdom.

Jews in Austria were being held captive by the German government. They were prisoners, just as if they were inmates in prison. The services Wang and I provided in issuing visas to Jews wishing to leave Austria and the horrible, irrational, ungodly actions being visited upon them was not merely some added expression of human decency. It was the least we could do and, more important to me, the least *I* could do and still claim membership in the kingdom of God.

As the days turned into weeks, news spread even deeper into the Vienna Jewish community that our consulate was willing to issue visas for those attempting to depart Austria. Day by day, the volume of visa applicants steadily rose. Yet even then, the increased volume was not so great that Wang and I were unable to keep up, though the response lengthened somewhat, requiring more and more applicants to leave their papers with us and return the next day to collect their completed documents.

Because we were not yet overwhelmed in our work, I knew we could handle an even greater volume of work. So I contacted several foreign Christian ministries working in Austria and asked them to assist us in notifying the Jewish community that visas were available from our consulate. Before long, information about our willingness to assist with travel authorization saturated the Jewish areas of the city as neighbor whispered to neighbor, "Get to the Chinese Embassy. They will help us."

Four weeks after Grace and Monto departed for New York, the number of people applying for visas at our consulate had risen to the point that Wang and I could no longer keep up within the space of a single day. Lines formed outside the consular compound with people who merely wanted to give us their application forms. At first, the lines formed in the morning and dissipated in late afternoon, but as time wore on the line lengthened, extending around the block. It was like the one I first noticed at the British Consulate, only our line never went away. People were present and waiting at all hours of the day and night, around the clock.

Eventually, Wang and I were forced to devote regular consular business hours solely to accepting visa applications. When the consulate officially closed for the day, we then worked through the night preparing the visas and related documents, but even then we could not keep up on a daily basis and a backlog developed in our office. To facilitate an even greater level of production, we resorted to sleeping on cots in the office, eating meals at our desks, residing in the building constantly.

Wang continued to raise questions about the sense of urgency with which we approached our task and the compelling reason for our actions. He did not, however, raise any questions as to the legality of our actions. That was because issuing visas for travel to

Shanghai, though irregular in the sense that they were not necessary from the perspective of Chinese immigration law, was not inconsistent with the policy of Chiang Kai-shek's administration or a Foreign Service precedent.

Historically, China's policy of openness and assistance to immigrants had been exhibited in the treatment accorded Jews in the city of Harbin, located in northeast China, when they fled to our country to escape the Russian pogroms of the nineteenth century. Precedent also had been set in the current period from the treatment accorded Jews in the Chinese-controlled portion of Shanghai. My friend Charles Berman had been a direct recipient of that openness and I had been a witness to the benefit that policy brought, both to Berman and to the city of Shanghai.

These matters now were settled Chinese law and policy and I was well within the scope of my authority in issuing the visas from the consulate in Vienna. However, Tsiang Qiz-hen, the Chinese ambassador to Germany and my immediate supervisor, had other ideas.

Having served as China's ambassador to Germany for many years, Tsiang enjoyed a warm relationship with his German counterparts in Berlin. That relationship afforded him a lifestyle of ease, access, and affirmation, a status he wanted to preserve for as long as possible. To facilitate that, he often made clear in memos and phone calls that he wished for us to extend favor to Nazi Party leaders who lived and worked in our region. Consequently, he was not in favor of assisting the Jews in any regard.

German officials had made their position clear on the future of the Jews, and Tsiang wished to take no other position pertaining to them.

With lines of visa applicants stretching around the block outside our consulate, it wasn't long before people began to notice. First, German soldiers appeared to investigate our activities and then to harass the Jewish supplicants. The soldiers dutifully filed reports with their superiors regarding what they observed, and soon Tsiang noticed us, too.

Before long, we received a tersely worded memo from Tsiang's office reminding us that our primary duty was to care for Chinese citizens who lived, worked, or otherwise traveled within Germany's borders and then to promote harmonious relations between Germany and China.

"You must comply with German law regarding all non-Chinese individuals," the memo read, "and apply German policy in accord with Foreign Service policy." I read the memo several times but it was clear from the first glance that what Tsiang really meant was that we should stop issuing Chinese visas to Austrian Jews. I ignored his directive.

The following week, Qui Houlan, one of Tsiang's closest advisers, visited the consulate in Vienna. I knew Houlan from my work in Changsha and in Ankara where I encountered him in the translation office. He had the intellect to become a capable public servant but was more interested in women than in doing his job. Tsiang enjoyed his company—Houlan was very entertaining—but hired him as an adviser in Berlin because Houlan's uncle held a ministerial post in Nanjing.

Based on my prior experience with Houlan, I was certain the decision for him to come to Vienna was one he suggested to Tsiang, rather than one that arose from Tsiang's own initiative. Equally transparent was Houlan's motivation. He was a man of leisure. A decision like this was motivated by a desire to party without concern that Tsiang might notice his conduct. Coming to Vienna on Foreign Service business also meant the government would cover his expenses, no doubt an additional factor in his reasoning.

That Houlan might have an ulterior motive or actually wish to scrutinize our consular operation was of no immediate concern to me. Houlan was not the ambitious type. I was more concerned that in his effort to justify the trip and preserve his favorable position with Tsiang, he might inadvertently say something that would create a problem for us where none had previously existed. Vienna under German occupation—with the Jews and the Germans and the Nazis and those who still favored an independent Austria—was a nuanced situation. Houlan was not a nuanced person.

Upon his arrival at the consular compound, Houlan noticed the lines of applicants waiting outside. Once inside the building, the stacks of files were unavoidable. Visa applications were stacked on every available surface. He sauntered through the outer room, glancing around with a curious look, and slowly made his way into my office. "Ambassador Tsiang," he began with an affected, imperious tone, "has heard rumors of what you are doing."

"We are conducting the work of the Foreign Service," I replied. "That is all."

Houlan took a seat in a chair across from me. "Issuing so many visas has not gone unnoticed by others, too."

"Oh?" I replied. "Who is that?"

"Don't be coy with me. You are starting to make news among the Germans."

"I'm sure they see us every day."

"Not the Germans here. The ones in Berlin." Houlan stood and walked to the window for a glance at the street down below. "Your Jews are creating quite a stir."

I did not care for his offhanded comment about the Jews but I didn't wish to unnecessarily antagonize him, either. Instead I asked, "Helping the Jews with their travel plans is a problem?"

Houlan turned away from the window to face me. "There is concern in Berlin that you might embarrass the government."

"The German government?" I asked.

"No," Houlan snapped. "*Our* government."

"My actions are lawful," I pointed out. "How could that possibly embarrass our government? Everything we do is in accordance with proper Chinese law and policy."

Houlan gestured to the stack of visa applications on my desk. "Are those proper forms?"

"Have a look for yourself. Why do you even ask?"

"They say you are issuing visas to Jews without a proper application."

"You mean that I am simply filling out the visa and handing them to people on the street?"

"More or less," he shrugged. "Are you?"

"No, all work is done according to correct law and proper practice." I gestured to the stacks of papers on my desk. "Check the files and you will see." I knew Houlan would not go to the trouble of reviewing each file.

"Good," he answered. "I will do that."

We set up a table in an adjoining room and brought Houlan several stacks of visa application files for him to peruse. As expected, however, he only looked at a few, then became bored and returned to his hotel. I did not bother accompanying him there or meeting with him that evening. I knew the real purpose for the trip and did nothing to hinder him from engaging in Vienna nightlife as he wished, though I was uncertain how entertaining it would be. Since unification, German soldiers were everywhere and normal life in the city was disrupted from its usual routine.

CHAPTER

ᴄᴏ 22 ᴄᴏ

THE FOLLOWING DAY, Houlan departed Vienna and returned to Berlin. I sent a car from the consulate to take him, but begged off from accompanying him to the train station. When he was gone, I brought another assistant, Soshana Schonborn, into the visa-processing operation in order to increase the volume. We also streamlined the process, turning a slow, deliberate review into a paper mill that churned out visas. Not quite as Houlan had suggested—we did not walk the streets with preprinted forms and randomly fill them in with information from passersby—but at my insistence we no longer held to the traditional processing format, though we continued to adhere to Foreign Service policy and Chinese law.

Wang and I reviewed the visa applications, checking for obvious incongruities, then turned them over to Soshana. She drew the names and relevant information from the papers and used it to prepare the visa form. Wang assisted her as his time permitted.

When the visas were ready for issuance they were brought to me. I reviewed the visa to assure the information conformed to Chinese law, then signed the final product. Working in this manner allowed us to produce as many visas as possible in the shortest amount of time. Although I did not perceive Houlan as a threat, I still was concerned that the report of his trip might have negative repercussions for our consular operations, particularly his view of whether we were disregarding the directive from our ambassadorial supervisor. Others had been relocated for much less and I did not want that to happen.

Regardless of the explanation I gave Houlan for our work, or the defense of it that I offered to Tsiang, our efforts to issue visas to Jews and assist them in leaving the country was unusual by any diplomatic standard. I had difficulty doing these things, though I prayed often for the protection of the Holy Spirit, but the irregularity of our conduct was a fact that Wang could not forget and he continued to raise the issue with me. He was particularly troubled by the knowledge that we were circumventing the wishes and direct order of Ambassador Tsiang.

"I have received many gifts from God," I explained, no longer interested in obfuscating my underlying motivation for my interest in the Jewish people. What I undertook to accomplish on their behalf I did in obedience to God and I was no longer interested in avoiding that topic. I added, "The things He did for me and the blessings He has bestowed upon me are not only for me exclusively but for others, too."

To my surprise, Wang seemed not at all put off by my response. Instead, he turned the conversation in a different direction. "But won't these things we are doing reflect badly on you with our superiors?"

Now I realized the thing that worried him most was not my reputation but his. "Is that really what you're worried about? Are you really concerned about my reputation in the Foreign Service?"

Wang was silent a moment, then said, "No. I am not worried about your Foreign Service career. I am worried about mine."

"I thought so."

"And Soshana's," he added.

From his tone of voice I knew his interest in Shoshana was more than altruistic. They had been friendly with each other as colleagues at first, but over the past few months I had noticed looks that passed between them which seemed to indicate more than a passing interest on both their parts. I did not mention it or address the manner in any way. They were good employees and conducted themselves always in a professional manner. I did not intend to address it as we spoke then, either, but asked, "What is your concern about her?"

An awkward look flashed through Wang's eyes, as if he wondered whether I actually knew the depth of his interest in her, but he recovered enough to explain, "Isn't she in danger from all that we are doing?"

"I hardly think so. She is merely following my direction. And she is not Chinese but an Austrian citizen."

"German," Wang corrected.

"Yes," I acknowledged. "German."

"If they are beating Jews in the street," Wang continued, "will they not beat those who help the Jews?"

"Perhaps."

"So you are exposing all of us to that risk, merely because you feel compelled to help them."

Having studied in Germany for an extended period, and studied international law in Chicago, I was certain that we were in no real danger. Adolf Hitler and German government officials were not so radical as to think they could survive without involvement with other countries of the world. And to do that, they still had to respect some aspects of international law. Diplomatic immunity and the established standards of the diplomatic profession were essential in doing that. In addition, the Nazis were not yet in a military position strong enough to disregard manipulation as a means of achieving their ends. For manipulation to be effective, they needed to establish an aura of cooperation and mutual respect, whether they really meant it or not. If we offended their sense of German dignity, the punishment would be our relocation or dismissal from the Chinese Foreign Service and expulsion from the country. I believed we were in no danger of interment.

As the days passed, we heard nothing more from the embassy in Berlin regarding Houlan's visit and inspection. As the possibility of repercussions from his report diminished, I became more focused than ever on our efforts to assist the Jews. At the same time, news of our willingness to help spread deeper into the Jewish community. The already long lines outside our consulate building grew even longer.

With so many Jews collected in one place, German soldiers could not resist the temptation to harass those waiting in line. At first appearing in ones and twos, soldiers soon came in squads to taunt those awaiting our attention, taunting them, spitting on them, and shoving them from one side of the sidewalk to the other.

Civilians noticed the conduct of the soldiers and soon joined in, beating some of the Jews who were waiting in line. Their actions were encouraged by the German soldiers, who laughed and applauded at the sight of it. There was such a commotion that drifted through the open windows of our building, and I went over to have a look for myself. When I saw what they were doing, I sent Wang outside to investigate. He returned with a troubling report and I was resolved to help alleviate the discomfort of those waiting for our attention.

"Tell the guards to allow those who are waiting to enter the grounds," I instructed.

Wang looked concerned. "That is a deviation from standard procedure."

"These are extreme conditions," I replied. "Tell the guards to open the gate."

"But—"

"Wang," I commanded sharply. "Do it now."

At my instruction, the guards opened the gate to our compound and directed those waiting in line to enter the compound grounds, inside the fence. By diplomatic accord and international law, the compound was Chinese sovereign territory. Any attempt by German soldiers to enter the grounds would be tantamount to a military invasion of China, something I knew they would never do—not as a first response.

Jews who had been standing on the sidewalk filed onto the grounds and quickly filled every available space. Still, as they entered the safety of the compound, more arrived to take their place outside the fence, enduring the harassment of the soldiers and beatings from civilians for the hope of receiving the documents necessary to permit their departure from the country. Even after nightfall, they continued to wait in line. I was impressed by their determination and stricken by the severity of their circumstance, but we had no other resources to allocate to their relief except to work as quickly as possible to process their documents, which we did with all our strength and effort.

A few days after we had opened the compound to those waiting in line, I was required to attend a conference on the status of foreign nationals living in Vienna following unification. The meeting was held at the Palais Coburg, the residence of a Habsburg descendant, and was conducted as a curtesy. Members of the diplomatic community were fully aware of German and international law as it applied to our citizens. I thought the meeting was a waste of time and did not wish to attend, preferring to remain at the consulate where I could devote my time to consular matters and the needs of the people standing outside our building, but I had been ordered to attend by officials at the embassy in Berlin. And so, I attended.

The palace was located on the opposite side of Vienna's central district from our consulate. Being too far away to conveniently reach it by walking, a driver took me there by car. On the way over, I wondered how many would attend; we all were extremely busy, but we arrived to find quite a crowd had assembled. Almost every country with a diplomatic presence in Vienna was represented. Almost. The United States did not send a delegate, nor did the French.

The meeting was divided into sessions and between the first and second, Henry Selby, the consul general from the British Consulate who was seated next to me, turned and commented, "I noticed the long lines around your building."

"Yes," I replied. "They have become quite lengthy."

"Someone told me you have allowed people to fill your compound."

"It became necessary for their safety."

Selby arched an eyebrow. "You are not concerned for your own safety?"

"Not at all. They only want to leave the country. They have no intention of causing trouble."

"I assume these are the same people who previously stood outside our facility."

"I imagine so."

"We have heard rumors about German plans to remove all Jews from Austria."

"By force?"

"Apparently. What we are hearing today is the public version of their policies. What they really want to do is move all non-Germans out of the country."

"Where would they go?"

"That's a very good question. One for which no one seems to have a clear answer. The Germans are building a camp at Mauthausen. A little way north of here. Presumably, according to our analysts, Jews from Vienna would be moved up there."

My forehead wrinkled in a frown. "All of them?"

"According to what we've heard, they want to remove all Jews from Vienna first. Then the others in time."

"That would be an operation of tremendous scale and complexity," I noted. "For what purpose would they do such a thing?"

"Well, as I said, I think removing them from Vienna is just the first thing they want to do. The initial stage of a much larger undertaking, as it were. I think they want to do that so they can make room for others they intend to bring in from outlying areas."

"Why would they do that? In stages? Move out the Jews who are here only to bring in Jews from somewhere else?"

"Perhaps they see it as a means of pacification."

"Pacification?"

"Maybe, to the German mind, gathering everyone and moving them from all the various areas is too random. Too disorderly. Most Jews in Vienna live in the Second District. If they begin there, they can collect people from outlying districts in an orderly fashion and account for them more exactly."

"Still, that would be a large operation."

Selby nodded. "But they have experience with this sort of thing."

"Experience?"

"They already have done this in Bavaria. Constructed a camp at Dachau for political prisoners, then expanded it and began removing Jews from the cities and towns of Germany proper."

The thought of such an operation and the misery it must inflict on human lives seemed overwhelming. "This is incredible," I sighed. "I have heard reports about them removing the disabled and elderly from nursing homes."

"We have confirmed that operation actually occurred. And now they appear to be moving on to address what they see as the Jewish problem."

I looked over at him. "Would they really do such a thing?"

Selby avoided eye contact. "I'm only telling you what I have heard."

The meeting lasted into the afternoon. When it concluded, I ordered the driver to take me through the Second District. As we made our way through the narrow streets, I saw crews building walls between a row of buildings with concrete block and bricks that stood along the traditional border of the Jewish Quarter. Others were busy installing fences across nearby streets. Two locations appeared to be under construction as entrances into the neighborhood and I saw what appeared to be very large steel gates yet to be hung.

At the sight of all that, the things I had heard from Karl Meitner and from Henry Selby became all too real. Jews who lived within the reach of the German Army were in serious trouble. And not just of enduring miserable treatment—they had faced prejudice and disdain for generations—no, this was much worse. The Nazis perceived them as a threat and they intended to do something about it. Their minds were made up. They intended to remove the Jewish population from Europe, one way or the other. And I was worried they might choose the worst possible means of achieving that desire.

All the way back to the consulate I brooded over what I had seen and heard, trying to make sense of it and wondering if a way could be found to speed up the emigration of Jewish people from Austria.

When we arrived at the consulate, the driver halted the car at the compound driveway while the gates opened to let us enter. The day was warm and the rear window of the automobile was open for ventilation. As we sat waiting, a man stepped quickly toward us. He held documents in his hand and when he was near the car he tossed the papers through the open window. The pages fluttered onto the seat beside me and in that moment the car started forward.

As soon as we had passed into the compound, the gate closed behind us and the driver moved the car to its place beneath a portico on the side of the building. Still seated in the car's rear seat, I gathered the documents and scanned over them and saw that they were visa applications, about twenty in total, submitted by Hans Kraus—a Jewish surgeon—on behalf of himself and his family members. The gravity of the moment, in light of what I had experienced already that day, seemed clearer to me than ever. I was not the only one who understood the threat to Jewish lives. The Jews understood it, too.

When I reached my desk upstairs, I read through Hans Kraus's documents. Satisfied by the content, I prepared the visa documents that day myself. After a final check for accuracy, I affixed my signature and placed the documents, twenty in all, in a large envelope.

Although the hour was late, almost sunset by then, I rode to Kraus's apartment in the Second District and knocked on the door. I was greeted by a woman about the age of my mother. She looked at me curiously, then glanced over her shoulder and called in Yiddish, "Hans, there is someone to see you."

A moment later, Hans Kraus, the man who threw the

documents to me as I arrived at the consulate, appeared at the doorway. He smiled, "You are the man at the Chinese Embassy."

"Yes." I introduced myself.

He ushered me inside, then closed the door behind me. "Please excuse the clutter."

The front room of the apartment was in disarray with furniture sitting askew, the drawers open, and the contents stacked on every available surface. At first I thought they must have been the object of a search by the authorities but then I noticed their belongings were in neat stacks. Those who search for contraband are not careful and fling things about wildly. That's when I saw the suitcase on the floor nearby.

"You are packing?" I asked.

"Yes. I knew you would help us. So I gave you the papers and came straight home to tell them. 'Pack,' I said. 'Our visas will be ready soon.'" Suddenly an awkward look of realization came over him. "Although, I did not mean to presume that you have brought them to us this quickly." Then his eyes focused on the envelope I was carrying in my hand and his countenance brightened. "Did you?" he asked expectantly.

"Yes," I replied. "These are your visas."

I handed Kraus the envelope and he raised the flap to look inside, then handed it to the woman who answered the door. "Give this to Gisela," he directed politely.

The woman took the envelope from him and hurried to the next room. I glanced around. "Packing is quite an ordeal."

"Yes," Kraus replied. "Sorting through our belongings, trying to choose what to take and what must be left behind."

"And your furniture?" I asked.

"That we must leave." He said the words with a smile but I could see the sadness in his eyes as he spoke. I felt sad, too, at the thought of them leaving so much.

"There is no way to send it?"

"We are leaving tomorrow by airplane. There is not room for much."

The walls held many pieces of art, some of which I was sure was of great value. And the room was filled with furniture—chairs, tables, a large sofa, and several bookcases filled with books. None of it would be making the trip with them.

After a moment I smiled at him. "That was a brave thing you did, tossing me your papers."

"We stood in line. All of us. I with my family, documents prepared, waiting for the chance to submit our visa applications. Soldiers harassed us. Some boys came and spit on us. We were afraid we would be arrested."

"How long did you wait?"

"We waited in line three days—then I saw your car turn into the compound and I saw you seated in back. When it came to a stop to pass through the gate, and the window was down, and you were just sitting right there, I thought, *Now is my chance.* So I tossed our applications through the car window."

"But how did you know who I was?"

"We saw you before, and some of the people in line with us also pointed you out. They knew you from Karl Meitner."

"Ah," I replied with a nod. "Karl is a good friend."

"He speaks well of you. I knew you would help us, but I did not expect you to deliver the documents yourself." He clasped my hand with both of his. "Thank you." And I could see his eyes welling up with tears. As were mine.

CHAPTER

❧ 23 ❧

EVEN THOUGH KRAUS was packing to leave, he interrupted his preparations to introduce me to his neighbor Samuel Neurath, who lived at the end of the hall in the apartment building. Neurath was a lawyer by training and had a thriving practice until the Germans took over Austria.

"Now with German law in place," Neurath explained, "I am prevented from practicing my profession."

We visited a few minutes with Kraus, then he excused himself and left. "We are flying out in the morning." He glanced over at Neurath. "You know what to do with our belongings."

"They will be in good hands before you reach the street on your way out."

Kraus clasped Neurath's hand. "Good-bye, my friend. Next year, we shall meet in Jerusalem."

Neurath smiled. "Next year in Jerusalem."

When Kraus had gone, Neurath looked at me. "He is blessed to be leaving, and even more so to be leaving by airplane. Many are sneaking out in the backs of trucks, the trunks of cars, hiding in rail cars with the refuse. Whatever they can do to get away."

"Will you be leaving also?"

"I am not sure," Neurath answered.

"Our office would be happy to issue visas for you and your family members," I offered. After what I had heard and seen, the thought of him, or any Jew, remaining in Vienna seemed more than unreasonable.

"My wife is not well," Neurath explained. "And someone has to be here to advise people on what they should do."

"They are sealing off your neighborhood with walls and fences."

"And soon we will need passes to enter and exit." He reached in his pocket and took out a card. "This is what they are giving us." He offered me the card. I took it from him and saw that it was a standard identity card. "Everyone has been issued one of these?"

"Not everyone," Neurath replied. "They are going block by block making sure every person is accounted for."

"A census," I whispered as I realized the Germans were putting into effect the plans Henry Selby had warned me of just a few days earlier.

Neurath nodded. "A census. Though I am uncertain what they intend to do with that information or how they mean to care for us. We are not allowed to work in our chosen field. There's a doctor on the next floor. A wonderful man. But he can no longer practice medicine. Last week, he worked as a street sweeper and was paid with loaves of bread." Neurath shook his head. "Others are being treated the same."

I knew precisely what the Germans intended to do with the census information, but I didn't have the heart to tell him. Instead, I told him I looked forward to helping him and his neighbors in any way possible, then I handed him my business card. "Come to the consulate at any time, day or night. Tell the guards I sent for you and show them my card. They will escort you to my office."

We talked awhile longer, visiting amicably over a cup of tea, then I departed. As I walked from the building, I saw a German Army officer standing beside my car. My driver was seated at the steering wheel and from the angle of my approach I could not see his face to know if we were in trouble or merely receiving serious questions.

"A rather long visit with your friend Hans Kraus," the officer smirked as I came closer.

"We are old friends," I replied, hoping that the information would somehow save Kraus from harassment when I was gone.

"You should be careful in this neighborhood," the officer continued. "It is very dangerous here at night."

The sun was setting just then, the last rays of light barely peeking over the horizon. "I am not afraid. These are my friends."

The officer came closer, his face next to mine. "You should be careful of the friends you choose." His voice was low and husky as he looked me in the eye. I did not respond but stared back at him. After a moment, he wheeled around on his heels and started up the street. I watched until he was out of sight, then opened the rear door of the car and climbed into the back seat.

Rather than deterring me, the officer's attempt at intimidation only spurred me to further interaction with the Jewish people of Vienna. Over the next several weeks, I returned to Neurath's apartment again and again, getting to know him, the community, and the challenges they faced in an intimate way.

As Neurath's confidence in me increased, he introduced me to key Jewish community leaders. Through them, I made friends with more and more Jews. Doing that took time away from the work of issuing visas, but the effort to establish deeper relationships among the Jews seemed important.

Wang Kai confronted me about it one day. "I thought your goal was to issue as many visas as possible."

"It is," I replied.

"Then why do you spend so much time with the Jews in the Second District?"

The tone of his voice hinted at a sense of irritation that I had noticed but let pass. "They are a people in need of many things. And they have become my friends."

"Wouldn't it be more helpful to them if you spent your time here, at the office, expediting their visa requests?"

"Perhaps," I acknowledged. Once again, his impertinence was

evident by the manner in which he spoke to me. "But I am hoping that, at least in some small way, I am able to ensure their safety while we prepare their documents. A window of safety that might last a little longer than merely handing them a piece of paper but to provide them an opportunity to actually leave the country."

Wang smirked, "I don't understand."

"The Germans know who I am, right?"

"Yes. I am sure they do."

"So, if they see me visiting in Jewish homes, might my presence deter the Germans from harassing or arresting them?"

"Yes," he replied. "But it might also put you in harm's way."

"The Germans are deliberate and methodical. Their policies are administered in an orderly fashion. They would not think of arresting me."

He shook his head. "I'm not so sure of that." Neither was I, but I did not say so.

✦

In spite of Wang Kai's questions and doubts, I continued to stop by Neurath's apartment at least once each week. On those occasions, he often took me to visit others or had guests already present when I arrived. One of those guests was a man named Tobias Goldstaub. "Until the Germans arrived, Tobias owned a clock shop a few blocks away from here."

"It was a good business," Goldstaub offered. "And I was known in the craft."

"Then the Germans arrived and now he can no longer work."

"They closed the shop," Goldstaub added. "Then gave the space to someone else."

"But you owned the shop?" I asked.

Goldstaub explained. "I owned the building, but they say we can no longer own property. So they forced me to sign a deed giving it to someone else."

"He got nothing for it," Neurath added. "Nothing."

"You wish to leave the country?"

"I wish the Germans had never arrived," Goldstaub grimaced. "And now that they are here, I wish they would leave."

"That is why I asked him here." Neurath turned to face me. "He insists on remaining, but he has children." He gave me a knowing look. "And daughters."

I understood his concern. "Mr. Goldstaub, there is no future for you here. The Germans have arrived and they aren't likely to leave anytime soon."

"But why?"

"There are many reasons why they came. And just as many for why they shall not soon be leaving. You, however, must."

Goldstaub looked at me with a forlorn expression. "I must leave?" he asked, standing as if to leave the apartment.

"Not the room." I corrected him. "The country."

Goldstaub's shoulders sagged. "My wife has been telling me this for weeks."

"You should listen to her."

"They say we need a visa."

"I can help with that. Bring me your passports and I will prepare the necessary documents."

Goldstaub sighed. "Very well, if that is how it must be."

Goldstaub left the apartment, then Neurath and I sat down to tea. Thirty minutes later, there was a knock at the door and when Neurath answered it, Goldstaub appeared. He held a cloth pouch and inside it were a dozen passports. He handed it to me. "Here. We will do as you suggest."

That evening, I prepared the documents necessary to permit Goldstaub and his family to leave Austria and immigrate to Shanghai. I delivered them to him at Neurath's apartment the following day. As I arrived at the building I noticed the German officer who had approached me before was standing on the corner. He watched me and as I glanced around, checking my surroundings, I saw three military trucks parked half a block away. I delivered the visas to Goldstaub and returned the passports to him without incident, but I was concerned for his safety and that of others in the building, including Neurath.

A few days later, I returned to check on Goldstaub and Neurath. This time there seemed to be no one home at Neurath's apartment, so I went to Goldstaub's. I was greeted there by a woman who introduced herself as Alma. "I am Tobias's wife. Tobias was arrested two days ago."

This was a concern to me. "And he has not yet returned?"

She was on the verge of tears. "No."

"Do you know where they took him?"

"They didn't say. They never say."

A glance over her shoulder revealed that the apartment was in disarray. Drawers had been removed from a chest and the contents were scattered on the floor. Clothes were strewn about, too, but I saw no luggage or boxes to indicate they were packing. "Your apartment has been searched?"

"Twice today. And many times before that."

"What were they looking for?"

"They didn't say." She looked down to avoid my gaze. "They never say," she muttered again.

Alma and I talked a few moments longer, then I made my way downstairs. As I stepped outside to the street, I saw the German officer was still standing at the corner, where he had been when I arrived. The thought of Goldstaub being arrested and hauled away infuriated me, and I was filled with boldness. Instead of entering the car and driving away, I walked up to the officer and stood near him, as he had done with me before. "Your men arrested Tobias Goldstaub. Where have you taken him?"

He sneered. "That is none of your business."

"Goldstaub has been issued documents approved for travel on a Chinese visa," I declared with conviction. "He is scheduled to depart for Shanghai. Tell me where you have taken him."

"Wolkersdorf," he replied tersely. He leaned in close and snarled, "You should leave him there. For your own good."

When I returned to the office I made phone calls and learned that Wolkersdorf, a village north of the city, was the site of a German detention center. I was not aware of such a facility but others in the diplomatic community knew of it and described it as a place to which the Germans took people who caused trouble for them or whom they feared might cause trouble in the future. It sounded like a vague process and I was certain that the vagueness was deliberate.

The normal diplomatic process for such instances involved filing a written inquiry with the German foreign minister's office, then waiting while they investigated. The process was usually quite lengthy and often the result was irrelevant by the time it arrived. Rather than endure all of that, I directed the consulate driver to take me to Wolkersdorf. We arrived in less than two hours.

Wolkersdorf Detention Center was little more than a net wire fence fifteen feet high surrounding a cluster of crudely constructed barracks buildings. The area inside the fence was filled with people, most of whom were men, who appeared tired, dirty, and listless.

A brick building stood near what seemed to be the compound entrance. The driver parked beside it and I went inside. An officer was seated at a desk opposite the doorway. "You are holding Tobias Goldstaub," I said without waiting to be greeted.

The officer looked up and glared at me. "Who are you and what do you want?"

"I am Ho Feng Shan," I announced. "I am consul general at

the Chinese Consulate in Vienna. I have come to collect Tobias Goldstaub."

The officer grinned mockingly, and gestured for me to step over to the window. "Look out there," he pointed. "Do you think I can locate a single person in that crowd at merely your suggestion?"

"I think you have detailed records of every person in your custody," I replied. "You can locate any person in this facility that you wish to find."

"And what makes you think that?"

"I have been to meetings with your officials who spoke in detail of how your government and military operate." I looked over at him. "I am here to collect Tobias Goldstaub. You will get him for me, please?"

The officer turned back to his desk. "And what do you want with a Jew?"

"Mr. Goldstaub is a guest of the Chinese government," I answered. That wasn't entirely correct but I cared little for exactness at the moment. I wanted Goldstaub released and was certain this would be my only opportunity to make that happen. "He has been issued a visa for travel to Shanghai. His presence there is required. I am here to collect him."

The officer took a seat and held out his hand. "Identification, please." The statement was delivered as a demand, not a request. I took my identification card from the pocket of my jacket and handed it to him. He glanced at it, then rose from his chair, pushed his way past me toward the door, stepped outside and disappeared.

A few minutes later the first officer returned with a second, apparently of higher rank. "What is this about?" the second officer demanded. "You are disrupting our operations."

"This is about Tobias Goldstaub."

"And what of this Goldstaub?"

"He is to travel to Shanghai on a Chinese visa. The Chinese government is most interested in his arrival there. Obviously, he was brought here by mistake. Perhaps an oversight on the part of a junior clerk. In any regard, I was hoping we could work this out among ourselves and avoid the necessity of telephoning our respective superiors in Berlin." I did not think matters would go that far but I was prepared to risk a call to Houlan, if that became necessary. Despite his self-promotional nature, Houlan was one who enjoyed a ruse, especially in situations such as this where we held the advantage of speaking openly. Few of the German soldiers we encountered were fluent in Chinese.

The two men huddled together near the desk. After a moment, the second man turned to me and ordered, "Wait here." Without further conversation, he placed his hat atop his head, opened the door, and stepped out.

A few minutes later, a soldier appeared with Goldstaub in tow. I placed him in the car with me and we returned at once to Vienna. It was almost dark when we arrived in the Second District and I saw that the fences and walls were almost complete. Soon the Germans would begin the process of removing the residents, a moment I dreaded.

As the car came to a stop outside the apartment building where Goldstaub lived, I turned. "You and your family should leave at once."

He clasped my hand tightly. "We shall not forget you." A moment later he was out of the car, through the doorway, and headed up the staircase.

We heard nothing further from Goldstaub, but a few weeks later a cousin in South America sent news through a friend that he and his family had arrived in Brazil. I wondered how they were able to get that far but it was merely a matter of personal curiosity. Their destination was of little concern to me, so long as it was somewhere other than Europe.

Not long after news arrived about the Goldstaubs, we received a cable from the Chinese diplomatic mission in Ottawa, Canada, indicating that Hans Kraus had arrived there with his family. In light of the previous report from Goldstaub, I was not surprised the family had gone in that direction. It seemed like a good move to me. With little effort he would be able to enter the United States and then would be set for life.

CHAPTER

∽ 24 ∽

A FEW WEEKS LATER, Anna Meitner—Karl Meitner's sister—came to the consulate gate and asked to see me. Although we permitted visa applicants to wait in the compound yard, guards still manned the entrances and kept them closed except to admit additional applicants as space became available. Anna was in such a distraught emotional condition, the guards at the gate were reticent to allow her into the compound. After pleading her cause multiple times, however, she finally persuaded them to send a messenger to my office. When I learned she was attempting to see me, I asked the guards to bring her to me at once.

"Karl has been arrested," Anna blurted out as she rushed through my office doorway. Her eyes were red and her face was pale, as if she had been crying for quite some time.

"When did they do this?" I asked.

"They took him this morning."

"Why did they take him?"

"He was selling on the black market. Cigarettes, I think."

After Austria was occupied by the German Army, the country's economic infrastructure was disrupted. Uncertainty prevailed throughout the country. As a result, economic production came to a halt. Very soon, shops throughout the country faced shortages of almost every kind. At first, the people endured the hardship under the assumption that the disruption in supply was merely temporary and that better days lay ahead. However, as weeks went by with no relief in sight, news spread through Vienna that the goods they needed existed, but only that they were being diverted by the German military command for use by the German Army and for the pleasure of those private individuals whom the Germans favored.

Upon learning of this, residents of Vienna began trading for goods on the street in order to acquire the essentials of daily life. Jews, who were forbidden by German law to own property or to operate a business of any kind, used the resulting Vienna black market as a means of obtaining cash, often for the singular purpose of paying the cost of passage out of the country. The irony that a man of Karl Meitner's credentialed professional accomplishment would be forced to participate in such conduct in order to survive seemed overwhelmingly cruel to me and I resolved to do something about it at once.

After my experiences in assisting Kraus and Goldstaub, I had made a point of developing contacts within the German military command and the Austrian governing apparatus. When Anna told me about Karl, I instantly knew the correct person to contact. His name was Franz Beck, a German officer who was sympathetic to the Jewish cause and who I suspected might be Jewish to some degree. I asked a servant to bring tea and refreshments to my office, which were served to Anna while I placed a telephone call to Beck.

"He was arrested near the train station," Beck reported after checking his records. "According to our sources, Meitner was attempting to sell onions in commercial quantity. Boxes of them, actually. He has been processed and sent to the camp at Mauthausen. There is nothing further I can do about the matter. It is out of my hands."

When I gave the news to Anna, she became even more upset than when she arrived. "Not Mauthausen," she cried. I was distraught, too, though I forced myself to remain calm. I knew of this camp's reputation from references made about it during the refugee conference I attended in France.

Opened shortly after the Germans arrived in Austria, Mauthausen camp was located near the Wiener Graben quarry, which was owned by the city of Vienna. Granite from the quarry was used to pave Vienna's streets. However, as part of unification, the city leased the quarry to the German Earth and Stone Works, a company owned by the Schutzstaffel—the Nazi

Party's paramilitary protection squad, better known simply as the SS.

Inmates at the Mauthausen camp were used as slave labor, extracting blocks of granite from the quarry. They worked under terrible conditions with little food or care and were driven like animals until their bodies were used up. Once they were no longer able to provide manual labor, exhausted workers were killed. Already by the time Karl was taken, the death toll at the camp had been reported to be quite high. Anyone sentenced to Mauthausen faced little hope of survival. Few lasted even for as long as a single year.

Sensing there was little time to waste, I withdrew a blank visa form from my desk and prepared it for issuance using information I gathered from Anna while she sat in my office. Usually, we simply stamped the visa in an applicant's passport. In this instance, that was not possible, so I used the form instead.

When I completed the document, I added my signature and impressed it with the official seal. Then, visa document in hand, I called for a driver, who brought the car around to the building's side entrance. An assistant notified me when it was in place.

"Come," I said to Anna as I prepared to leave. "We will take you home now."

"No," she replied in earnest. "I do not want to go home. I want to get Karl out of that camp."

"I will address that situation," I assured her. "But you must not participate in this."

"He is my brother. I want to help."

"You have helped already," I replied. "You have done all you can do. Any more and you will be in great danger."

"I don't care about the danger."

Anna's devotion to her brother was touching and I tolerated what might have otherwise seemed to be an impertinent attitude, but I could not permit her to accompany me. "Then let me suggest," I said calmly, "that your involvement from this point forward will only endanger Karl. It will not help him." She seemed to understand what I intended and when we reached the first floor, she walked out to the car without further protest. We sat together in silence while the driver took us to the Second District.

When we arrived, we found the gates that previously had lain to one side were now fully in place and manned by German soldiers. Anna glanced over at me. "I do not think you can go inside now."

"How long have the gates been in place?"

"Only since yesterday. They locked them in place last night."

"We were not informed of this development," I noted. "German authorities have been diligent about informing us of similar matters in the past."

She gave me a serious but knowing expression. "I think things have taken a turn for the worse for us."

The driver opened the rear door of our car and I assisted Anna in alighting from it. She made her way to the guards, showed them her identity card, then moved through an opening in the gate without turning back to wave or note our presence. As she disappeared from sight, I returned to the car and we proceeded on our way out of the city.

Unlike the camp at Wolkersdorf, which had been hastily constructed by German soldiers, the camp at Mauthausen was part of a commercial enterprise. Although an asset of the Nazi Party, it nevertheless functioned as a business designed to provide construction materials for Nazi projects. In addition, inmates from the camp were rented out to other corporations, businesses, and enterprises of various kinds.

The main administrative building was a two-story structure. A guard was posted outside the entrance. He opened the door as I approached and I went inside to the desk of a young clerk. Perhaps twenty-five years old, he wore the uniform of a German officer but I was certain from the way he carried himself that he never had seen combat of any kind.

"What are you doing here?" the clerk asked with a thinly veiled surly attitude. "We do not allow civilian visitors."

"I am not a civilian," I replied as I took my identity card from my jacket. "I am the Chinese consul general from Vienna. I wish to speak to someone in authority about one of your prisoners."

The clerk glanced at my card. "We have no Chinese prisoners."

"He is not Chinese."

"What is the prisoner's name?"

"Karl Meitner."

The clerk came from behind his desk and walked to a table a short distance away. What appeared to be large record books lay there and he opened one, ran his finger down a page, then turned to me and said, "Meitner has been assigned to the quarry detail."

"Will you retrieve him for me, please?"

Just then, another officer appeared from a hallway that led off to the right. This man, however, was taller, older, and more dignified. He had two rows of service ribbons on the chest of his jacket and he had a presence that indicated he was a person of authority. I later learned his name was Riegler, the camp commander. "What is this?" he asked, glancing at me with a wary expression.

"He is asking after one of the prisoners," the clerk reported.

Riegler turned to me. "What is the nature of your inquiry?"

"I am the consul general from the Chinese Consulate in Vienna," I explained. "I have come to collect Karl Meitner."

"Collect him?" Riegler had an astounded expression. "You want to collect one of the prisoners?"

"Yes," I reiterated.

"I'm afraid that is impossible."

"Apparently, Karl Meitner was arrested by mistake," I explained. "He has been issued a visa for travel to Shanghai. Our government is expecting his prompt arrival. This is a matter of utmost urgency."

"I was not informed of this." Riegler now looked irritable. "Did you go through proper channels?"

"I *am* the proper channel," I replied boldly. "Meitner is traveling under our protection. I am the government's representative in this matter."

"This is highly irregular." Riegler glanced over at the clerk. "Get Berlin on the phone." Then he whirled and disappeared down the hallway.

A few minutes later, I heard Riegler's voice from down the hall, as if he was talking to someone on the telephone. There was a pause, then he called for me and as I entered the office, he handed me the telephone receiver. I took it from him and placed it to my ear.

The person speaking from the other end of the call was Cai Youmei, a functionary from our embassy in Berlin. I knew him as a colleague—he was with us for a short time in Turkey—but our various assignments did not require us to work together in great detail. Cai and I conversed in Chinese and I had little fear of anyone in the office realizing the meaning of what we said.

"What is this about?" Cai asked.

From my experience with his work, I surmised that Cai knew nothing of what I had been doing in Vienna. Consequently, delving into that topic would only lead to an argument between us regarding proper policy and Tsiang's directives. Instead, I avoided the question and asked, "Is Houlan available?"

"He is absent today. What is this about?" Cai asked once more.

Again, I ignored his question. "Then please allow me to speak with someone who shares Houlan's duties."

There was silence for a moment, then to my great delight the voice of Hou Shei came on the line. He was my friend from the time when I lived in Shanghai. I had not heard from him since the day he took me to the train station for my return to Changsha.

Still speaking in Chinese, I quickly explained the situation to Hou Shei, gave him the details about Meitner, and schooled him in what he should tell Riegler. He took great delight in the ruse I suggested we play, and when all was set I handed the phone to Riegler.

After a brief conversation with Hou Shei, Riegler hung up the phone and motioned for me to follow him. Without a word to me, he instructed the clerk to have Meitner brought to the office and then released to my custody.

An hour later, Meitner appeared at the administrative building. He was dressed in drab gray attire that was covered with granite dust and sweat stains. He had a sour smell about him, his skin was pale, and he stood silently before us with his hands clasped together at his waist. He looked down at the floor the entire time.

The clerk gave me a form to sign, which I did, then I walked outside with Meitner. He hesitated when we reached the car, as if entering it was forbidden or wrong, but I nudged him forward and he climbed inside. I got in beside him and told the driver to take us away quickly.

No one said a word as we drove from the camp, nor even for a great distance thereafter. When I finally turned to look at him,

I saw tears streaming down Meitner's cheeks.

"You are safe for now," I assured.

He looked over at me. "Thank you, but I am not sure I shall ever feel safe again."

"You must leave the country immediately," I warned. "You and Anna."

He nodded his head. "I know that."

"I will arrange your travel."

Meitner turned away and stared out the window. "Do you know what they are doing back there?" he asked in a soft voice.

"I have some idea. but I think if I saw it for myself I would be unable to remove the images from my mind."

"No," he sighed. "You would not. And neither shall I."

The hour was late when we arrived at the consulate, too late to retrieve Anna from the Second District. Karl bathed and we found clean clothes for him from a closet downstairs, then we ate dinner and he slept on the cot I had been using. I slept in a chair that sat in the corner opposite the bed.

The next morning, I sent a driver to get Anna. They were reunited at the consulate and remained there while I arranged travel for them. That proved easier than I thought and early the next day, I accompanied them to the airport where they boarded a flight that took them to Switzerland. They were to be met there by a member of our diplomatic mission who would assist them in traveling on to their destination. I had made travel arrangements that would take them all the way to Shanghai but left directions with our Swiss staff to make certain the Meitners were given the option to change those plans. They had an uncle who lived in New York and I was sure they would have preferred to go there instead, though I did not press the matter with them.

Obtaining Karl Meitner's release from the camp at Mauthausen had been a harrowing experience for me and I was certain it would lead to repercussions with the diplomatic staff in Berlin, perhaps with the German authorities. I was not afraid of what they might do to me; sending me home to China was the standard procedure for addressing such incidents and if that was the price I paid for Meitner's freedom, then so be it. I only hoped Hou Shei did not suffer from it for having assisted me.

CHAPTER

∽ 25 ∽

AS THE WEEKS WENT BY, travel in and out of Vienna's Second District became even more restricted and problematic than it had been when the Meitners lived there. Still, I was able to enter and exit during the day as often as I desired, though I was scrutinized by the guards at the gate and my passage in each direction was noted in the guards' log. This treatment did not deter me, however, and I continued to go to the second district regularly, as I had many contacts with whom I wanted to work.

Samuel Neurath remained a resident there, too, and I wanted to make sure I did as much for him as possible. He was determined to care for his neighbors for the duration of the German occupation, though I attempted several times to convince him that the occupation might be lengthy and the end for him more than unpleasant.

A few blocks from Neurath, Margarete and Julius Rosenberg lived in a building that sat four or five blocks from the river. Julius was an executive with an American corporation and they lived a comfortable life in one of the neighborhood's largest apartments. I was introduced to them at one of Mrs. Littlejohn's English club meetings but we became better acquainted through the Chinese-Austrian Cultural Association, a group of about twenty from various backgrounds who met for an occasional weekend retreat at the Südbahn Hotel, a luxurious facility in the mountains at Semmering. During those gatherings we discussed Chinese and Austrian culture, reviewing the aspects of each and attempting to deduce ways that individuals from the two countries could work together for their mutual benefit. Of course, that was before the Germans arrived. After they took over, no one any longer went anywhere without permission.

Not long after the Meitners departed from Austria, the Rosenbergs approached me about rendering assistance in leaving the country, too. They had arranged for payment of the embarkation fees but had been unable to obtain a visa. Both were Austrian citizens and held duly-issued passports, which the Germans continued to recognize. However, without a visa allowing them entry into a destination country, they would be unable to leave. I gladly provided the necessary authorization for travel to Shanghai simply by stamping the requisite visas on the pages of their passports. With those documents, and with the assistance of the corporation for whom Julius worked, the Rosenbergs obtained tickets for air travel to Switzerland, the first stop on their way to a new life.

On the morning of their scheduled departure, I went to see them at their apartment in the Second District to say our final good-byes. When I arrived, I found their luggage stacked near the door but their rooms were in utter disarray. As I glanced around with a look of bewilderment, Margarete informed me that Julius had been taken into custody by Nazi agents.

"Why did they take him?" I asked.

"They did not say, but they searched the house. Supposedly looking for contraband."

"Radios," I suggested as I followed her up the hallway to the sitting room.

"Radios?" she asked with a glance over her shoulder in my direction.

"Often they search for radios. They want to control the flow of outside information reaching Austrians."

"To keep us from hearing the truth."

I nodded in agreement. "To enhance your sense of isolation."

"Well," she sighed, "their techniques are working."

While we continued our conversation, there was a knock at the door. Margarete rose from her seat by the window and went to answer. As she did, I heard a gruff voice say to her, "Step aside, Jew. We're here to search your apartment."

"It was searched this morning already," Margarete replied.

"Well, it's about to be searched again."

From the sound of their footsteps I knew that whoever was there had pushed their way past Margarete and were coming up the hallway toward the sitting room where I remained. A moment later they appeared in the doorway, two men wearing business suits with rumpled white shirts and dark ties. Their hair was short and neatly trimmed but their shoes were scuffed and unpolished.

The first one looked over at me. "Who are *you*?" he asked in a demanding voice.

"I will tell you," I replied, remaining seated and motionless in my chair. "But first, you must tell me who *you* are."

He stepped closer and glowered over me. "You think you're going to tell *me* what to do?" He jabbed the air with his finger for emphasis.

"No," I replied, unfazed by his bullying antics. "The procedures tell you."

"Procedures?" he scoffed. "What do *you* know about procedures?"

"Tell me who you are and I will tell you all about proper procedure."

"I am an agent of the Third Reich," he roared. "That's who I am."

"I doubt it," I countered, my eyes focused squarely on his.

He seemed taken aback by the directness of my response but continued to rale. "I don't care what you doubt. This is the home of a Jew. In the land of the Reich. I can do anything I want in here and there isn't anything you can do to stop me."

I casually straightened the leg of my trouser and replied in an even tone. "You should know to whom you are speaking before you make a threat like that."

He stood there a moment, hands on hips, apparently unable to think of anything else to say. Finally, frustrated that I did not cower in his presence, he turned away and started up the hall toward the front door. The second man followed after him and as I heard the door open, one of them said, "Who is that man?"

"He is the Chinese consul general," Margarete replied.

"Why didn't you tell me that before?!" the first man shouted, then he stepped out to the building corridor and I heard him tromp away with a heavy step.

Not long after the agents left the apartment, Julius returned. We were glad to see him and after celebrating his return I said, "You both should come with me now."

"And go where?" Julius asked.

I glanced at my watch. "To the consulate. You've missed the plane and I think you should not stay here while we figure out what to do next. You can stay at the consulate until you leave the country."

Margarete looked concerned. "You think they will return?"

"I do not know. But I don't think you should take the chance."

Julius took a seat in the chair where I'd been when the agents arrived. He looked tired from the day's ordeal. "You think they are focused on us," he said, more as a statement than a question.

"I think whatever brought them to you brought them past many others on their way," I said, recalling a statement Father repeated often. One he adapted from something Confucius said.

"You mean they wanted us in particular?" Margarete asked.

"Yes."

Julius seemed to agree. "A servant with the company where I worked informed on me," he said.

"Informed on you? For what?"

"They said we lived an extravagant life."

It seemed an odd claim. "Extravagant?" I asked. "What does that mean?"

"Actually," Margarete shrugged, "it means they are interested in locating things of value and they think some of it might be here."

Julius nodded. "Artwork, mostly. Silver service. Gold coins and jewelry. Things they can sell or trade. . . or reduce to bullion."

"And they think because of your position you might have items of interest."

"That was the contraband they came to find," Margarete explained.

"And did they?"

"Did they . . .?" Julius asked, looking up at me.

"Did they find anything?" I elaborated.

"No," Julius replied. His eyes darted away and I could tell by the expression on his face that he was withholding something he did not wish to discuss, but I did not press to find out more.

A glance around the room told me there were bare spaces on the walls. An outline made by the glare of sunlight against the interior finish indicated the size of the items that once had hung there. No doubt, they had been secreted away and though the Rosenbergs did not admit it, I was sure they had taken steps to conceal anything of value they may have owned. I imagined they had done so at the first sign of trouble. That's the kind of person Julius was and the kind of attention that had made him successful in business.

At my repeated urging, Julius and Margarete returned to the consulate with me and remained there for the next two days while we worked out alternate transportation for them. Finally, after numerous phone calls and several favors, they boarded a train for Zurich and headed toward the border. As the train departed he station, I whispered a prayer for their safety and a blessing on their future.

As news spread among the Jews of our efforts to free detainees from the Germans, it also spread among the Germans, particularly after the release of Karl Meitner from the camp at Mauthausen and the confrontation with Nazi agents at the Rosenberg apartment. In the days that followed, German authorities redoubled their pressure on members of the Chinese diplomatic corps in Berlin. They threatened Tsiang Qiz-hen, our ambassador in Berlin, with the loss of personal privileges that had been extended to him beyond the normal courtesies and initiated steps to expel almost half of our diplomats operating in Germany.

At the same time, the German Foreign Ministry filed a demand with the Foreign Service in Nanjing, calling for us to reduce our administrative staff at all Chinese facilities in all lands held by the German Reich. Even more onerous than ordering diplomats to leave the country, curtailing our support staff would seriously inhibit the effectiveness of our programs at every level. As we already were operating without support staff in Vienna, these measures were of no significance to us and we continued to issue visas to all applicants who contacted our consular facility.

When remedial measures proved ineffective in deterring our actions, Joachim von Ribbentrop, Germany's foreign minister, called Tsiang Qiz-hen to his office and confronted him directly. "You are aware your consul general in Vienna is issuing visas to Jews?"

"Yes," Tsiang replied. "We are aware of his conduct."

"And you are aware that Jews are nonpersons under German law."

"Quite aware."

Ribbentrop took a file from the drawer of his desk, opened it, and removed a single document. He handed the document to Tsiang. "This a formal letter of protest. You must stop your consul general in Vienna from issuing visas."

"I would be delighted to accommodate your demand," Tsiang

replied as he quickly scanned the document. "And I have communicated this to him in many ways. Unfortunately, he is operating within the authority of his office. If I direct him as you request and forbid him to do the things to which you object, I would be acting contrary to official Chinese policy."

Ribbentrop's jaw was tense and his eyes bore in on Tsiang. "You are telling me that it is the official policy of the Chinese government to provide assistance to the Jews?"

"No," Tsiang responded quickly. "It is our policy to respect the autonomy of our consular officers."

"Are you not his supervisor?"

"Yes, but consul generals are appointed by the Foreign Service minister. Not by me. As such, they have their own portfolio. I direct those serving in Germany as the authorities in Nanjing instruct me, but I do not have the authority on my own to restrict their portfolio."

Ribbentrop placed his hands on the desktop, leaned forward, and lowered his voice. "I only have one superior to whom I am accountable. And that person is the führer himself."

Tsiang nodded. "I know this."

"He is beginning to think that what Ho Feng Shan is doing for the Jews is really executing your policy." He jabbed with his finger to emphasize the point. "That your consul general is doing these things at *your* insistence and direction."

"I assure you, his efforts to assist the Jews of Vienna is not a result of any policy promulgated by me or my office. And he is not acting at my direction. I cautioned him before and sent someone to talk to him about this very thing."

"Well, it hasn't done any good," Ribbentrop snarled.

"I will try again," Tsiang promised.

Ribbentrop stood, indicating the meeting was over. "If you cannot resolve this matter," he advised as he moved toward the door to escort Tsiang out, "we will resolve it ourselves."

When Tsiang returned to the embassy he phoned my office at once. "Did not Houlan make our policy clear to you?" he shouted into the phone.

"I understand Chinese policy very well," I calmly replied.

"Issuing visas to the Jews is antagonistic to our host country." He was still shouting. "You must stop issuing visas to them immediately."

"The Germans do not wish to have Jews living among them. I am helping the Jews leave. Why do German authorities object to my actions? I am helping the Germans solve their problem."

"What you are doing is damaging relations between our countries," Tsiang continued to shout angrily.

"What I am doing does not violate our government's stated policy or the policy of the Foreign Service."

"I will take care of the Foreign Service," Tsiang blustered. "You stop issuing visas. You are about to get us all killed." I heard the clatter of the phone as he slammed the receiver onto its base.

In spite of Tsiang's anger and frustration, I resolved more firmly than ever to ignore the order from Tsiang just as I had ignored him in the past. In the days that followed, I issued even more visas, upping the volume to a frenzy, certain that I would soon be forced to quit, either at the point of a gun or, more likely, by removal from my position.

One week after Tsiang's phone call, German troops arrived at the consulate and surrounded our compound. They snapped the locks off the gates and dispersed the Jews who were waiting on the grounds. With their own soldiers manning the entry posts, officers from the detail disarmed our guards and forced them to move inside the main building. When I came down to confront them, the officer in charge handed me a document. Among other things, it informed me that we had two days to vacate the premises.

The officer ordered in a stern voice, "If after two days you are still here, you will be arrested and taken into custody as a revolutionary against the Reich."

The German soldiers withdrew to the compound perimeter but forbid anyone other than staff to enter. I watched them from the window of my office and placed a phone call to the embassy in Berlin. When Tsiang came on the line, I reported the German action.

"I warned you." I could hear the satisfaction in the tone of his voice. "I warned you that things would get serious."

"This is an outrage. And I demand that you lodge an official protest with the German government."

"No," Tsiang replied. "This is what happens when you ignore

our policies and directives. If you had followed my direction, none of this would have happened."

"Has the Foreign Service decided to close this consulate?"

"Not yet. I have not taken up the matter with the ministry yet."

As minster of European affairs, Chen Rong was our supervisor. I knew he would never agree to close the consulate. Tsiang knew it, too, which is why he had not requested it and why he never would.

"Then what are we to do?" I asked. "We have two days and then we must be gone from this building. Am I authorized to rent space elsewhere?"

"Yes, you may rent alternate space." Tsiang had no choice but to permit me to do this, as contacting the Foreign Service regarding the loss of our building would reflect badly on him. "But," he continued, "all of this must be worked out within the budget you have already been allocated. There is no more money to add to it."

"But we have already spent the amount allocated to lease a building in Vienna."

"Then you'll have to make do on your own until the next budget allocation."

That afternoon I phoned a friend, Alan Rohan, who showed me a building in Vienna that had space for rent. "Two rooms with an entryway," he advised as he opened the door to allow me inside. The space would be marginally adequate as an office, but our existing facility had three stories with a basement. It had been in operation for many years, in the course of which we had accumulated numerous records. However, with a two-day deadline facing us, we had few options at our disposal and so I agreed to take the space, paying the first month's rent from my own money.

Working frantically, we moved files regarding all pending matters and as much of the furniture as seemed practicable into the new space. Everything else was assigned to a moving company for shipment to Berlin.

"Do you think they are prepared to receive all of this?" Wang asked as he surveyed the truckloads of items to be moved.

"Tsiang can take care of it himself," I snapped. "We have no other option. Either we destroy it all, which I do not think is wise, or we send it to Berlin."

Aside from a lack of room for equipment and records, we also faced cramped space for personnel. Consequently, I dismissed Soshana Schonborn and sent her home. We no longer needed guards or groundskeepers, either, and they were dismissed as well. We kept the driver and one car, though I was certain the Germans wanted it and him, too.

At the same time, I closed the house Grace and I had rented as a personal residence and shipped our belongings to Hu Yi in Changsha. I kept only my clothes and one or two personal items with me. Free of that, I moved into one of the rooms at the new location and took it as my living space. Wang Kai joined me there and shared the space with me. This left only one room for consular operations, but greatly reduced our monthly expenditures.

As German authorities directed, we were gone from the original consular building within the two-day limit. On the third day we opened for business at the new location and began receiving visa applications from anyone who wanted to apply, encouraging those who came to our office to spread the news of our new address. As we waited for the volume of new applications to increase, we worked diligently to process the applications that were pending when we had been forced to vacate the larger facility.

CHAPTER

∾ 26 ∾

IN 1939, HITLER BEGAN agitating for control of the Polish city of Danzig, a port city on the Baltic Sea. Once part of the German Empire, Danzig had been severed from Germany as part of the Treaty of Versailles, the agreement that ended World War I. The city, however, had a predominantly German population and reuniting it with Germany had been a much-discussed idea in the years following the Great War.

At first Hitler attempted a negotiated arrangement, suggesting the establishment of a so-called Polish Corridor—a strip of land across northern Poland that would geographically connect the city to Germany. European countries in the region were agreeable to that, but Poles found it unacceptable, as the area of the proposed connection held a predominantly Polish population.

Various other ideas were offered; many of them put forward by Neville Chamberlain, the British prime minister whose appeasement policies had attempted to avert war over the recent Germanic aggression. One of his major achievements had been the arrangement of an accommodation of the invasion and annexation of Austria and the Sudetenland. This time, however, Chamberlain's offers and ideas fell short of establishing widespread support and Hitler resorted to bluster, advancing the German Army toward the Polish border and, finally, concocting alleged acts of aggression against the German people being held "captive" by the Poles.

All was set for a German invasion in August, but a last-minute flurry of diplomatic activity resulted in a postponement. None of those efforts proved successful but in the negotiations, accommodative suggestions made by representatives from England and France convinced Hitler that neither country would fight to stop him from moving against Poland by force. As a consequence he ordered the invasion to go forward and on September 1, 1939, units of the German Army crossed the border into Poland.

One of the last-minute attempts to avert war included a mutual defense treaty between Poland and France, with an addendum that obligated England as well. Leaders of those countries thought the threat of a widened conflict would deter Hitler from any rash action. Their hopes were quickly dashed, however, and when the German Army crossed into Polish territory, England was forced to come to Poland's defense. France was obliged to join as well, and a state of war was declared between those two countries—Allies once again, as they had been for the Great War—and Germany.

News of events in Poland was kept from the Austrian public, but regular updates arrived at our offices by cable and diplomatic courier. We also read of it in newspapers smuggled to us from France. With conditions in Europe having festered for quite some time, and with Germany exhibiting such aggressive behavior since Hitler's rise to power, I expected the war would soon involve all the nations of Europe. I expected Asia to be embroiled in war, too, as Japan had been equally as aggressive there. Perhaps even the United States would be drawn into the fighting, although it was geographically removed from the conflict and separated from it by two oceans.

With events in Austria now shifting toward wartime, even more so than before, I expected our foreign office to react by ordering us to close the consulate and withdraw from Vienna. This was standard practice for countries with diplomatic staff assigned to areas embroiled in conflict of the nature we faced.

Of more personal concern to me, however, was the rising level of opposition to our work. Tsiang's abuse of Foreign Service policy was a nuisance, and Ribbentrop's accusations against me were not the first. However, the two of them together posed considerable risk, as they both had a penchant for ignoring the rules. Sentiment had been strongly against me in Berlin for quite some time, but now that sentiment had merged with the potential for genuine harm.

In light of that possibility, and the realization that I could do little to change my circumstances, I did my best to quicken the pace of visa issuance. At least by doing so I could accomplish some good for others, regardless of the outcome for me. With only Wang as my staff, this required us to strip the process of all but its essential components.

For those applicants who held Austrian passports, I merely stamped the form onto a page of their passport booklet without preparing a separate document. For those who had no passport, I issued a visa form that they could either proffer on its own or insert in other travel documents they might acquire. The formal application process served only to provide us with the necessary names and detailed information required by the visa form. With armies on the move, chaos would not be far behind, and they might have a chance to slip through with the barest of documentation. And as an added matter, no one would have time or care to follow up on the correctness of our work. Only the documents in the hand of the traveler mattered and I prayed silently over each one as I worked.

Not long after Germany invaded Poland from the west, forces from the Soviet Union attacked from the east, forcing the Polish Army to defend on two fronts, which was an impossible task. For France and England, there was no means of intervening that did not entail great loss of life and material. The speed of the German advance, however, made even the bravest defense of Poland a nonissue as the country fell into Nazi hands within a matter of weeks.

With Poland lost, England and France attempted to use Norway as a means of blocking the German Army's advance across northern Europe. This involved an elaborate scheme, one that did not account for the possibility that Germany would invade Norway, too. This, of course, was precisely what happened and the Allied forces that were deployed to Norway in the effort were forced to withdraw in great humiliation.

Failure of Chamberlain's earlier appeasement polices, followed by his failure to execute a successful strategy in the war's earliest months, placed great strain on Chamberlain's government. By April 1940, his political support had begun to unravel and there were calls for his removal from office.

That same month, a note from Chen Rong was delivered to me by diplomatic pouch. "My dear friend," the note began. Reading those words my heart sank as I knew that whatever followed would be difficult. "No longer able to sustain your position. Request that you return to Nanjing by the end of the month or upon the arrival of Qui Houlan, your replacement, whichever first occurs. See me upon your return. Our office will arrange travel details."

By then more had occurred than merely my efforts to issue visas. In Asia, Japan had expanded its control over more of China, using a brutality unknown previously to impose its will over the

Chinese people. Our agents working in Japan and Europe determined that Germany and Japan were in secret negotiations to form an alliance—perhaps one that included Italy as well—that would present a global front of opposition to the West. From sources inside China, I learned that our inability to counteract the Japanese was viewed by the Communist Party in China as exposing fatal flaws in the Kuomintang government, flaws that left our people vulnerable to outside exploitation and exposed the Kuomintang to internal political challenges.

Because of this, I did not desire to return to China. I had lived through both the earlier Kuomintang and the Communist uprising and did not wish to repeat that experience. Consequently, I replied to Chen Rong and asked if there were alternatives to returning to China that might be available to me. A few days later, a cable arrived with Chen Rong's response, ordering me to transfer to the United States where I was to assist the Chinese delegation in New York in reporting on US war preparations.

Not long after I received the final cable from Chen Rong, Houlan arrived to take my place as consul general of Vienna. Wang Kai collected him from the train station and brought him to the office. I was busy when he arrived and did not look up as he entered. He came and stood near the corner of my desk, placing his hand on a stack of files and papers that rested there. "This is quite a lot of work," Houlan noted as he leafed through the pages.

"We do our best," I replied without making eye contact.

"And these were all duly issued?"

The comment caught my attention and I glanced up from my work. Wang looked in my direction but quickly turned away. "Duly authorized," I replied curtly. Houlan nodded politely and I continued to prepare visa documents, applying the official stamp and adding my signature with as much speed as my tired fingers could muster.

"Do you think they will get to use those?" Houlan asked, gesturing to the document that lay before me.

"The travelers?" I asked.

"Yes."

"They cannot go anywhere without it," I noted.

"But will they have the opportunity even with it?" he asked.

"One does not know the answer to that question." I laid aside my pen and looked up at him, at last focusing my full attention on him. "Do you intend to continue this practice?"

"Of issuing visas?"

"Yes."

"I will consider any request," Houlan assured. "But I cannot say as to whom or how long that practice may be extended. Whatever Berlin tells us to do, that is what we shall do." He gave a dismissive wave of his hand. "This is not really any of my concern, though."

"Not your concern?"

"The Jews and how they are treated by the Germans. It is not an issue that captures my interest."

"As I suspected," I said with disdain.

"You know," Houlan offered, "even your friends think you have lost your way."

"My friends?"

"You still have friends in the Service. But they do not agree with what you have done."

"None of them?"

"None of them in Berlin."

"And have they taken measures to counteract or nullify my work?"

Houlan shook his head. "No, and they will not. In fact, we have received reports that some of the Jews from Vienna already have arrived in Shanghai, though I'm not certain how long they can remain there, with the Japanese advancing."

The advance of Japanese forces toward Shanghai was a problem I already had considered, but it was not really a concern for anyone except those who lived there. My primary consideration in issuing visas was that as many Jews as possible should escape from German clutches. Once free, they could travel to any location that would have them. Many, I assumed, would actually go to the United States or to Palestine. Those seemed the two likeliest locations.

Later that afternoon, Houlan went to a hotel to spend the night. Wang Kai and I remained at the consulate office, issuing still more visas as the hours ticked past. "I know you have not agreed with me," I noted. "But I appreciate your service in doing as I instructed."

"I did not understand at first," he admitted. "But now I see the importance of what we have done."

"Will you continue to issue the visas after I am gone?"

"I suppose I shall be obliged to do as Houlan instructs," Wang Kai answered.

"That is understandable, but you must do all in your power to see that the visas we have issued thus far are delivered to the parties who requested them."

"Yes," Wang said. "I shall."

The next morning, I gathered my belongings into two suitcases and prepared to leave for the train station. Wang Kai walked with me downstairs where the car was waiting. As he opened the door for me I stepped out to find a line of people waiting to enter the office. They stood one behind the other all the way out to the street and down to the next corner.

"So many yet to be served," I said.

"Yes," Wang Kai replied. "They keep coming every day."

With so much to do those final weeks before my departure, I had rarely gone out of the building but sat at my desk issuing documents constantly. I was astounded that so many applicants remained. "You must help them," I whispered to Wang.

"I will do what I can."

I turned to face him. "No! You must do it. You must press the matter forward. Do not leave it to Houlan to direct you. He will allow you to do as much as you choose, but he will not direct you to do anything. Press the issue," I repeated. Wang Kai nodded in response, then turned away and started back up the steps toward the office.

The driver helped me with my luggage, then held the car door for me as I slid into the rear seat. We drove to the train station without incident. I alighted there, said good-bye to the driver, and made my way to the ticket window.

A few minutes later, I boarded the train for Trieste, Italy, where I took passage on a ship bound for New York. Before we set sail, I sent a telegram to Grace and Monto to indicate the name of the ship on which I was traveling, along with the date and time of my expected arrival.

Once aboard, I spent most of the daylight hours in a chair on the deck, staring out at the water, watching the waves as they slipped past the hull of the ship. Although they passed by my location constantly, there always was another to take the place of the one that faded from view and for as many waves as we passed in one day, there were an equal number the next. They set the rhythm of the day, wave upon wave, moment by moment. Lulled by that repetition, I recounted the events of the past two years.

For most of my time in Vienna, I had issued visas to people who were attempting to flee a ruthless Nazi regime. As news of my willingness to be of assistance spread, more came to our offices seeking help. For every visa we issued, two more requests took its place. And still, after months and months of round-the-clock effort to address their needs, as I left the office for the final time I passed applicants standing in line from the building to the street and up the block. As much as we did, there always was more to do. And I began to wonder if I had done anything at all. If my life had made a difference. If I really had helped anyone at all. There were so many. . . . But there was more I could have done, too. I could have stamped one more passport. Issued one more document. If I had slept less. Eaten less. Spent less time in the District and more time at my desk. Or if I had taken the office *to* the District. If. . . if. . . if.

The question of had I done enough troubled me all the way to New York and even as we sailed into the harbor, with the Statue of Liberty on one side and the towering buildings of Manhattan on the other, I wondered what difference it had all made. What difference I had made. Whether my life meant anything at all.

❧ ❧

As I expected, Grace and Monto were waiting for me when the ship reached the dock. They rushed forward to greet me as I came down the gangway. Grace was prettier than I remembered and I took her in my arms right there to kiss her as I had when we said good-bye before. Only, now I hoped we would never be apart again.

Monto seemed to have grown a foot taller and twice as confident as when I saw him last. His English was very well developed, too, and we conversed freely with no need of resorting to Chinese.

After gathering my luggage, we took a taxi over to Brooklyn where Grace had rented an apartment. It had two bedrooms with a sitting area, kitchen, and bathroom—offering far more comfort than we would have enjoyed in China and I knew it suited her well to be there. We spent the remainder of the week getting reacquainted, enjoying each other, and a night or two out at a play and a restaurant.

On Monday of the following week, I took the subway to Manhattan and reported for duty at the Chinese delegation's office on Forty-Second Street, not far from the docks where our ship had arrived less than a week earlier. I knew no one who worked there but quickly became acquainted with them all. Most of my time was spent reading American newspapers, government reports, and information about exports and imports from the country's major ports. I used that information in an attempt to deduce the amount of goods the free world economy was producing, the amount it could produce if asked to do more, and gauge the willingness of US industry to retool production for a wartime effort. I was unsure who would make use of that information, we had few in China with the expertise to make future projections based on that kind of data, but I enjoyed the work, so I applied myself diligently.

From my work there I came to realize that while most Americans viewed events in Europe with a wary eye, few realized the threat looming in the East. Americans seemed disarmed by the exotic nature of Asian culture and were lured by the seemingly conservative lifestyle modeled there, most likely from the lifestyle they experienced when engaging Asians who resided in the United States; a decidedly conservative and industrious group, particularly among the Japanese. We who experienced them in China knew a different side: A cunning, ruthless, and brutal side with an arrogant sense of superiority that I was certain would lead many to seriously miscalculate American ability and resolve.

Life in the United States was comfortable—luxurious by comparison to what most people in other parts of the world endured—and I settled into it quickly. The sense of futility and questions about the meaning and worth of my life's work that had plagued me as I departed Vienna receded to the background, but they did not disappear entirely.

By November 1941, I had grown accustomed to the daily routine of arriving early for work, then taking a stroll at noon during which I purchased something for lunch from one of the many street vendors that catered to the Manhattan workday crowd. Often I ate while seated on a bench where I watched the pedestrians as they passed by, rather like I watched the waves slipping past the ship on the voyage over from Italy.

One particular day, the sun was bright but the temperature was cool, the air brisk, and I did not sit long but ate quickly, then started back to the office. As I made my way along the sidewalk, a man approached. He looked familiar but I could not place him at once, though he seemed to recognize me and was grinning from ear to ear as he walked up to me. When he was a short distance away he reached out with both hands and took hold of me by the shoulders. "Ho Feng Shan!" he exclaimed. His sudden appearance and impulsive action startled me, but before I could react he wrapped his arms around me and pulled me close in a tight hug.

After a moment, he released me and I stepped back to look at him. That's when I realized: he was Hans Kraus, the Jewish surgeon from Vienna who one day tossed his visa applications to me through the window of the car as we returned to the consulate compound.

"Ho Feng Shan," he repeated at a slightly lower volume. "Don't you remember me?"

I smiled, "Yes, but I did not expect to find you here."

Kraus draped his arm across my shoulder and walked with me up the street. "When we got to Switzerland," he explained, "we met a guy who helped us come to Canada. And from Canada, we made our way here."

"You are in practice now?"

"Sort of," he replied, though I knew from the tone of his voice that his position was not entirely to his satisfaction. "I have applied for a license, but right now I'm working at a hospital in Queens. What are you doing here?"

I explained my work and we talked awhile longer but I had to get back to the office, so we made plans to meet again that weekend. "Come to our apartment," Kraus urged. "Bring your family. It's almost Thanksgiving. We can celebrate early. Some of the others are living here, too. I'll see if they can join us."

"The others?"

"Yeah," he replied. "Some of the others who got out of Vienna at the same time. I'll ask around and see if they can meet us." He gave me his address and I agreed we would come on Saturday for a visit, then we parted ways.

That Saturday, Grace, Monto, and I made our way to the apartment building in lower Manhattan where Kraus lived. We located the correct door and I knocked on it to announce our arrival. When the door opened, there was Kraus, grinning as broadly as the day I saw him on the sidewalk earlier that week, and behind him was a room full of people. Before once more giving me a hug, he glanced sideways over his shoulder and called in a loud voice to those in the room, "They're here!"

As we entered the room, those who were gathered in the apartment began shouting, clapping, and cheering. Then one of them pushed past the others toward me and I saw that it was Karl Meitner, the man I had retrieved from the camp at Mauthausen. He grabbed me in a hug and squeezed me as tightly as Kraus had earlier, only this time I was so relieved to see him I hugged him back.

After a moment, he pulled away, still with one arm on my shoulder, and gestured to the room with a broad sweep of his free hand. "Everyone here in this room is alive today because of you."

Quite by surprise, tears filled my eyes and before I could stop them they trickled down my cheeks. The thought that these were women, men, and children whom I had saved from the Nazis, who had a life now they might never have known otherwise seemed overwhelming and I was overcome with emotion. I relaxed my weight against Meitner, turned my face against the cloth of his jacket, and sobbed.

A NOTE ABOUT
HO FENG SHAN

ᏸᎧᎴ ᎧᏣᎴ

THE STORY you have read is a work of fiction loosely
based on events from the life of Ho Feng Shan, a diplomat for
the Republic of China who was stationed in Vienna during the
German occupation of Austria. According to Yad Vashem, he was
thought to have issued thousands of visas to Jews attempting to
flee Nazi persecution. Through his efforts, thousands were saved
and for his devotion to the cause of their rescue, he has been listed
as one of the Righteous Among the Nations—non-Jews who risked
their lives and futures to save European Jews from the Holocaust.

Information drawn from varying accounts of Ho Feng Shan's
early life and from portions of his career in the Chinese Foreign
Service have been combined with events recounted by others
from the era to form the structure of our story. Those events have
been portrayed as realistically as possible, but with an eye toward

creating an entertaining and engaging work of fiction. Characters, events, and locations in this book are the work of the author's imagination and have been arranged and compiled to provide a hopefully poignant glimpse of the devastating effect Nazi injustice and racial hatred had on so many.

Our hope is that in viewing events through the lens of this story you will be inspired to read further on the subject of the Holocaust, the need for justice in the world today, and the difference that can come in the lives of many through the work of only a few, perhaps even you.

ACKNOWLEDGMENTS

My deepest gratitude and sincere thanks to my writing partner, Joe Hilley, and to my executive assistant, Lanelle Shaw-Young, both of whom work diligently to turn my story ideas into great books. And to Arlen Young, Peter Glöege, and Janna Nysewander for making the finished product look and read its best. And always, to my wife, Carolyn, whose presence makes everything better.

BOOKS BY: MIKE EVANS

Israel: America's Key to Survival

Save Jerusalem

The Return

Jerusalem D.C.

Purity and Peace of Mind

Who Cries for the Hurting?

Living Fear Free

I Shall Not Want

Let My People Go

Jerusalem Betrayed

Seven Years of Shaking: A Vision

The Nuclear Bomb of Islam

Jerusalem Prophecies

Pray For Peace of Jerusalem

America's War:
    The Beginning of the End

The Jerusalem Scroll

The Prayer of David

The Unanswered Prayers of Jesus

God Wrestling

The American Prophecies

Beyond Iraq: The Next Move

The Final Move beyond Iraq

Showdown with Nuclear Iran

Jimmy Carter: The Liberal Left
    and World Chaos

Atomic Iran

Cursed

Betrayed

The Light

Corrie's Reflections & Meditations

The Revolution

The Final Generation

Seven Days

The Locket

Persia: The Final Jihad

GAMECHANGER SERIES:

GameChanger

Samson Option

The Four Horsemen

THE PROTOCOLS SERIES:

The Protocols

The Candidate

Jerusalem

The History of Christian Zionism

Countdown

Ten Boom: Betsie, Promise of God

Commanded Blessing

BORN AGAIN SERIES:

Born Again: 1948

Born Again: 1967

Presidents in Prophecy

Stand with Israel

Prayer, Power and Purpose

Turning Your Pain Into Gain

Christopher Columbus, Secret Jew

Living in the F.O.G.

Finding Favor with God

Finding Favor with Man

Unleashing God's Favor

The Jewish State: The Volunteers

See You in New York

Friends of Zion:
   Patterson & Wingate

The Columbus Code

The Temple

Satan, You Can't Have
   My Country!

Satan, You Can't Have
   Israel!

Lights in the Darkness

The Seven Feasts of Israel

Netanyahu (a novel)

Jew-Hatred and the Church

The Visionaries

Why Was I Born?

Son, I Love You

Jerusalem DC (David's Capital)

Israel Reborn

Prayer: A Conversation with God

Shimon Peres (a novel)

The New Hitler

Pursuing God's Presence

Ho Feng Shan (a novel)

COMING SOON:

The Daniel Option (a novel)

The Good Father

TO PURCHASE, CONTACT: orders@TimeWorthyBooks.com
P. O. BOX 30000, PHOENIX, AZ 85046

MICHAEL DAVID EVANS, the #1 *New York Times* bestselling author, is an award-winning journalist/Middle East analyst. Dr. Evans has appeared on hundreds of network television and radio shows including *Good Morning America, Crossfire* and *Nightline,* and *The Rush Limbaugh Show,* and on Fox Network, *CNN World News,* NBC, ABC, and CBS. His articles have been published in the *Wall Street Journal, USA Today, Washington Times, Jerusalem Post* and newspapers worldwide. More than twenty-five million copies of his books are in print, and he is the award-winning producer of nine documentaries based on his books.

Dr. Evans is considered one of the world's leading experts on Israel and the Middle East, and is one of the most sought-after speakers on that subject. He is the chairman of the board of the ten Boom Holocaust Museum in Haarlem, Holland, and is the founder of Israel's first Christian museum located in the Friends of Zion Heritage Center in Jerusalem.

Dr. Evans has authored a number of books including: *History of Christian Zionism, Showdown with Nuclear Iran, Atomic Iran, The Next Move Beyond Iraq, The Final Move Beyond Iraq,* and *Countdown.* His body of work also includes the novels *Seven Days, GameChanger, The Samson Option, The Four Horsemen, The Locket, Born Again: 1967,* and *The Columbus Code.*

✦ ✦ ✦

Michael David Evans is available to speak or for interviews.

Contact: EVENTS@drmichaeldevans.com.